EVERY HIDDEN
FEAR

ALSO BY LINDA RODRIGUEZ

FICTION

Every Broken Trust

Every Last Secret

POETRY

Heart's Migration

Skin Hunger

EVERY HIDDEN
FEAR

A Mystery

Linda Rodriguez

MINOTAUR BOOKS

A THOMAS DUNNE BOOK
NEW YORK

A THOMAS DUNNE BOOK FOR MINOTAUR BOOKS.
An imprint of St. Martin's Publishing Group.

EVERY HIDDEN FEAR. Copyright © 2014 by Linda Rodriguez. All rights reserved. Printed in the United States of America. For information, address St. Martin's Press, 175 Fifth Avenue, New York, N.Y. 10010.

www.thomasdunnebooks.com
www.minotaurbooks.com

Design by Omar Chapa

The Library of Congress Cataloging-in-Publication Data is available upon request.

ISBN 978-1-250-04915-5 (hardcover)
ISBN 978-1-4668-5028-6 (e-book)

Minotaur books may be purchased for educational, business, or promotional use. For information on bulk purchases, please contact Macmillan Corporate and Premium Sales Department at 1-800-221-7945, extension 5442, or write specialmarkets@macmillan.com.

First Edition: May 2014

10   9   8   7   6   5   4   3   2   1

To my daughter, Crystal Lynne, with greatest love

ACKNOWLEDGMENTS

I am fortunate to be a member of the Novel Group. Jacqueline Guidry, Judith Fertig, Robin Silverman, and Deborah Shouse are constantly there for help, support, and celebration. The Latino Writers Collective is my writing familia and dear to my heart. My fellow bloggers at Writers Who Kill and The Stiletto Gang are always a help and support. Julia Spencer-Fleming has been incredibly generous to me in so many ways and introduced me to my other wonderful friends at Jungle Red Writers.

I am truly grateful for my fantastic agent, Ellen Geiger. I am also fortunate to have a great editor, Toni Kirkpatrick, and a terrific publicist, Sarah Melnyk. I have been lucky in my professional colleagues, and I sincerely appreciate them.

For valuable technical assistance, I would like to thank Harry Hylander, retired after many years with the campus police force of the University of Missouri–Kansas City; Gayle Reese, retired after years as both a city police officer and a campus police officer; and Chato Villalobos of the Kansas City, Missouri, Police Department. I am also grateful for the advice of Luci Zahray on poisons. What I have right is their doing. Any mistakes I have made are my own.

I am also grateful for my tremendously supportive family, Crystal Rodriguez, Don Shull, Niles Rodriguez, Denise Brown, Joseph Rodriguez, Gustavo Adolfo Aybar, Erika Noguera, Becquér Francisco Aybar, Sam Segraves, Becky Ross, and Patrick and Andrew Ross. Most of all, I thank my husband, Ben Furnish, my true partner in absolutely everything.

EVERY HIDDEN
FEAR

CHAPTER 1

I had dead leaves and cobwebs in my hair and stuck to my face. I couldn't wipe them away because my glove-covered hands were digging wet, smelly leaf slime out of the gutters while my tough old grandmother scolded me for letting my house get into such bad shape. I'd had better afternoons chasing down murderers.

I'd planned on a quiet, restful day for a change, since Brian was off with friends. I didn't get those very often any longer with Gran and my ward, Brian Jameson, both living with me, especially lately with Brian's grumpy mood. I'd thought I might read a book for pleasure or sit on the front porch and knit in the unseasonably warm weather. One of the advantages of giving up a hard-hitting career with the Kansas City Police Department and moving to a small college town as head of campus police was the slower pace of life here right outside the city. Perhaps I might take Lady, my collie, for a nice, leisurely walk through town and window-shop on our way to the park. Until I caught that hardheaded old woman up on a ladder, getting ready to clean my gutters. Eighty years old and climbing a ladder as if she had no more sense than a squirrel!

So nothing would do but to give up my peaceful afternoon and climb up to do the job myself with Her Toughness holding the ladder steady and calling out orders, complaints, and warnings while a train hooted its way through the heart of Brewster, Missouri. I just wanted to get finished and off the ladder—I'm not fond of heights—and wash up. But Gran was not a person to be satisfied with a lick and a promise, so I could see I was going to be stuck up there all afternoon, moving slowly around the house.

"You can't neglect things like this, Skeet." Gran's voice was stern as I pulled loose a Virginia creeper vine that had somehow made it all the way to the gutter. "If you're not constantly watching and taking care of little things with a house, all kinds of things will fester in the dark and grow out of sight to damage it until they pull it down on your head."

I sighed. I was a little shocked at how much junk had collected in my gutters, and from this height, I could see more Virginia creeper around the corner and heading for the roof. But I really didn't think I was in danger of my solidly built ninety-year-old house collapsing on my head imminently any more than Gran was going to collapse in a Victorian faint at my feet.

"Those clogged gutters'll lead to leaks in the roof and in the walls, if you don't take care of them. Water's your enemy when you own a house. It'll rot the wood and weaken your whole structure." Gran shook her head as I threw another clump of leaf slime down to the ground, a little too close to her feet. "It's the stuff that's out of sight and hidden from view that does all the damage."

I rolled my eyes as I turned back to the gutter. I was taking care of it, wasn't I? No need to go on and on about my sins of neglect.

"Okay. I just never owned a house before, Gran. I didn't know all this stuff. Now that you've told me, I do. And I'll take care of things." I didn't see why I couldn't hire someone to clean out the gutters and things like that, giving some guy who needed it work and saving my few peaceful afternoons off for myself.

She ignored everything I said. "After this, we'll have to go to the hardware store and get some caulk for the windows. It's going to be Thanksgiving soon, and you haven't winterized this house. Normally, we'd have had some snow or ice by now, or certainly hard freezes."

"It's the good thing about global warming," I teased as I leaned as far as I could along the front of the house before having to climb down and reposition the ladder. "We're becoming a milder climate here in the tornado-blizzard zone."

"Hmph! Human messes always screw up the earth. No respect, at all." She dodged another handful of twigs and leaf slime. "But the earth is going to slap back. Got a big, bad storm on its way. Need to be prepared."

"Gran, all the weathermen and the weather station say this mild weather's going to last through the holidays. We shouldn't get any real winter weather before New Year's Day. Wouldn't be the first time our first real snowstorm didn't hit until New Year's."

I caught myself after reaching too far and started to climb down the ladder. This was the part about heights that I really hated, climbing down backward, so I concentrated on my feet and the next rung.

"I don't have to listen to *yonega* weathermen. I hope I have enough sense to read the signs all around me like I've been doing for eighty years, like my grandmother taught me and I tried to teach you." She waved away my attempt at protest. "And the signs all around tell me we've got a blizzard coming, a bad one."

I set my first foot on the ground and breathed a little relieved sigh. "Meteorologists have—"

"Meteorologists! Why are they looking at meteors when the signs are here in the caterpillars and squirrels and foxes and trees and other living beings?" She snorted with disgust and moved away from the ladder as I stepped off the last rung.

"Gran, I don't want to argue with you on such a nice day. Let's take a break and go in for some coffee and some of those cookies you made last night. We can bring them out to the porch here and relax for a minute before doing the rest of the gutters." I reached to take her arm but dropped my hand after seeing the odorous junk from the gutters smeared on my glove. "And I could clean up a little."

"Hmph! You just want to get out of cleaning the rest of those gutters. Don't think I don't know it." A spark of mischief appeared in her dark eyes. "But those were good cookies last night, and they'd go well with some hot coffee."

Before I could agree enthusiastically and lure her on into the house, a noisy, bright green car pulled up in the street in front of us. We both turned toward it just as Brian leaped out of the back of clean-cut quarterback Noah Steen's car and slammed the door. Brian's best friend, Angie Melvin, had one tattooed arm hanging out the passenger window, and she stuck her head with its burgundy and blue hair out as well. "Bye, Bri. Call me later. Hi, Skeet. Hi, Mrs. Whittaker."

Angie had first-named Gran one time only in the first days after Gran moved herself in with Brian and me. Gran put a stop to that in no time, and she was the only adult in town that

Angie didn't call by first name or some sarcastic nickname. Mine, when she was pissed at me, was Supercop.

Brian nodded and waved, then turned a scowling face in our direction as Noah and Angie drove off.

"Didn't you have fun with Angie and Noah?" I asked. "You look like you lost your best friend."

"Maybe that's because I have," he snapped back at me. "Angie just hangs on that stupid jock's every word and ignores me. I don't know why they ask me to come along. Sometimes I think she doesn't want me there at all. He's the one who always asks. Just trying to get in her good graces. Like he's so sensitive and caring. Hah!"

"Whoa, Brian. She didn't sound like it just now, asking you to call her later and everything."

"That's just so she can go on and on about handsome Noah and every little thing he said and did. 'And isn't he just wonderful, Brian? Isn't he the greatest?' The most boring phone calls in the world."

I opened my mouth to try to make things better somehow, but Gran jabbed me in the side with her bony elbow and frowned at me, so I just shut my mouth and focused on Brian the way I would focus on witnesses in silence to lead them to say more than they intended when I was investigating crimes. Brian stood in frowning silence for about half a minute. Then the technique worked its magic.

"Sometimes I don't think Noah really likes Angie. Not that way, you know. I think he's just playing a game with her, and she's going to get hurt real bad." He lowered his eyes and shook his head impatiently. "And I don't think I can stand it because she's already been hurt so much. I don't see how she'll survive it. I'd like to hit him, but he's older and bigger and a jock, and he'd probably wipe up the floor with me. Then he'd just take Angie off and hurt her anyway."

He swiped at his eyes angrily. "She deserves better than him. I can't see what she sees in him. She's usually so smart. Just brilliant. But right now, she's being so dumb."

"She can't see that there's a great guy, smart and talented and honorable, who would treat her much better, can she?" Gran asked quietly.

Brian stood in silent shock. "I don't . . ." He shook his head furiously and ran up the porch steps and into the house, banging the screen door behind him.

I started after him, but Gran laid her hand on my arm. "Let him go. He needs to cry it out and hit walls, and he won't be grateful to have any witnesses to that later."

"He's in love with Angie? That can't be! He's too young. Only fifteen. I know he thinks the world of her. But that's just friendship. He can't be in love at his age. Can he?"

I'd had custody of Brian for less than a year since his parents died. Pretty soon, the adoption would be final, if nothing got in the way. I had a bad feeling love might be one of those things that could derail it.

"Skeet, his age is when the worst of love hits. And he won't know what to do with it. He feels totally out of control."

That sounded like love at any age to me—or at least my experience with it. I was not a fan of Cupid.

Gran went on over my thoughts. "It was bound to happen. He's always thought the sun rose and set on Angie, so when the hormones kicked in, she's where all his feelings ended up."

"Oh, shit! Hormones. Sex. Please, no. Not to my boy. Brian's too young to handle all that. Hell, I'm too young to handle all that, so how can a kid manage? And how on earth can I help him?"

I couldn't guide a kid through first love. I'd made a mess of my own love life, marrying an exciting, handsome fellow cop, who made me laugh and thrill with passion, only to find that he couldn't handle a strong woman who made a success of her career and that he had to manage his fears by being verbally abusive and sexually unfaithful. I had nothing to teach poor Brian, except the lesson I'd learned—avoid romance and love.

"Give him room for one thing, Skeet. A lot of the love miseries a person's just got to sort out on their own." Gran shook her head. "He's right. Angie's already had a lifetime of hurt, and she doesn't need more. And he's probably right about the other boy's feelings. Brian's a good observer."

I wanted to throw something. Angie had had such a rough time lately. I'd been glad to see Noah show up and some color and happiness come back into her cheeks once she'd healed enough physically to go back to school. She'd been through hell, and recovering from physical injuries and surgery to remove her spleen had left her bereft of a lot of her admirable strength and vitality.

"This is all too complicated." I gestured with my stained glove toward the front door. "Let's go clean up and figure out what to do over coffee."

"And cookies," Gran added, as she started up the porch steps.

As that same train gave a mournful whistle from the far side of town, I followed her, wishing I could go back to being on the ladder wrist-deep in gutter muck and blissfully innocent of the problems roiling beneath the surface of my life. Gran was right. What you couldn't see could destroy you. I suspected that the way water was your enemy if you owned a house, love was your enemy if you wanted a happy, peaceful life.

The next day was a bright, clear Sunday, and Gran talked Brian into going fishing with her and my old friend, Sid Ambrose, our part-time county coroner in his retirement from the medical examiner's office in Kansas City. Sid got a kick out of Gran, and she enjoyed having a fishing buddy up here. I was glad to see Brian off to spend some time with two of the wisest people I knew.

I had a lazy morning sitting in my pajamas and knitting in the company of Lady and Wilma Mankiller, my scrappy street cat that I'd brought with me from Kansas City. Wilma used to constitute my immediate family, but it had since been expanded to include Lady, Brian, Gran, my dearest friend Karen, and others. I had to shake my head sadly when I remembered those days of just Wilma and me in a drab city apartment.

She seemed much happier now, too, as she batted around at the pink yarn moving past her head or thrust that head under my hand, demanding petting. Wilma was not the shy and retiring type. She went after what she wanted.

Eventually, I dressed and drove to the Clubhouse Restaurant located on the public golf course next to River Walk Park. They had a great Sunday brunch buffet, and if I was lucky, we'd get a table overlooking the river where I could watch eagles and herons, as well as the constant ripple of the Missouri's powerful current. I'd promised to meet Pearl Brewster, last descendant of our town's founder, for a lunch meeting with my friends, Miryam Rainbow and Annette Stanek. Pearl had a project she wanted us to help her with, probably something to do for teens. Pearl was the local champion and mentor of teens with any kinds of problems, and her projects were usually useful and sensible.

As I left my car, I could hear another train in the distance, the regular background music of Brewster, Missouri. Train tracks ran through the heart of town to a station on the edge of the wide Missouri River. As one of the earliest river ports, we'd always been a natural stopping place for trains, with tracks leading both north to Omaha and Des Moines and south to Kansas City and beyond to Oklahoma and Kansas. Passenger trains no longer held much importance in American life, and the old station was now a hip restaurant, but freight trains still ran in both directions through Brewster night and day.

The train moaned off into the distance, and I saw Joe Louzon, Brewster's chief of police, walking toward me. I gave a little moan of my own. He'd asked me to have lunch with him that day at the Clubhouse, and I'd been happy to claim a previous commitment. You'd think he'd have known I'd never agree to go to lunch, just the two of us. That would feel too much like a date, something I was definitely not doing.

"Skeet, did you change your mind?" he asked eagerly, a bright smile lighting up his broad, muscular face.

"No, I'm meeting friends for lunch. Just the way I told you." I had to stop my forward motion because he planted his stalwart body directly in my path like the defensive end I knew he'd been back in high school football. "It so happens we're eating here."

Joe'd been good for a long time about not pushing his desire for anything beyond friendship. He knew my ex-husband was still in my life because we shared care for my ailing father, but that never bothered Joe, who always seemed secure and rock-solid sensible.

"What friend exactly are you meeting?" he asked with intensity. "Don't bother with some little white lie. I saw your hired-gun pal, Heldrich, go in just a second ago."

I rolled my eyes and sighed. It was only when Terry Heldrich came into town that Joe suddenly became jealous and down-right pushy about wanting more from me than I could give. It wasn't fair when we'd never been more than friends, and I'd made it clear I wasn't ready for anything else. Besides, Terry meant nothing to me. He might have had other ideas, but I just avoided him. Still, I felt like I'd lost a good friend in Joe.

"I imagine you've seen a number of people go inside recently. Some of them might be the people I'm having lunch with, but Terry's not one of them. Would you please move out of my way? I'm going to be late."

He tightened his mouth into a straight line with a little skeptical pursing of the lips at the center. I missed the days when he used to smile warmly at me and make me feel that he was happy with me just the way I was. I missed my friend.

He stepped to the side and gestured me to go ahead with his strong right arm. His eyes, half-sad, half-angry, followed me as I passed.

I couldn't help turning to tell him, "I'm meeting Pearl, Annette, and Miryam, honestly."

He rewarded me with a halfhearted smile, neither one of us getting what we wanted.

I shook off the sadness the encounter caused me as I entered the dark, fragrant interior of the Clubhouse Restaurant with a crush of people, most of them coming in off the links after playing rounds of golf. I wouldn't let it ruin my day. I looked forward to hearing what Pearl had to say and to getting the reaction of the others. I liked old Pearl, and no one knew this town her great-great-grandfather had founded better than she did.

In front of me as we moved through the walnut-paneled halls, some of the town politicos chatted with the local sensation, wealthy developer Ash Mowbray, who'd apparently played a round of golf with them. Ash had one of those big, deep voices that dominate a whole room, as if the owner never learned as a child how to use his indoor voice.

"Don't tell me it's a cinch if it isn't, Harvey," he blared. "You're the mayor. You should know whether you have the votes or not."

I noticed poor old Harvey Peebles turn a sickly shade of yellow, almost the color of the big gold tie pin he always wore because it had been some award. He looked up and rushed to reassure the much-taller Ash in a smaller, more civil voice.

Behind me, someone set a gentle hand on my shoulder, and I turned directly into Terry Heldrich's chest, covered in a dark T-shirt under a battered leather bomber jacket. Immediately, I bounced away in embarrassment, brushing off his hand.

"I'm sorry," he said, looking down at me with a grin that gave the lie to his words. It lit up his dark eyes above those cheekbones other men might have paid for, if they could have. "Didn't mean to startle you. I just wanted to say hello."

His employer, Walker Lynch, swept past us imperiously in another group of golfers without a break in his conversation, even when they were directed to a table.

"Hello," I said. "You'd better catch up to your party. Your boss may want you for something."

Terry knew I didn't approve of who he worked for and what he might or might not be doing for Walker, but he kept showing up in my path anyway. I had to give him points for perseverance, if not sensitivity.

I could tell the first time we met that he was nothing but trouble for any woman, especially me. When we had to run background checks on him as part of a murder investigation, we kept coming up blank. He had a military special-forces background that was classified before he did some mercenary work that also seemed classified and then some government work that was—guess what?

He should have disappeared back to Kansas City shortly after with his wealthy employer, Walker Lynch, but to my dismay, Terry rented an apartment in Brewster and commuted to the city—like a growing number of people. Brewster was in danger of becoming just another Kansas City bedroom community and losing its charm and identity.

Annette waved at me from the bar, tall enough that I could see her red head over the crowd. I knew the shorter Miryam and Pearl must be with her.

"There's my party. I'd better be going, and so had you." I started out toward my friends.

"Skeet," Terry called as I pushed on through the crush of people in the lobby. I turned toward him. His grin had subsided into a tight-lipped smile, and his hands rested on his hips. "I'm still expecting you. To come see my new apartment. Have you lost the address?"

I shook my head. "I haven't lost your address. I wouldn't hold my breath if I were you."

He laughed out loud, throwing his head back and showing perfect teeth. "But that's the wonder of it. You are so very not me." He brushed the tip of his hat in salute, and I marched away from him to where Annette and the others stood waiting. I could feel him staring at me, a heated area between my shoulder blades where his gaze rested. He thought he was so funny—and so hot. I'd continue to ignore him, and he'd eventually take the hint and leave me alone.

"Pearl, how are you?" I asked as I reached my destination.

I learned at Gran's knee that you always greet elders first. Among the Cherokee, elders are highly respected and valued. Not the way most of American society functions. I figured when I got old, I'd better move back down to the Cherokee Nation of Oklahoma to live where I'd still count for something.

"I'm doing well, Skeet. Well enough to be sorry I haven't just played a round of golf." Pearl was only six or seven years younger than my grandmother, but like Gran, she was physically fit and active, more so than a lot of her younger colleagues. They just made women tougher in those days, I think. Pearl entered a lot of golf tournaments, where she was a prized partner because her teams usually tended to win or come in high in the running.

"Annette. Miryam. How are you guys?" I smiled at them, a little uncomfortable as they both hugged me. We're good friends, but I've never been much of a hugger or cheek-kisser. Not a lot of call for that as a police officer.

"Great, Skeet," Miryam said with a flip of her blond curls. I knew most of the male eyes in the room would be focused on Miryam, and so did she. "Looking forward to having lunch with you and hearing what Pearl wants to rope us all into now."

Pearl called over a waiter and arranged for our table. Within a few seconds, the waiter came back and led us to a table at the back of the dining room by the windows that overlooked the river, a prime location thanks to Pearl's status in town. Unfortunately, it was directly next to the big table where the politicians and Ash sat.

On the other side of Ash's table sat Bea Roberts, owner of Aunt Bea's Antiques and Collectibles, with Peter Hume, owner of Creative Home Design, and his young companion, Dante Marcus. That was a bad juxtaposition. Bea and Peter were very vocal leaders of the opposition to Ash Mowbray's plans to build a huge shopping mall (financed in large part by Walker Lynch) out by the wealthy Wickbrook neighborhood. Bea and Peter both owned shops on Brewster's courthouse square, as did Miryam, and all three believed that Ash's development would destroy the square and all its stores.

Bea had run against Harvey Peebles for mayor and barely lost to him. She was revving up for another campaign, determined to defeat him, especially after he fell right in with Ash's mall plans. Peter, who'd always seemed a quiet, laid-back guy before, had transformed into an enraged, aggressive quarreler once Ash appeared to be finding traction for his project. I knew with those two tables of enemies right next to each other, someone wouldn't have an enjoyable meal, and I was afraid it might be us.

In fact, Harvey looked downright sick as Bea and Peter glared at him, though Ash himself seemed oblivious. The two city council members with Harvey, Professor Aldo Lutz and Ian Parguenter, fidgeted and shifted in their seats, as well.

"This is my treat," said Pearl as she opened her menu. "So order something you've always wanted."

"Oh, my." Annette chuckled. "You must be planning on seducing us into a hell of a lot of work, Pearl."

We all began to consider our menus and make our choices.

"Everything's so fattening," Miryam complained.

"Nonsense! You're not a model or actress anymore. You don't have to adhere to those stupid, unhealthy diets any longer." Pearl shook her head vigorously. "Eat something so you can build muscle. Like Skeet here. You won't age well, if you don't."

Miryam opened her mouth to defend herself but was overridden by Bea's angry voice.

"You're just letting him buy this town, Harvey. Lock, stock, and barrel. What happened to your backbone? Don't estate lawyers have one? Can't you stand up to Ash Mowbray and Mr. Deep Pockets Lynch behind him? What happened to your principles? Or didn't you ever really have any to start with?"

"Now, Bea. That's uncalled for." Harvey's voice sounded almost like a bleat. "Besides, this isn't the place for that. We're not here on business. Just having lunch after a game of golf."

A waiter hovered between the two tables, making calming gestures.

"And how many of your fellow citizens did you sell out during this game of golf?" Peter demanded. "How much did they slip into your pocket to betray our interests?"

"That's just out of line, Peter," said Aldo Lutz in the voice of a professor calling a student onto the carpet. "You, too, Bea. You don't agree with the position Harvey and the rest of us are taking. You've made that clear. Honest people can disagree on the issue. But don't throw personal accusations around like that. You're verging on slander there."

"Yes," Harvey agreed in a small voice.

"Oh, it's just the old town elite carrying on in its death throes." Ash's big voice boomed out into the room. "Modern times call for modern solutions—and modern men." He grinned as he held up his hands, as if to show off himself as an example of the modern man.

"I don't like that man Walker's brought to town," muttered Miryam under her breath as the hostess decorously headed in the direction of the trouble.

"You don't have to worry about these toothless old relics, Harvey and Aldo." Ash waved his hand as if brushing away a mosquito or gnat. "Just ignore them. They'll wither away in no time. Their day is long past, and deep inside, they know it."

A wordless squeal of rage burst from Bea's mouth. I stared

as her face turned red and swelled. I wondered if she would have a stroke or heart attack on the spot.

"You! I remember you, Ashton Mowbray!" Bea's voice was loud, with a hard, mean ring to it. "Son of a drug-dealing crook and a drunken whore. A charity case all your life. We all remember who you are. White trash of the worst sort. A bad seed. You ran away from here, where people knew who you were, but you couldn't leave that behind. You still carry your dirtiness with you, no matter how much money you have now."

"What's she talking about?" I whispered to Pearl, who always knew all the gossip in town.

Pearl frowned. "Ash Mowbray grew up here, like she said. Poor. With worthless parents. The only thing he ever had going for him was his athletic prowess."

Ash's self-satisfied smirk faded as Bea's words shot out. His mouth set in a hard line. The politicians at his table all looked aghast.

"You crusty old bitch!" Ash's voice blared out so loudly that the entire dining room turned to stare. The hostess was hurrying to reach the back of the dining room now. "Don't forget, I know the secrets of this crummy town, too. I know which upstanding citizens liked a little dope from my old man or a little slap and tickle from my mom—and which old ladies liked a young boy's body in their beds after he mowed their lawns and got all hot and sweaty." Bea gasped, and her eyes widened in shock at his words. "Better keep your mouth shut, old woman, or you'll get more than you bargained for." He'd all but come out and accused Bea of seducing him when he was a kid, and everyone was staring wide-eyed.

At that moment, I'd have been glad for Joe's presence, so I

wouldn't have had to try to keep the peace. But since I'd turned him down for lunch, he wasn't around. I sighed and stood up. "None of this stuff from Bea or you does anyone any good, Ash. Let's just shut it down. You're both disturbing the peace."

"You're picking the wrong team, Skeet Bannion," Ash said in a threatening manner. "These old bigwigs are on the way down. They're crashing, and if you side with them, you'll crash with them."

"I'm not siding with anyone, Ash." I kept my voice emotionless. "I'm just trying to get all of you to settle down and let everyone else in the restaurant have a pleasant lunch. But if you and your friends would rather I call out the city cops, I can always do that."

I looked over at Harvey and his councilmen, who were shaking their heads and waving their hands wildly in negation. "That what you want me to do, Harvey?"

"No, Skeet. No! There's no need for anything like that." Harvey turned in appeal to Ash.

"We don't need any trouble just now. Right, Ash?"

Ash smiled. It transformed his whole face. "I'm not one to cause trouble, Harvey. You know that." Then he shot a suddenly hateful glance at Bea and Peter. "But if trouble comes, I'll always be the only guy who walks off the field at the end. My motto is 'Take no prisoners.' All you old-timers should remember that from my football days."

By this time, Harvey and Aldo each had one of Ash's big arms in their hands as if they seemed to be begging him to behave. It was amazing the crap people would put up with from someone with lots of money.

As the hostess arrived, breathless, Peter threw down his

napkin and stood. "If we have to sit here and be threatened by this piece of trailer trash, I'm leaving. Come on, Dante. We can find some place to eat with a higher-quality clientele."

"That's not necessary, sir," the hostess said. "I can move your table to the other side of the dining room, if this person is bothering you."

"I don't want to leave, Peter," Dante said. "And I don't want another table. I like this one with the view of the river, thank you very much."

In frustration, Peter turned to the hostess. "Why do you have to move us when this cretin is the problem?" He pointed at Ash. "Why don't you move—or remove—him?"

"Peter, you and Bea started this whole shouting match." Aldo Lutz stood now, as well. He turned to Harvey and the others. "I think we'd all better leave and find another place where we can eat in peace." Harvey and Ian Parguenter nodded and stood, shoving back their chairs.

"And sell out your fellow citizens?" Bea asked with a curled lip.

"Are you coming with us, Ash?" Harvey asked, and Ash shrugged and moved out from the table to join them.

"It's not necessary for anyone to leave," the hostess said in desperation. "We can rearrange the seating. This is a large restaurant."

"Let's go," said Ash, and the three politicos followed him toward the front door.

Miryam looked troubled as we all watched them file out of the restaurant. Her hand shook when she picked up her glass of water.

"Are you all right, sweetie?" Annette asked, as Miryam soaked up water from the tablecloth with her napkin.

Pearl smiled. "She's probably just a little stunned, that's all. So much anger. Almost a violence in the air."

Miryam nodded. "You're probably an empath like me, Pearl. I'm full of toxic energy now from that scene. That Ash Mowbray is the most hostile creature I've ever encountered. Leave it to Walker Lynch to bring such a beastly guy to town." She looked up at me. "Maybe we should leave, too, Skeet. I think I need to lie down away from all this negative influence."

Pearl seemed about to disagree when she looked at Miryam, who really did look distressed. "You don't look well, dear. I suspect you're right. It's probably put us all off our feed. We'll just reschedule and try to make sure none of those idiots battling over the mall are around when we do."

Annette stood. "That's fine, Pearl. Do you want a ride home?"

Pearl stood slowly, and I was reminded that she was almost as old as Gran. "Yes, if you don't mind. I don't really feel like walking, after all that. Isn't it amazing how emotional outbursts can take more out of you than physical exertion?"

Miryam stood as well and moved to offer Pearl a little support at her elbow.

"I'm sorry this messed up your lunch party, Pearl." I looked at the table with its menus still spread out on it.

The old woman shrugged and gave me a tight little smile. "I'll just set up another one to finagle you all into my little project. Don't worry. You won't escape me." She turned, seeming slightly more fragile than usual, and Miryam and Annette walked with her toward the door.

I couldn't blame Miryam and Pearl. All the shouting and threats left everyone unsettled, even me, and I was used to them—just not in peaceful little Brewster. Ash Mowbray obviously had some grudges against the town, and he seemed determined to cause as much trouble as he could as a way of getting a little of his own back from the town that had obviously looked down on him in his younger days. I thought of the hate in Bea's voice, the rage in Peter's, and the threat in Ash's. Ash had come back intending to stir things up apparently, and he was definitely getting his wish. A dangerous wish, it seemed to me.

CHAPTER 2

At the end of the day when Gran and Brian returned from fishing, exhausted and happy, I took us all to Pyewacket's for supper, so Gran wouldn't have to cook. We'd become spoiled since she came to live with us. I didn't think my simple beginner cooking would go down as well, now that we were used to her cooked-from-scratch meals.

On the courthouse square in Pyewacket's, surrounded by sixties album covers, movie placards, and a giant Jimi Hendrix Revolution poster, we were seated near Pearl and the Steens, the family of Angie's heartthrob. Noah Steen and Brian nodded awkwardly to each other. Noah, his mother Chelsea, and father Elliott lived across the street from Pearl, so it wasn't unusual to see them at local eateries together. The town thought they were good neighbors for taking pity on Pearl's single state. That thinking bothered me because I hate the idea that a woman alone is somehow less than whole and must be pitied. Maybe because of my own single state.

At any rate, we settled in next to a Brady Bunch poster and two vintage *Tiger Beat* magazine covers for a delicious dinner, while Brian told me the pathetic jokes with which Sid had amused him and gave a blow-by-blow account of Sid's and Gran's battle for fishing whopper supremacy. I loved seeing his old pre-in-love-with-Angie self and began to think Gran was wrong, that we had nothing to worry about.

Contented, I looked around the dining room as the tie-dyed waitress hurried off with our order, only to frown when I saw Ash Mowbray leaning over the far corner table in deep conversation with two banker types who weren't locals. As I scanned the room for Bea or Peter and came up empty, my frown faded. We shouldn't have a repeat of the earlier clash over the mall proposal.

Loud laughter came from the table where the Steens and Pearl sat. Dark-haired, broad-shouldered Noah and his slighter, sandy-haired dad were fooling around, half-wrestling in their chairs. Chelsea admonished them, but I could tell from her face she didn't really disapprove. In fact, it was the warmest look I'd ever seen on her usually reserved face. I wasn't a fan of Chelsea Montgomery Steen. A mover and shaker in Brewster with her expensive, perfectly matched wardrobe on the bony figure she exercised and dieted rigidly, I always found her a little too cold and controlling for my taste. So her obvious de-light at the silly horseplay of her husband and son was a pleas-ant surprise.

"You haven't told us how your day went, Skeet," Gran said as the waitress brought out our meals. "What did Pearl want?"

I took my bowl of spicy buffalo chili and the basket of pop-overs for the table that the waitress handed to me. Gran had ordered the special, Trinidad stewed chicken over rice, which looked and smelled so rich I almost regretted my own choice, and Brian could hardly wait to bite into his sausage-mushroom-pepper calzone.

As the waitress headed out to bring Brian another lemonade, I replied, "I'm afraid Pearl didn't get to tell us about her new project because of a big fight that erupted——"

I broke off when I heard Ash's big voice drawing near as he and his tablemates left. I didn't want him to overhear me detail his verbal brawl. With that hair-trigger temper, he might start shouting at us in front of the whole restaurant.

He passed us but stopped at the Steens' table and said something in a low voice. I hoped he was apologizing to Pearl for his earlier behavior. But it was Chelsea who shook her head impatiently in reply, without ever looking up at him. He frowned and set his hand heavily on the back of her head.

His voice rose to its usual loud volume. "Don't ignore me, Chelsea."

"Take your hand off me." Chelsea's voice, usually stony and restrained, sounded shriller than usual, surprising me. She never moved her head to glance at him.

Instead of removing his hand from her head, Ash gripped a handful of hair, pulling her head back so that she had to look up at him. "You know better than to ignore me."

That brought me to my feet, and Noah also leaped up, knocking his chair backward, but his father laid his hand on the boy's muscled arm and rose more slowly and carefully. "Ash, Chelsea told you to let go of her. You're out of bounds. Be a gentleman."

"I'm out of bounds?" Ash laughed. "You don't know anything at all about her, do you? Be a gentleman? You think I'm the one who's trash here?"

Chelsea's always unflappable face reddened. "Let go of me."

Elliott nodded and said softly, "There's no need for this kind of crude talk. Just calm down." He gestured with his hands for Noah to sit.

Ash turned his head slowly to glare at Elliott. "You'd like me to shut up, wouldn't you? What is it they call a bird that raises another bird's egg?"

Chelsea's eyes widened, and the red left her face, taking most of her normal color with it.

Elliott's face blanched. "I only want some reason and calm to prevail. It isn't good for your business to go around making scenes or harassing women."

"Don't you tell me how to run my business, you imitation of a man. Living all these years pretending my son was your very own. The town should have known when Noah turned out handsome and a football star that he couldn't have been your blood."

Ash directed an evil grin down at Chelsea's face as he released her hair. "I don't need to harass women. They come to me. Right, Chelsea? Still as sexy as when you were a hot little teenybopper. You still like to go out to that old barn outside town to get a little? Who'd you go with after I left? Because it's obvious this stick of a man couldn't keep a hot-blooded thing like you satisfied."

The last of the color fled Chelsea's face, turning it gray. Her eyes rolled up, and she slid bonelessly out of her chair to the floor with a thump that seemed loud for someone so small and thin.

"You shut your dirty mouth!" shouted Noah as he leaped to his feet again and flew across the floor at the man who'd just publicly proclaimed him illegitimate. "You don't talk about my mother and father that way, telling stinking lies."

Pearl and I both moved to help Chelsea. We picked her up off the floor easily, since she weighed hardly anything, a hollow-boned bird brought down by Ash's shot of harsh words. Elliott came around the table to take her into his arms, holding her upright.

Noah was right in Ash's grinning face with his fist cocked, ready to punch him, a younger, stronger, less dissipated version of Ash when seen so close together.

I called out. "Noah, come help with your mother. She's ill. We need to get her to the car and home. Now!"

He twisted to look and saw his father holding his mother's unconscious form. Ash threw his arm around his shoulders, and Noah hurled it off with a wild-eyed look.

By this time, Gran had joined us, and she planted herself between the two, pushing Noah in the direction of his parents and away from Ash. "Go help your dad with your mother," she said gently.

"That's not his father," Ash insisted. "I'm his father. Chelsea told me she was pregnant before I left town. All you have to do is look at the resemblance."

"Be quiet. Just stop." Gran glared at Ash, giving him the mean-eyed glance that had stopped bullies cold for generations down Tahlequah way.

Noah had reached his father and helped to support Chelsea's limp body as they headed toward the exit.

"I've come back to claim you, son," Ash called after him in his big voice, despite Gran's evilest stare. I had to admire his guts, if not his brains. "You're my son and heir. You'll have everything you could ever want."

Noah turned his head back to look at him. "Over your dead body. I'll see you in hell, you lying asshole."

Elliott murmured something to his son, and they turned back to carry Chelsea out the door.

Pearl stood next to me with a grim face. "I'm afraid he came back just to make trouble. I think this mall project is his excuse to pay off old scores. I had hopes for him when he was young, but I guess blood really does tell." She reached to take Chelsea's purse that hung from a chair back. "I'll take this to Chelsea." She shook her head. "What a nasty mess!"

"Is it true?" I asked.

Pearl shrugged. "It could be. He was a handsome boy. Noah has those same strong facial features. He actually looks a lot like Ash did then. Ash's yearbook photo could be of Noah, now that I think about it." She shook her head, as if in disbelief at her previous blindness. "Chelsea's reaction makes it seem true, doesn't it? What kind of monster deserts the mother of his child and then comes back years later to try to claim him when another man's done all the work of raising the boy? He needs to leave before he causes even more ruin than he already has.

"Elliott loves that boy, and he's done a good job raising him, no matter whose blood runs in his veins." Pearl's lips tightened into a line. "That man had better watch out. He's made threats and stirred up the whole town. Some people might not be inclined to wait calmly for him to destroy their lives."

Monday morning dawned still damp from a middle-of-the-night thunderstorm that hadn't given us as much rain as it did thunder and lightning. I was slated for a breakfast with Annette and Miryam. It seemed weird to meet at our regular time without my best friend Karen, who'd brought us all together in the first place, but Karen had been tied up for a while nursing her

Chilean shepherd back to health after he nearly died saving her life. The rest of us tried to keep the routine we'd established going, so that Karen would be able to slide right back in again when Ignacio was completely recovered, but I had to admit these mornings had lost a little of their shine for me with Karen's absence—and I suspected it was the same for Annette and Miryam.

We'd just settled in at the Herbal, taken a good breath of the mint- and anise-scented air, and ordered full, cooked-from-scratch breakfasts when Ash Mowbray walked in with Harvey, Walker Lynch, and Terry. I almost got up and walked out when I saw them. I'd had my fill of Ash Mowbray the day before and had no desire to hear him bully someone else in my town. I wondered if Walker realized what a liability he was.

By the angry look on Walker's face, I guessed he did. He seemed to be laying down the law to Ash in clipped, hushed tones as they walked past our booth to a nearby table, and I was glad to see someone doing it, even if it was my nemesis. Terry was on the job, an alert panther walking through the jungle listening and sniffing for threat, ready to deal out his own brand of danger on a second's notice. Way too dark, exotic, and lethal for little Brewster, Missouri. Maybe between them they could keep Ash in line and let me get out of here without another meal ruined by the man's temper and determination to cause trouble.

"There goes my appetite," said Miryam, losing her cheerful grin. I knew she had some dire history with Walker. I'd witnessed a confrontation between them in the summer, with Miryam terrified and Walker toying with her like a cat with its prey before it snaps it up.

"I refuse to let that creep ruin another meal," Annette

announced. "Ash Mowbray kept me from ordering something luscious at Pearl's expense yesterday. He will not mess with my breakfast this morning, or he'll face the wrath of a hungry art school dean." She made a ferocious face and curved her hands into claws, growling softly.

I laughed. "I think we're safe. It looks as if Walker and Terry have it covered."

"Oh, God! Don't look now, but Bea Roberts just walked in." Annette's hands uncurled and dropped to the table. "She's out of control about this mall. I hope she doesn't start anything again."

"Annette, you are aware that this mall project of Ash's spells death for all the courthouse square shops, including Bea's and mine, aren't you?" Miryam's voice rose higher and higher as she completed her question. "Is it so wrong for us to hate the men who're doing this to us and to want to fight them tooth and nail?" She was almost shouting.

Bea walked over and sat down with us without any acknowledgment that she was intruding and hadn't been invited. "You tell them, Miryam." Her voice was loud enough to be heard all over the coffee shop. "People don't understand the stakes and how high they are for us—and how high they are for the town. Because with the square shops gone, this won't be the same town at all."

I thought Bea was probably right about that last, and it made me sad to think of losing the distinctive qualities that made Brewster so special. But it didn't make me feel welcoming to sharp-tongued Bea as she invaded my breakfast with friends. I'm selfish. Sue me.

"Could we please not have a repeat of yesterday's brawl?" asked Annette. "I just want to eat my breakfast in peace before

I start a hellish day at work. My faculty members have the knives out for me today. I don't need to add hostility or violence to this day before it begins."

I could sympathize. Midmorning I'd be going into KC to a federal human trafficking task force meeting filled with all kinds of federal agents and high-level Kansas City cops—testosterone, aggression, and competitive one-upmanship galore. I hardly needed to begin my day with any of that.

At the thought of testosterone and aggression, I found my eyes drawn to Terry, who'd been sitting, back to the wall, dark eyes watching Walker verbally blast Ash, obviously tensed to leap up and pull Ash off his boss if Ash got violent. No fool, Terry. He could see that Ash was a guy with impulse-control issues.

At Bea's raised voice, however, Ash and Walker had stopped their argument and turned their sights onto the booth where we sat. Just what we needed—the attention of a couple of already angry, hostile men. I knew, if things got out of hand, it would fall to me to stop them and settle them down again. It was easy to stir things up when you weren't the person who'd have to deal with the resulting mess.

"You still got a problem with me, old woman?" called Ash in a threatening voice. "I've warned you, but I guess you're too dumb to figure out what's in your best interests—and what's really not."

"Don't you threaten Bea!" Miryam put her arm around Bea's shoulders, as if her soft, little blond self could protect the plump older woman. "You have no right to come into our town and make threats to our citizens. There are laws against things like that."

"Shut up, Miryam," ordered Walker. "You can't afford to get involved in this."

Miryam shrank back at his voice but replied nonetheless. "I can't afford not to get involved in this. All the money I have is invested in my bookstore. If you drive all of us on the square out of business, I lose everything."

"Then you'll just find some other rich old man to seduce money from," Walker said in a tone of contempt. "It wasn't your money in that store anyway. It was Harry's."

He leered at her. "You know you can always come to me for money."

Miryam was pressing herself against the back of the booth, as if she hoped to bore through it and disappear from Walker's sight. Her eyes were huge and horrified at his words, and she whimpered a little at his last statement.

I couldn't watch Walker toy with her until she was almost catatonic again, so I stood with a sigh.

"Let's see if we can't start over here. It's morning in a public place. Could we all calm down and go back to our own business—you all over there and us over here—and just have a meal in peace?"

"I told you, Skeet Bannion, not to try to stand against me," Ash growled. "You're choosing the wrong side."

I sharpened my own voice. "I'm not choosing any side, Ash. I'm just sick and tired of having you ruin my meals and everyone else's with your bullying and temper tantrums. This will make the third meal in a row that you've spoiled, and I'm getting sick of it."

"I'd watch out if you make Skeet mad, Ash." Terry put a slow drawl into his voice that wasn't usually there. "She carries a gun and has marksmanship medals. I understand she's an ace at hand-to-hand combat, too." He tapped his hat with a finger in salute. "Not a woman you want to piss off."

"If you think I'm afraid of you," Ash yelled at me, "you're nuts. Whatever, you're still just a woman, and I'll beat you to a pulp."

People all over the café were staring at us. Walker noticed and frowned. Harvey cringed.

"Do not physically threaten women," Terry said in a soft, quiet voice that sounded deadly. "I don't like that, Ash."

Walker indicated the door with one hand. "Get him out of here, Terry, before he does any more damage."

Terry walked over to Ash. "Let's go."

"What if I won't?" Ash asked in a belligerent tone.

"You will leave this place," Terry said in a matter-of-fact voice. "We're just negotiating whether you leave damaged or undamaged. If I were you, I'd choose the latter."

He reached for Ash's arm in a sudden movement and pinched the nerve inside the elbow.

Ash squealed and stood up. "Okay. Okay. Walker, call off your goon."

The four of them walked to the door, Ash constantly throwing glances at Terry, who walked behind him, allowing him no chance to turn and come back into the room. As they passed through the door, Terry looked back at me and winked. I rolled my eyes in irritation.

"You two just had to get Ash started, didn't you?" Annette said furiously to Miryam and Bea when the door closed behind him. "I told you I didn't need this kind of crap first thing in the morning." She threw her napkin down, stood, picked up her coffee, and headed for another table. "I'm going to eat breakfast in peace. Skeet, you can join me. No one else."

Miryam still looked like a frightened child after Walker's insults. Bea looked indignant.

"Well, thank you for the support—or lack of it." Bea flounced back into her chair, turned to Miryam, and said in a softer tone. "Thank you for yours, though. At least, someone has some guts around here."

I felt sorry for Miryam, but I'd had enough of Bea myself, so I grabbed my coffee and went to join Annette. A breakfast in peace sounded good, but I thought it was probably too late for that for any of us. I had a sour taste in my mouth as I thought of Walker and Ash and what they were doing to my town.

By the time I finally hit my office at Chouteau University that morning, word of the earlier altercations had spread through the entire population. It was one thing I disliked about the move to Brewster—the scandal grapevine. Don't get me wrong. Cops in the city can gossip with the best of them, but it's a lot easier to keep personal, off-duty business private in a sprawling metropolis. Twelve miles away in a small town, everyone knows all your business almost before it happens. I finally had to tell my secretary Mary that I didn't want to hear any more speculation about Noah's parentage or Chelsea's morals or Elliott's and Ash's comparative virility, that we had real work to do and could we please get to it?

Fortunately for the warm relationship Mary and I had developed since I came to the university, I had to leave at 10:00 A.M. with Lieutenant Gilbert Mendez for a federal task force meeting in Kansas City. Gil's my top investigator and basically my strong right hand, even though Frank Booth outranks him as a captain. Frank and I manage to get along somehow, although it didn't look like we would at first, but Gil and I are partners, a true team. I dread the day he leaves for more opportunity with KCPD or the feds, but I know it has to come sooner or later.

So why was I bringing him to the attention of the federal task force on human trafficking? Because it was so hard to prove any connection between the low-level traffickers and the wealthy and powerful businessmen who were their employers. The trail was too carefully obscured. Money was our best bet for leading us to the top guys and proving their involvement, and Gil, with his double degree in accounting and criminal justice, was an ace at tracking financial connections and collusions.

I'd attended the task force meetings alone the first few times. Then Gil accompanied me once to explain some oddities he'd encountered in his financial ferreting. He also answered other questions highly placed task force members had about the money side of the business. They requested that I bring him with me from then on.

After a contentious meeting, we left the federal courthouse conference room where the task force met, and Elizabeth Bickham, U.S. Attorney for Western Missouri, pulled me aside. I told Gil to wait in the hall.

"He's good," she said, pointing after Gil as he walked out in a group of agents—FBI, IRS, DEA, ATF—and police officers from various metropolitan departments.

I nodded glumly. "I expect one of you will snatch him away from me real soon."

Towering over me in her four-inch stilettos, Elizabeth laughed. "I don't know about that. He seems doggedly loyal to you. Ferg from IRS has already made tentative expressions of interest and gotten nowhere." She looked around to make sure everyone had left the room but the two of us and closed the door. "What progress on Walker Lynch's trail?"

I sighed. "It's a long tangled mess. We're having to untangle it one strand of money at a time, and we're still on the outer ones. I think it's going to take a while to get to any of the inner strands."

She flashed me her great photogenic smile. "It'll come, Skeet. If we can hang in there long enough." Her smile faded. "You know, before I hit high school, I knew I was going to law school and into politics. I was going to wield power to make a difference and counter all those rich people with power who stomped on most of the world."

I smiled at her and patted her thin shoulder. "And, boy, you sure have."

She gave a sigh, and her almond-shaped eyes focused on a distant point I couldn't see. "Of course, what you learn later as an adult is that, to get political power, you sometimes have to lie down with scorpions and snakes and try to get up again without being poisoned. So far, I haven't died from any of their bites. Not yet, but I know it's just a matter of time. I want to make that difference before they carry me out frothing at the mouth. I want things to be better because I was here exercising power for a time."

I frowned. "Elizabeth, is there a problem?"

"It's our old friend, Walker. Some of his political operatives have been sniffing around and talking with some of the people who are my supporters." She shook her short Afro, as if to clear her head. "It's nothing yet."

"But it's enough to worry you." I didn't like the sound of it because I knew this woman could smell shifts in the political power structure before others had any idea things were happening.

Her brilliant smile was back. She pointed a perfectly manicured finger at me. "It doesn't matter. Not if you and Gil can untangle things, and we can nail Walker and stop these trafficking ventures. If we have time to do that, it'll be long enough." Her face took on a determined look. "And I've had to lie down with vipers before. I've got enough poison in my system to keep me immune for a while at least. Got some fangs of my own, too, if they don't watch out."

I wished there were some way I could defend her against attack, but when it came to politics, I was pretty damn helpless. "What can I do?"

"Just keep at it, Skeet." She laid her long, strong hand on my back. "Don't give up. Help me put him away."

"That's a given." I wanted to do more to keep her where she was doing so much good.

She put a finger alongside her nose. "And no worried look when I open the door and we go out. We need to be laughing like we were engaging in girl talk."

I pasted a smile on my face, and she threw her head back, loudly hooting with laughter. It was such a goofy, happy sound that it made my smile genuine, and when she opened the door to the hall where all those guys were still gathered in paranoid clusters, we did look as if we'd just been giggling and telling dirty jokes about them.

I gathered up Gil and headed for the car. Then we drove through bright, warm sun south to Gil's favorite restaurant, which had become our accustomed lunch place on task force days. I'd worried the first time he directed me there. Chelly's Cafe is in south Kansas City on Eighty-fifth Street, on the outskirts of the inner city before you hit the suburbs, and I was used to looking for good Mexican food much farther north on Southwest Boulevard and elsewhere on the Westside. But Gil kept saying, "It'll be worth the drive. You'll love the food." And he'd been right.

When we walked into Chelly's brightly colored interior, the owners, Norma and Ruben Campos, called out an enthusiastic greeting from their positions at the bar. Norma was mixing a margarita for some lucky person, and Ruben had been going over some papers with her. After our exchange of greetings, he vanished shyly back into the kitchen. We followed Norma to our booth and settled in with the menu.

"Those task force meetings always leave me starving," Gil said with an uneasy laugh. "I'm going to get carnitas. I need meat after being with the carnivores. All those big city cops and agents are pretty hard-core, aren't they?"

I smiled. "You'll get used to it. They're all basically lone wolves, but they can cooperate when they're hunting. And this time they're hunting really big prey. That should keep them from going after each other's throats, at least for a while."

He dropped his eyes when I spoke about them going for each other's throats. "What are you getting?"

"I'm trying to decide between the sopes and the tomatillo chicken. They were both so good, and you can't get them anywhere else that I know of." I shook my head at my indecision. "But I think I'll do the tomatillo chicken today."

"Good choice." He took a sip of his soda and looked around at the walls, one of hot pink, one of rich orange, one of purple, and one of lemon yellow, then up at the deep blue of the ceiling. He rested his eyes on the ceiling for a second or two. I could tell something was troubling him.

When he looked back at me, it was to ask, "How did you do it? Work all those years with those guys with their huge, screaming egos? Man, even their jokes had razor-sharp edges."

I shrugged slightly. "It wasn't easy at first, but I had an advantage. I'd grown up with one of them, a failed version, it's true, but just as competitive and domineering. You get used to it. You can't give way to that kind. Not ever. You always have to stand up to them, even on the little stuff. If you don't, they lose respect for you and try to steamroll right over you.'

His face fell. "Sounds exhausting."

"It is. Stressful and exhausting. But you can't get them to act any other way because they're too afraid to lose that predatory edge they've worked so hard to develop." I looked directly at him without saying anything for a second. "They are the best at what they do. Currently. But there are women and men coming up who've chosen not to put on that armor that leaves you and everyone around you sliced to shreds, and they're becoming the new best."

He tried to laugh. "I can see why you came to Brewster and Chouteau U. Frank should have to go sit in meetings with those guys. He thinks he's such a tough guy. Let him see how it's really done."

I did laugh, loud and long. Before I could reply, our food arrived, and we tucked in to our lunch.

"Think we'll get him?" Gil asked after a few minutes. "Walker Lynch."

I sighed and set down my fork. "That's why we brought you on board, so that we can finally prove what some of us believe—that Walker's behind this huge trafficking venture. These guys are the best. They'll bring you hints and clues to send your investigations in the right direction, and eventually, yes, we will shut him down. You're an ace at what you do, too, Gil. That's what I think."

I turned back to my green-sauce-covered chicken and

savored the delicate flavor of the sauce and the tenderness of the meat. I hoped to hell my little pep talk would turn out to be true. I wanted Walker Lynch out of business and behind bars. He was a dangerous and corrupt man, a true sociopath. I worried about how far he would go. I worried about having defenseless people vulnerable to him and what horrors that temptation might lead him into.

And now he'd brought Ash Mowbray back into Brewster and was stirring up huge trouble there. I had a bad feeling about that whole situation.

So I wasn't happy later that afternoon when Mary ushered Chelsea into my office with the look of a saint escorting a leper. "You have time to talk to Chelsea, don't you, Skeet?"

I frowned at this breach of our usual procedure, established in my first days in the position. No one was to come in without Mary checking with me first to make sure I wasn't busy or on the phone or sitting with confidential documents spread around on my desk. The feds are bugs about student confidentiality, and a lot of what I deal with impacts student information that's classified.

"I'm sorry," Chelsea said. "I'll just take a little of your time, I promise."

"Of course. Have a seat. Mary, would you please see that we're not disturbed?" I swiped the papers off my desk and stuffed them into the empty top drawer I keep for just that purpose.

"Sure, Skeet." Mary turned to Chelsea and paused for a second. "I'll be praying for you and your family," she said in a rush and hurried out of the room, inadvertently slamming the door.

I closed my eyes in frustration for a second. Mary was an

excellent secretary, but she was also president of the Women's Missionary Union of the Brewster Baptist Church. "I'm sorry about that, Chelsea."

Chelsea sat, as exquisitely controlled as ever. "Mary means well. At least she sees me as a victim as much as a slut, and that's more than most in town are willing to do. Especially when I'm driving Noah's bright green, loud jalopy today while mine's in the shop. I suspect some people think I'm advertising." She gave me a sardonic smile.

"Surely not?" I shook my head as the words left my mouth. "Stupid of me. Of course, people jump to the worst conclusions. I'm sorry. It has to be ghastly."

Chelsea's lips tightened the tiniest bit at the corners for less than a second. It was so minute and fleeting I wouldn't have noticed it if I hadn't been trained in observation and reading facial expressions. "It is what it is." Her voice was unemotional, and I wondered what she'd had to sacrifice for that control—and what had driven her to it.

"What can I do for you then?" I asked, relieved that I wasn't expected to make her feel better, something usually expected of women, at which I sucked.

"Give me your best professional advice." She folded her hands together on my desk and leaned slightly forward. "I've been the victim of a kind of crime, and I don't know if I should report it or if that's something I'd regret. I'd like you to tell me what would happen if I reported it."

"In general, I strongly urge victims to report crimes and press charges." I leaned forward myself. "If you don't, it strengthens the hands of criminals."

"A sentiment with which I happen to agree, usually," she said, "but this situation is a little more complex."

Aren't they all? I wanted to say but didn't. "You really should be talking to Joe Louzon, you know? I don't have any jurisdiction over things that don't happen on the campus, and I imagine this didn't happen here at the university, did it?"

"No, but I'd rather not talk about this to Joe." She hesitated slightly. "I've not found him the most sensitive or . . . insightful person."

I remembered hearing that she and Joe had disagreed over some civic situation just before I moved to Brewster. Couldn't remember what it was. Not sure I ever knew.

"But why come to me?" I was genuinely puzzled.

"Angie." She smiled slightly. "We see a lot of her now that she and Noah are dating, and she's always singing your praises."

I choked a little. "Angie? Sing my praises? I think you must have misunderstood."

She shook her head. "Not at all. She says you're the bravest, smartest police officer around. She even calls you Supercop."

I snorted. "She doesn't intend that as a compliment, believe me. Angie really doesn't care much for me."

She shook her head just slightly, every movement controlled. "You're wrong. She does. You saved her life."

I shrugged. "Any cop would have done that in that situation. She just doesn't realize that."

"Nonetheless, that's why I've come to you. Angie has had a difficult life. You know that. She's had to learn to watch and judge people. I trust her judgment of you." She nodded in a definitive motion as if there was to be no more argument on the topic.

"Okay. Tell me about this crime."

She hesitated. She obviously didn't want to speak of it to

anyone. This didn't surprise me. People either wanted to tell everyone around them they'd been victimized and repeat the details ad nauseam, or they didn't want to put it in words to anyone ever. I watched her in silence, knowing that, with most people, this would prompt them to start pouring out the words.

Her one hand tightened slightly on the other as the silence stretched out second after second.

"Ash Mowbray's been blackmailing me ever since he showed up in Brewster," she said calmly. "He's been threatening to tell my son about his true parentage."

I tried to keep my expression steady, showing no surprise. "And now he has. Even though you paid him what he asked?"

"Yes. Much as I hated it." Her voice remained cool, detached from what she was saying.

I nodded. "It's always a bad idea. Blackmailers either bleed you dry eventually and go public, or they go ahead and make good on their threats even if you continue to pay. All part of the personality type that goes in for blackmail."

"I don't want him to get away with it," she said with a little more emotion than usual. I figured for Chelsea that was close to a scream of rage.

"Report him and file charges." I spread my hands wide above the desk. "Once it goes to trial and he's found guilty, not only will he face jail time, but you'll also be able to file to recover the money from him. Punishment and restitution both."

She gave me a tiny bitter smile. "It wasn't money he demanded. I'll never get back what he took from me."

I froze, staring at her expensively highlighted hair and her perfectly made-up face, and wondered what emotions they hid. "Sex, I suppose?"

"What else? He hardly has the imagination to want anything but sex and money." She'd regained total control over her voice and face, but I know you don't experience forced sex without serious emotional damage. I wondered what would happen when she couldn't shove the memory down and contain it any longer.

I shook my head. "It sounded like he wants your son."

"No, he'll never lay his hands on Noah. I won't allow that. Ever." Her voice turned to ice.

I looked at her with skepticism. "If he's Noah's father—"

"Elliott is listed as Noah's father on the birth certificate. That means he is legally Noah's father, and Ash has no power over my son." Her voice took on the slightest shrill edge that again signaled to me the emotion beneath that disciplined façade.

"What if he takes you to court, and DNA evidence shows his paternity? The courts will take that into consideration."

Color fled her face, and I worried that she might faint again. She'd obviously not considered that Ash might demand DNA testing. Her hands unfolded and then clenched into fists on top of my desk. "I won't allow him to do that."

I shook my head slightly. She was fooling herself. She didn't have the power to stop it. Ash was rolling in money and could afford a slick lawyer, who'd immediately see that DNA was the way to go.

"Well, what he did to you will probably be considered sexual assault because he was threatening you, even if it wasn't a physical threat," I said, trying to get back to our original topic. "The district attorney's office would have to decide for sure, but I think it's likely. It's actually a much more serious crime than blackmail for money. I recommend that you report him immediately and file charges. Don't let him get away with it."

She smiled tightly. "Don't worry. Whatever happens, that man isn't going to get away with anything. He's going to pay."

The buzz of the intercom interrupted us.

"What, Mary?" I asked impatiently.

"Chelsea's son is out here with Angie and Brian." Mary sounded rattled. She did better when the day's events fell into a smooth routine. Don't we all?

"Oh, I'm driving his car today," Chelsea explained. "I told him I'd be here and he should meet me."

I nodded. "Send them on in, Mary."

A few seconds later, Brian came through the door, followed by Angie and Noah. The change in handsome Noah was shocking. Obviously, he hadn't slept in the night just past, but the dark circles under his eyes should have taken weeks of sleepless nights to create. His skin, always a golden tan, looked faded and loose on his facial bones. He looked like an ad for that old movie *The Lost Weekend*.

"Hey, Supercop," Angie said with casual scorn. Because of what Chelsea had said, I wondered for a second if I could be wrong about Angie's attitude toward me, but her tone of voice made it all too clear that I wasn't.

"Skeet, was it okay? All of us coming to the office this way?" At least Brian took my job seriously.

I gave him a big smile and nodded. "As long as you guys don't decide to spray graffiti on the walls."

He grinned back at me. I noticed his T-shirt was getting too tight in the shoulders. We'd have to take a shopping trip this weekend.

"What's up, Noah?" I asked, trying to keep the tone of the

conversation light. "I thought you had football practice after school. Did coach cancel, or are you playing hooky?"

If he had been, the football coach would've turned a blind eye. Noah was widely viewed (in our part of the state, certainly) as the best high school quarterback in Missouri. Universities were already scouting him.

"I'm not on the football team any longer," he said. "I quit today. Who wants to be one of those idiots anyway?"

"What—?" Chelsea started to ask.

"Jimbo Garns said some stupid shit in the lunchroom," Angie explained, naming the second-string quarterback.

"Everyone started laughing and pointing," Noah said in a numb voice. "Whispering about the crap that Mowbray creep said."

"It wasn't everybody." Angie slid her hand up and down his arm soothingly. "Besides, Brian gave that stupid Jimbo something to suck on. When he finished, everyone was laughing. But at Jimbo. Not at you, Noah."

Brian blushed slightly, and I gave him a nod of approval.

Noah nodded, too. "Yeah, that was great, Bri. I appreciate you having my back that way. It was pretty ace the way you destroyed him. But it was like that all day, every class. And the guys from the team, the ones I should have been able to count on to back me up—they were some of the worst. If I'd heard any more of that, I was going to hurt someone and get kicked out of school forever. So why should I knock myself out? Let them go win games without me."

Chelsea looked deathly ill. "But you love football."

"Not anymore, I don't." Noah shook his head firmly to convince her.

"They'll be back crawling, begging your forgiveness, when

they realize they can't win without you." Angie gave his shoulders a quick hug. "You'll see."

As Brian watched Angie hug Noah, his face fell into such a sad look that I almost cried out in protest. He turned aside for a second.

"Oh, Noah, I'm so sorry," Chelsea said softly.

"Don't worry, Mom. Haven't you been reading all that stuff about concussions to me lately? I think I'd rather grow up with all my brain cells functioning anyway." He reached out a gentle hand to stroke her hair and forced a smile on his face. "It's just a game. It doesn't matter."

"But it does. To you. I know it does." She turned away from all of us.

"No, Mom. It doesn't. Not really." He moved up behind her to put his arms around her tiny body. "You matter to me. You and Dad and what that son of a bitch is doing to both of you." His jaw tightened, and the tendons in his neck bulged with tension. "Death isn't good enough for him. He's the kind of person torture was created for." He rested his chin on her head. "We'll get through this. Together."

Brian had moved closer to me while Noah spoke, and Angie looked forlorn since Noah had left her side to go to his mother. His gentleness toward his mother surprised me. I'd always seen him as the quintessential homecoming king, handsome, athletically gifted, reasonably smart, but essentially shallow. I could see I'd have to reassess.

Chelsea made no sound or movement that I could tell, but Noah saw or felt something. "Are you crying, Mom? Don't cry. I've never seen you cry before. Ever. Oh, Mom." He wrapped his arms tighter around her until she disappeared behind his bigger body.

The rest of us felt awkward and embarrassed, witnessing what should have been private grief. Someone needed to do something, and I supposed it needed to be me since I was the grown-up among us. The problem was that I didn't really know what to do. Part of me felt that probably the best thing that tightly controlled woman could do was cry out some of her pain, but I knew how I hated to lose control and cry. I knew I'd want someone to give me a way to stop and get out of there to someplace where no one else could see or hear.

"Noah, why don't you run your mom home?" I finally said. "It's been a long day for everyone. I can take Brian and Angie."

Angie opened her mouth to protest, but I frowned at her and shook my head, and Brian leaned over to whisper in her ear. She didn't look any happier, but she closed her mouth.

Noah looked back at me. "Yeah, I'll do that. Thanks, Skeet." He turned back to Chelsea. "Let's go home, Mom."

When Chelsea turned to leave, no trace of tears showed on her face. Her makeup was still immaculate. But her skin was grayer and looser, as if she'd instantly lost more weight, and she had lines that weren't there when she sat down across the desk from me.

"Thank you, Skeet, for your advice," she said in a formal voice. I sensed that would be her preferred way of dealing with me from now on—formality.

They walked out of my office, with Noah's strong arm wrapped around her shoulders. I suspected it was the only thing, other than her own will of steel, keeping her on her feet. I tried desperately to send a telepathic order to Mary not to say anything to them.

Mary's voice proved I had absolutely no psychic powers.

"I'm praying for you, Chelsea, and for your family. We all are at church."

The only reply was an inarticulate growl of rage from Noah as they passed out of the department.

CHAPTER 3

The next day was Tuesday, and I was determined to get back on track with my routine, which had been thrown off by Sunday's and Monday's dealings with Ash Mowbray and the fallout from his activities. So I was out at River Walk Park at first light for my usual solitary run alongside the river's hushed rippling. Only a few feet into my run, though, I encountered something I'd never expected to see—Miryam awake early in the morning and outside in the natural world.

A small, huddled figure, she sat on a wooden bench at the edge of the river, and she looked distraught, her blond curls disheveled, face oddly barren of makeup. I left the running path and walked over to her as a train moaned in the distance.

"Miryam, what's up?"

She turned with a start and relaxed when she saw it was only me. "You scared me. I didn't think anyone else would be out here this early."

"Why are you out here? It's not exactly your thing." I waved a hand to include the whole outdoor scene. A couple of eagles were floating in the air on the other side of the broad river, looking for prey or just enjoying the thermals that kept them aloft with little effort. "And it's not exactly your time, either."

She gave a sad, little laugh. "I'm not famous for my early rising, for sure." Then she stared out across the river into some spot of infinity she seemed to find.

I sat down on the bench beside her. "Trouble sleeping?"

She nodded. "It's fear keeping me awake. I know that. Fear of losing everything I have if this mall goes through. Even more, fear of Walker Lynch." She turned to me suddenly. "Why is he still hanging around Brewster, Skeet? Why did his henchman, that Terry, move into an apartment here? Why can't I be free of him?"

"I think Walker hangs around because Liz Richar is still here." I smiled at her, trying to calm her. "They've got some kind of thing going, and I think they're grooming Randy to marry her and make him the next attorney general or governor or something like that."

Liz was Angie's nasty stepmother, and Randy Thorsson was a state senator who used to be our incompetent district attorney. The idea of him holding any high-level political office was ludicrous, but he seemed to be achieving it.

She peered into my eyes. "But why would Terry Heldrich move here to live and commute into the city?"

I felt my face grow warm. "I think he just fell in love with the town. Lots of folks are moving here and still working at their jobs in KC."

She frowned and shook her head in disbelief. I'd have to come up with a better answer for why Terry was here—without mentioning that it might have something to do with me. "Why do you think Walker and Terry are still here?"

"I'm afraid to even think about it." She shuddered. "Walker's such a bad man, Skeet. Stay away from him and anyone that's part of his empire. He seems smooth and charming, but there are sharp teeth behind all that. He's bad, and a bad man with lots of money is just hell." She wrapped her arms around herself, as if she was suddenly cold.

I reached out to her but stopped my hand short of touching to reassure her. "Miryam, what has he done to you? I can tell he's hurt you in some way, and you're terrified of him. What happened? How can I help?"

She shook her head, making the curls that drew so many men's eyes fly. "You can't. There's nothing anyone can do."

I tried to think of something to say to ease her fears. "If it's any consolation, I don't think he's coming around so much because you're here. I really do think it's Liz and their political plans. I think they want to control all the top politicos in Missouri before they're through."

She scowled. "Oh, yeah. More power. Just what that bastard needs."

The train that had been in the distance now roared and clacked through the heart of the town, hooting to warn away any early risers out on the roads. Two crows in a tree to our left began to call out to each other in harsh voices.

"I would do anything, legal or not, to make Walker Lynch leave this town," Miryam swore, staring out again at that nowhere spot beyond the river. "I just don't have any idea what I could do." She looked back at me again with anguished eyes. "I hate to be so helpless around someone so powerful and vicious."

I patted her shoulder lightly. "You need to go home and get some sleep, instead of sitting out here making the horrors bigger than they have to be. Joe's a good cop, and he's not going to let Walker do anything to you. And neither will I. When Walker gets tired of Liz or his political games, he'll stay back in KC and we won't see him around here anymore."

"Not if Ash Mowbray has his way and they start this mall. We'll be stuck with beastly Ash and monstrous Walker for a long time."

I had to admit she had a point.

She looked at me with her pretty chin stiff and her jaw rigid. "I can't let that happen. I have to stop it somehow."

"Go home, Miryam. Drink some hot cocoa and get some much-needed sleep."

She nodded and stood up from the bench, and I joined her. "Thanks for listening to me. I think I might try to go to bed again."

We hugged, and I watched her walk back to her car. Somehow I felt I needed to make sure nothing bad happened to her on that walk. Probably just the screwy things we'd been talking about.

As she drove off, I waved and began my run again, this time with a head full of questions about Walker Lynch and Ash Mowbray. Why was Miryam so terrified of Walker? What had he done to her?

That evening I drove home from work with a different worry. The city council meeting on Mowbray's mall-development proposal was scheduled for early evening, and I worried about what it would do to young Noah Steen who'd seen his whole world brought down in ruins and very public shame.

I'd told Brian I was proud of him for standing up for Noah the day before. It was strange to see him suddenly on the same side with Noah, who'd been his rival for Angie hours before.

My boy had a strong sense of justice and empathy for the underdog.

Knowing that, I should have been prepared when Brian and Angie both greeted me as I pulled up at the house in my Crown Vic after work, the sound of another train disappearing in the distance of another unusually warm autumn day. Not that it was uncommon for Angie to join Brian, but they immediately made it clear they had an agenda as they followed me to the front porch.

"The city council's meeting on that mall thing today," Brian said with no preamble. "We need to go to that."

"Oh, no," I replied. "That's going to be a fiasco. I wouldn't be surprised if it turned into a slugfest. Feeling's running so high on that issue."

"Ought to be better than a movie with all that fighting and scandal going on," added Gran, as she joined us on the porch, drying her hands on a dishtowel tucked into her belt. Unlike the stereotype of grannies in long skirts and lace collars, mine was usually found in jeans and flannel shirts.

I widened my eyes and shook my head at her, trying to get across that this was a bad idea.

"That's why we have to go, Skeet," cried Angie. "Noah's going to support his parents, who have to be there. Everyone expects them, and Noah says if they don't show everyone will think they're too ashamed. Noah says they've got to go to this if they ever want to hold up their heads in this town again, and he's not going to let them face it alone."

"Good boy," said Gran.

"We're not going to let him face it alone," said Brian, though he didn't look happy about it.

I found myself wondering if he really hoped I would make them stay here, but before I could decide, Gran pulled the dishtowel from her belt and hung it on one of the wicker chairs on the front porch.

"Well, let's go then." She headed toward the car, with both kids trailing behind.

I rolled my eyes and locked the front door before hurrying back to the car to chauffeur idealistic kids and scandalmongering grandmother to our little town's version of the Roman forum. I had a bad feeling about this whole thing.

By the time we arrived, the place was packed. Usually no one showed for city council meetings unless there was some contentious issue under discussion—like trash pickup or a sales tax to support a new animal shelter. Then, you might get ten or twelve citizens. This time, it looked like everyone in town, except the college students, had shoved their way into the boxlike municipal building that held the council chambers and mayor's and city treasurer's offices, as well as the police department and the department of public works.

I would have been happy to stand in the hall outside the council chambers until Brian and Angie got tired of it and decided to go home, but Gran was in the lead and shoved her way through the doorway. I had to elbow my way through the cluster of people filling the door frame to follow and make sure she'd be all right—and that she didn't hurt anyone if they gave her any trouble.

Just past the door area, the crowd thinned out. I could see a few empty chairs down near the front, and Gran was heading for them. Harvey Peebles introduced Ash as I followed Gran to the seats next to Bea Roberts.

"Ashton Mowbray has come back to his hometown to invest money and provide jobs. He's here to tell you all about it and answer any questions. Let's give him a hand."

A sparse handful of the audience loudly applauded while

53

Harvey shook Ash's hand and turned the podium over to him. Others hissed, and Peter Hume loudly booed from where he sat with his lover, Dante Marcus, at the end of our row. Ash grinned at Peter as if he'd given him a standing ovation. He looked as if he was having fun while all the faces around him, supporters and detractors alike, showed nervous or furious expressions.

"Thank you all for coming out today," he began. "As I explained in the interview that ran on the front page of the *Brewster Mercury*, this project will create a hundred and twenty jobs in Brewster and bring in three hundred and forty-seven thousand dollars annually for the school district and one hundred and thirty-nine thousand a year to city and county coffers. It will be a major addition to the city infrastructure and will draw other new income—"

"Lies! All lies!" cried Peter, standing and shaking a fist at Ash before he turned to face the audience. "Ask him how many jobs and tax dollars we'll lose when all the courthouse square stores have to close. And those tax dollars from store owners on the square are all paid into the city budget, not with hundreds of thousands forgiven or deferred for decades through this tax increment financing."

A clamor sprang up in the room while Harvey picked up his gavel and knocked it against the table in a futile effort to silence the protest. "Peter, you're out of order."

Peter paid no attention. "Harvey, we know this isn't a problem for you. You're a lawyer and your clients are mostly dead people anyway." Harvey was an estate lawyer who specialized in estate administration. "But you're the whole town's mayor and you should be thinking of what this will mean to the courthouse square shop owners and to the town itself."

Dante grabbed at his shirtsleeve, trying to get him to sit,

but Peter ignored him. "And when those courthouse square shops are closed and shuttered, what will this town have to offer anyone who drives out here but another shopping mall with big-box stores like all the malls in all the suburbs all around KC? People come here for the wildlife refuge and the quaint small-town atmosphere. There won't be any of that left if Ash Mowbray and Walker Lynch have their way with this town. I'll bet those income numbers are based on what we're doing now with tourists and day-trippers. We'll lose them if this goes through, and what will the real numbers be then?"

"Afraid you'll lose your handsome young stud if you lose your business and your money, Pete?" Ash heckled, as if he didn't see Harvey trying to calm the situation down. It seemed Pearl was right about him caring more for settling old grievances than building his and Walker's mall.

Peter clenched his fists and glared at Mowbray as Dante hauled him back into his chair. At the same time, Bea leaped to her feet on the other side of Peter.

She turned to face the crowd behind us and shouted, "If we allow this aging delinquent who's nothing but a front man for Walker Lynch, a big Kansas City developer, to destroy the courthouse square, it will change us from the town we all know and love into nothing but another suburb of Kansas City, just another piece of KC sprawl. Is that what we want to do with our town? I know I don't!"

Harvey hammered his gavel harder and faster as if that would stop the storm of angry voices that had swept over the room. Neighbors argued with neighbors in clumps all over the council chamber, and the members of the council on the dais looked frustrated and distressed, no matter which side of the issue they favored.

"Stop this! Right now!" A piercing voice screeched out over the noise, the kind of voice you can hear over everyone else in a noisy restaurant.

The room grew quiet for a second, everyone too shocked to speak. Then Chelsea walked to the front. Noah's mother had been one of the most influential people in town, following in the footsteps of her parents—before Ash's revelation at Pyewacket's on Sunday. I wasn't sure how much clout she still carried. She wore a plain black dress that was too simple and ordinary for Chelsea, probably the closest thing to sackcloth and ashes her expensive closet contained.

When she turned her back on the dais and Ash to speak to us, her voice dropped half an octave but retained its carrying quality. "The question goes beyond a matter of jobs and taxes. The real question is what kind of a town are we? What kind of town do we want to be? And what kind of town do we not ever want to turn into? It's that simple, and we have to live with what we decide."

Ash dropped his happy act and glared at her. "You think people will still do what you tell them, Chelsea, like they did with your folks? Not anymore. Not when they know you're not so high class but just another slut."

Chelsea never moved or wavered. Two bright spots of red appeared on her cheeks but didn't go any further across her face. She stood before us, head high, immovable. I still wasn't sure I liked her, but I had to admire her courage and class.

Noah raced forward, with Elliott right behind him. Elliott caught his son's arms and pulled him back before he could leap up and attack Ash. Angie and Brian ran over to Noah's side and took his arms from his father, trying to calm him.

Elliott walked over to Chelsea, facing her and, above her,

Mowbray. "Ash, you need to leave these personal attacks out. Chelsea hasn't said a thing about you. She's only spoken about the town's need to consider what it chooses to become."

"And just what'll you do if I don't, little man?" Ash laughed unpleasantly.

"If you don't leave my family alone, you may find out to your regret just how far I'll go to protect them," Elliott said slowly and a little solemnly.

It should have sounded pathetic, coming from a fair, slight, older businessman in a suit and tie with no more heat in his voice than if he discussed insurance plans, but somehow it wasn't. There was something chilling about the low-key, determined way Elliott made his threat. I found myself wanting Ash to back off and let everything and everyone calm down before he forced Elliott into anything. Because, I realized, Elliott wouldn't bluster or rage, but he'd do whatever he believed he had to do to protect his family.

Ash snickered and waved Elliott away, as if he was less than nothing, a fly or a gnat. Behind him, I saw Walker Lynch grimace and lean over to speak into Harvey's ear. He didn't look happy with his front man. That didn't surprise me. I disliked Walker immensely, but I knew he wasn't stupid.

"It doesn't matter what he says about when I was a teenager," Chelsea said firmly, looking out over the crowd, still. "As citizens, we have to decide what kind of town we choose to live in. And we will have a long time to live with that choice. That's what we should be discussing. What kind of lives do we want to have here in Brewster? That's what we're here to decide."

The red spots faded from her cheeks as she stared out at us with a challenging look. As her steely blue eyes passed over the crowd, all the voices died down. I had never seen someone hold a crowd's attention and mold its mood with such control.

Ash opened his mouth, but before he could say anything, Harvey and Terry Heldrich were on either side of him. Harvey leaned into the microphone, as Terry pulled Mowbray back from the podium. The developer looked as if he might try to struggle against Terry, but one look at the dangerous expression on Terry's face, and he subsided. I knew I wouldn't want to take on Terry when he wore that businesslike look that said violence was his business.

"And it's good to ask ourselves questions," Harvey said with a slight quaver in his voice. "Thank you, Chelsea. In light of the high feeling in the room, I'm going to close this meeting. We'll reschedule for another day and hope we can have a more civilized discussion."

Voices began to protest behind us, and Joe Louzon moved toward the front of the room as a couple of his officers fanned out among the crowd to keep things under control. I wondered where they'd been earlier when things had grown so rowdy. It wasn't like Joe to let things get so out of hand. The complaints began to die down, and the council members vacated the dais more rapidly than I'd ever seen them move before. Bea caught Harvey by the end of his tie and and his big tie pin, holding him as she harangued him and others gathered around until Joe broke them up and freed Harvey from Bea's angry grasp.

"That's okay," said an indignant voice in my ear. "Chelsea's words will be the last they remember. They'll go on thinking about them. What a class act!"

I turned my head to find Pearl Brewster leaning over the back of my chair. "Pearl. Where were you?"

She straightened and gestured to the back of the room. "I was sitting with the Steens. I rode in with them."

I nodded. "I was surprised not to hear you add your opinion. I'm sure you have one."

The older woman shook her head. "No need. Bea and Chelsea said everything I'd have wanted to say. Except don't trust that big son of a bitch."

I was surprised to hear her swear. I'd never heard Pearl utter any cussword before. "I gather you really don't like Ash."

She shrugged. "I used to have hope for him when he was a kid. I even contributed a little money when he was raising some to leave town and take a football scholarship he'd been offered. Never knowing he'd gotten poor Chelsea pregnant and just dumped her." She sighed. "No good deed goes unpunished."

"I wouldn't say that," Gran added, leaning into our conversation. "The good you do creates more good. So does the wrong. Sometimes we just can't take a long enough view to see it, though."

"I don't think there's a long enough view to make this come out right," Pearl said, with an edge of irritation in her voice. "If I'd known that then, I'd never have helped him escape his responsibilities to that poor girl."

"And she'd have had a much worse husband than she's had and the boy a terrible father," Gran said matter-of-factly. "Helping him get away was probably the best thing you could have done for her and her baby."

Pearl frowned. I changed the subject quickly. I was used to folks not seeing things the same way Gran did. She looked at the world through a different tradition, and though I liked that tradition better than the world's, I knew the world thought it was cockeyed.

"I think we'd better go help Angie and Brian calm down poor Noah. Excuse us please, Pearl."

Pearl nodded as we slid out of the row to where the kids still held Noah's arms.

"Man, it's not worth it, Noah," Brian said. "That guy's just trying to make trouble. It's what he wants."

"Bri's right," Angie said, patting the arm she held gently. "Don't let him get to you. See how strong your parents are being. That's pissing him off. Give him some more of that. Be strong and unreachable. Drive him crazy."

Noah had stopped straining and struggling. I thought their holds on his arms were more for reassurance at this point than anything.

"That asshole," he said in a voice that rang out as the noise was dying down. I saw heads turning our way. "I ought to kill him. For what he called my mom. For what he did to her. For what he said to my dad. He needs to be dead."

"Don't do anything stupid!" Angie cried. "Don't be what he wants you to be."

"Don't worry. I'm nothing like him. No matter what he says." Noah looked at his parents who still stood facing each other as the crowd broke and flowed around them. They could have been two statues turned to stone. He pointed to them. "That's my dad. That's who I'm like. Not that freak."

"That's right," Gran said. "By your age, you choose who you'll be, what pattern you'll follow in life. And you've chosen a good one there. Stick with it."

Noah looked at her in surprise, then nodded abruptly. He peeled off Brian's and Angie's hands. "I gotta go see to my parents. This is hard on them."

He walked off toward Chelsea and Elliott, leaving Angie reaching out after him and Brian staring at her before shaking his head and turning away.

"Okay, let's go home," I said. "Enough drama. Who's up for pizza?"

Brian grinned. He lost his grin as he turned to Angie. "What do you say? You want some pizza?"

Angie still stared after Noah. "Sure, sure. I guess." She turned back to Brian and gave him a weak smile.

"Great. Let's go then." I ushered them toward the back of the room and wondered if Brian and Angie weren't both going to get their hearts broken. It was clear that all three of the Steens had already had theirs smashed. Love silently wreaking havoc again. I wished I could bust old Cupid in the chops, but I'd found out long ago that the only thing to do when faced with him was to run as fast as I could in the other direction.

I rose at my usual early hour and left the house to greet the dawn and run along the River Walk through the park between the golf course and the Missouri River. Years of growing up and going out with Gran to see the sun rise and watch her make her morning offerings to the four directions had left me an early riser, even when I didn't have to be.

I hadn't had a good night. Too much trouble witnessed in the evening. I looked forward to my morning run to clear my head and set me on course for the day. I'd run my circuit and then sit watching the water move past until my thoughts and mood were cleansed. *Oldest medicine in the world*, Gran said.

I parked in the lot at the entrance to the park and got out to start stretching before I set out. Joe's cruiser pulled up beside mine, and he got out, dressed in running shorts, T-shirt, and athletic shoes. I'd never seen him dressed like that in the almost two years I'd known him. Joe wasn't a runner. Not his style.

"What are you doing here?" I asked with a sinking feeling that he was there because he knew I would be.

"Thought I'd join you for a run," he said with a deliberately casual manner. "I need to do something like this for exercise."

What could I say or do? I shrugged and kept on stretching. I'd leave him in the dust early on, and that would put an end to the whole plan. He stood awkwardly, shifting from foot to foot, obviously uncomfortable in the skimpy shorts, watching me stretch, while a train thundered through the heart of town, whistling and hooting.

I took off and left the parking lot for the River Walk at a slow pace, Joe right by my side. He started to say something, and I held up my hand. "Don't talk. Run."

I slowly increased my pace as I always did, and at first he kept up with me, but I could tell he was having trouble with his breathing as I moved faster and faster. I figured he'd drop behind pretty soon and I'd have my morning run to myself the way I liked it. We were running past the golf course at that point when something caught my eye and made me slow down to take a better look.

It looked like a man sleeping on the ground. We get our share of drifters who ride in on the trains and find places to crash until Joe and his guys move them along. Sometimes they try for an arrest, so they can spend some time in jail with reliable food, showers, and heat. Winter was coming on, even though the weather was so mild. This might be one of those.

"Hell!" Joe had spotted him now. "Another vagrant to fill my cells when I don't have enough room to do the job as it is." He'd chafed for a long time at the limited space he had to share with the rest of the town's government in the municipal building.

"Maybe we can just roust him and send him on his way," I offered. "Wait! Something's wrong. That looks like a golf cart. That's not a tramp. Someone's been taken sick."

We ran over to the fence between the golf course and the park. It was just white wooden posts with two widely spaced crossbars running between them. Easy to squeeze between. It didn't take long to jog over to where the figure was lying to see if we could help.

It was the big, beefy form of Ash Mowbray. Joe had his phone out to call as soon as we saw the situation. There was a strong smell of alcohol, and I saw a fifth of Southern Comfort at my feet. My mouth pursed at the thought of the sweet stuff. It affirmed my belief that Ash had no class. I wondered if we'd only surprised Mr. Wealthy Developer sleeping off a drunk. But as we came closer, another smell told a different story.

"Is he dead?" Joe asked.

"Sure smells like it. Blood, feces, and all. We'll have to check, though. He might just be really sick or hurt."

I ran over to Ash while Joe followed more slowly, calling for medical assistance and one of his officers. As I came closer, I saw the bloody mess on the side of his head above the ear. I didn't think he'd need anything the EMTs could do.

Looking around for the weapon, I saw a golf club at a distance, as if it had been thrown. Kneeling, I checked for a pulse on the big man but found nothing. I walked over to the golf club. I didn't know what kind it was because I didn't play golf, but it had a big bloody head, and the shank was bent.

Joe walked over. "That what did it?"

I nodded. "Sid'll have to say for sure, but it looks like it."

Joe shook his head. "I never realized a golf club could be a weapon."

"Joe, anything can be a weapon if someone wants it to be, if they're pissed enough about something. And this guy went out of his way to piss off a lot of people."

"Half the town." Joe looked distressed. "But I'll have to start with the Steens."

And there it was, the thing I'd been trying not to think or see ever since I realized it was Ash lying there. Had young Noah Steen made good on his threat? Or had Elliott decided in a cool, clear way that Ash was too much of a threat to his family? I had the feeling this death had been caused by love. Too much could be as deadly as too little.

CHAPTER 4

Once Joe's officer, the EMTs, and finally the county crime scene techs arrived at the golf course, I left Joe to supervise the crime scene, glad it hadn't happened in my jurisdiction. I'd had enough of that recently.

Brewster was a placid college town on the outskirts of the greater metropolitan Kansas City area, but it had been discovered by well-to-do professionals in KC, who were turning it into a bedroom community for the city and, in the process, bringing a lot of the city's problems with them. Well-off folks always wanted to move out to someplace quiet and safe, but then they wanted to have all the conveniences and excitements they'd left behind in the city, and that meant people not so well-off had to move out to work the crappy jobs that provided those, and crime followed both the wealth and the despair.

Not that there hadn't already been crime out here. Witness what Ash had said about his parents' activities. Drugs and prostitution had been problems of small-town America long before urban sprawl was. But I'd dealt with more than my share of violent crime lately and was happy to leave this one to Joe and his crew.

Gran was pulling biscuits out of the oven when I arrived home with Wilma Mankiller winding about my feet and scolding me vocally for being gone longer than usual. Brian wandered in, toweling his hair dry after a shower.

"That smells great, Gran," he said. When Gran first arrived, he'd struggled with what to call her, trying "Mrs. Whittaker" at first, until Gran told him since he was mine and I was hers that he should call her Gran just as I did.

She smiled at him and frowned at me. "You're late. Wash your hands and sit down to eat. You can take your shower after breakfast. I'm not going to have everything get cold because you lost track of time this morning."

She slammed the oven door with one hand, startling Lady who lay curled on her bed in the corner, and she set the pan of biscuits on the counter with the other. I avoided Wilma once more and headed to the sink to wash up.

"I didn't lose track of time. Found a body on the golf course while running along the river. Had to call it in and wait until the crime scene techs got there." I dried my face and hands on the dishtowel and tossed it on the counter, pulling a clean one out of the drawer to hang in its place before Gran could scold me.

"Was it anyone we know?" Brian asked.

Gran set a baked egg and cheese casserole, a plate of bacon, and a covered basket with the biscuits on the table in front of us. "Brian, get the butter and jelly and that bowl of fruit out of the fridge. Skeet, get the serving spoons."

I held open the refrigerator door for him after I got out the spoons and grabbed a cup of coffee on my way to the table. "It was Ash Mowbray."

"Ash? what—" Brian began before Gran interrupted. "Sit down and say grace," she said sternly. "Before you start talking about evil things like that, bless your food and give thanks for it."

I dropped my head a little in acknowledgment that I'd violated one of her cardinal rules. Gran believed it was important to start the day off right. What you did at the beginning of the day could determine what kind of day you'd have. That meant a good, hot breakfast, and it also meant you said your prayers before you mentioned anything messy. I'd gotten out of the habit of following that particular rule the way I had as a kid.

We all sat at the table and bowed our heads while she prayed. "Creator, thank you for another day of breath and for this food. Bless it to strengthen and nourish us. Help us to say and do right things in the right way. Amen."

Gran might welcome the dawn with cornmeal to the four directions, but back home she was also an active member of the D. D. Etchieson United Indian Methodist Church and never saw any contradictions.

We filled our plates and started to eat—I began with a big gulp of burning coffee, of course—but Brian couldn't contain himself any longer.

"What happened to him? Wish whatever it was had happened before he screwed everything up for Noah and his folks." He shook his head in disgust. "He was a mean old creeper."

"He's dead now, Brian," I reminded him gently.

"Sorry," he muttered and took another biscuit, slathering it with butter.

"Why should you be?" Gran said in a matter-of-fact voice. "Being dead doesn't change the fact that he was a nasty piece of work. Or that he did hurtful things to your friend."

I looked at her in surprise. It had been her daughter who'd scolded me as a child for speaking ill of the dead, and she'd never said anything then.

"How did he die?" Brian asked, scooping up more egg casserole and snatching another couple of strips of bacon while he was at it.

He handed one strip under the table to Lady who'd wandered over. I made a face at him, and he shooed her back to her place.

"It looks very much as if he was murdered."

"Wow!" His hand froze in midair on the way to his mouth with another piece of bacon. He frowned. "Have you told Noah?"

"No. Joe will take care of that when it's time. You're not to say anything to anyone at school. I know it will be all over town in a flash. But not from this house." I reached for more of Gran's fruit compote and paused to give him a stern look. "Okay?"

He shrugged. "Sure. Last thing I want is to be the guy who's got to tell Noah that his real dad who he never knew about and cussed out all over the place is dead." He shook his head. "Talk about stuff that could warp you!"

"People in this town like to talk, especially about something like this," I said. "There will be all kinds of gossip and speculation once the word gets out. I just don't want any of us adding to it."

"You mean I can't talk about it, even after they all know about it?" Brian sounded incredulous.

"No, of course not. But don't speculate. Don't help build it up any worse than it is." I sighed and drank some more badly needed coffee. "People may think you know more than you do because you live here and I found the body. Just be careful when you talk about it."

"Are they looking at Noah and his family?" asked Gran as she polished off her single piece of bacon.

I shook my head at her, but Brian had stopped eating to stare at me.

"They won't think Noah did it, will they?"

"They have to look at everybody who had any grudge against him." I got up to pour myself more coffee and refilled Gran's cup, as well. "And he went out of his way to give a lot of people grudges against him. So they'll be looking at a lot of people for this."

I leaned back against the kitchen counter for a minute. "They'll probably question Noah and his folks, but that doesn't mean anything in a case with this many people angry at the victim."

Brian nodded, looking relieved, and turned back to the food. "Do either of you want the last piece of bacon?"

Gran leaned back in her chair and looked up at me. "That man's going to keep on making trouble for everyone, even from the grave, isn't he?"

When I made it in to work, shift change was already over. Although as an officer I worked technically eight to five, I liked to get in early enough to catch at least a part of the shift change from nights to days. If I wasn't in a meeting, I was usually around for shift change from days to afternoons (which actually lasted until 11:00 p.m.), but I never caught the change from afternoons to nights, so I liked to catch up with those guys when they passed things off to the day shift. I just like to stay on top of things and know what's going on before it catches me off guard.

Getting in too late for that started my day off on the wrong foot, and I doubted it would get better. Gossip about the murder was already starting to make the rounds of my department, so I knew those in town without law enforcement contacts would be hearing soon. I had about an hour before I had to head out for a deans' and directors' meeting that would probably take all morning, and I had counted on having more time to put together my report.

I grabbed coffee at the food table and looked a little too long at the box of doughnuts, even though I'd just had a hearty breakfast. Stress always makes me want caffeine and sugar, and I take my coffee black. I headed into my office, greeting those in the squad room this morning on my way. If I knocked out this report, I'd let myself have one doughnut. I held that thought out before me to motivate myself.

"Mary, hold all calls, please. I've got to get this report done for the meeting this morning."

"Okay, Skeet, but Sam's already called. It's about Charlie. He wanted you to call him as soon as you got in."

"Shit," I said under my breath. My ex-husband Sam and I shared care for my father, Charlie, while he was recovering from a stroke. That was part of the reason Gran had come up to stay with me. She thought I needed help with Brian and Charlie, but no one could really help with Charlie, unless they managed to knock some actual sense into his head. Probably this was going to be about Charlie misbehaving in some way, but the dread was always there right beneath the surface that one of these days he'd have another massive stroke that would do him in.

I closed the door and dialed Sam, sending out a prayer that this wasn't anything too serious. His voice was angry when he answered the phone, and I could breathe again. This was just going to be another Charlie-acting-up problem, not a Charlie-dying one.

"Skeet, he did it again, dammit! I didn't want to call and bother you with it last night, thought I could get him to see some sense, but I don't think it's going to work."

"What happened, Sam? What did he do?"

"Marie—that damned Marie!—came around again, and he went off with her for almost the whole day. Erika was so upset that she couldn't stop them. As if she could. She's tiny compared to either of them. I told her we didn't expect it of her."

"It's certainly not in her job description. Nursing's what she's hired for, not bodyguarding."

I could feel my head starting to tighten toward headache, and I tried to massage my scalp with one hand while I held my phone with the other. Marie had been Charlie's home nursing help for two days, but we'd had to get rid of her because she let him—encouraged him, in fact—to break his diet and to drink. Since my dad was a newly recovering alcoholic and at high risk of stroke and heart attack, those were pretty dangerous things for him to do. She kept coming around, though. Charlie thought it was because she liked him. I figured it was so she could get back at us for firing her.

"What did he say?" I asked. "After we told him we wouldn't have anything to do with him if he did this?"

"I know. I know. He said he couldn't let his stroke and us unman him. That if he did, he might as well take his old service revolver out and shoot himself. I didn't know what to say to that, Skeet. He's got a point, but at the same time, I think she wants to marry him, get his money, and help him kill himself."

"I know. I don't know what to do, either, Sam. But I know what I'm going to do tonight. Gran keeps offering to help out with Charlie, and I find reasons not to because they don't get along at all. But tonight I'm going to ask Gran to go in and get him ready for the night. Because if I do it, I know we'll have such an explosion that we'll never recover from it."

"You're too much like each other," he said. "That same temper."

"I don't know why I had to get all his bad qualities. I could have gotten Coreen's sexy phone voice or Gran's ability to grow things instead."

"Hey"—his voice softened—"you know I've always thought you had a sexy voice, phone or not. Along with a lot of everything else."

"No, don't," I warned. If Sam started his patented charm offensive this morning, I might explode. I tried to have patience with him and just keep putting up the barricades. He was a good guy, just not a good husband, but I couldn't help it that he didn't want to let go of what we'd once had. After all, he'd worked pretty hard to kill it.

"Just have to keep my hand in," he said quickly, then paused. "I'll tell Erika that there'll be someone new tonight. Poor Charlie. I almost feel sorry for him. I imagine your grandmother will give him hell."

I smiled a little. "She'll make him behave. She has no patience with bad little boys, no matter how old they are."

"You know she terrifies me. Always has." Sam had once said that he felt like Gran's eyes opened him up and laid all his thoughts and plans out in plain sight. For a schemer like him that must have been a terrifying feeling.

"She should. I told you she's got no patience with bad boys. No matter how good-looking or charming they are, either."

And Sam was both, but Gran had seen right through him the first time she met him. I'd sensed she wasn't happy that I'd hooked up with him. When I asked her about it, she just told me we all had to get these things out of our systems, and it was better done when young. I'd been insulted then. Now I just shook my head at how wise she'd been.

"What's she think of your new bad boy?" Sam's voice took on a bitter tone. "What's his name? Terry? The one who showed up all kitted out in assassin's gear when you were taken hostage."

I exhaled loudly into the phone in exasperation. "What are you talking about? I hardly know the man. I've only occasionally run into him since then. Don't know him. Don't like him. And this conversation's gone south, as they usually do, so I'm getting off the phone. Tell Erika that Gran will be there tonight."

I hung up as he started to apologize. I gulped some coffee to see if the caffeine would help keep me from a headache. Then I pulled some Advil from my purse and swallowed two with coffee. Somehow I had to concentrate and write this report when everything that had happened this morning had set my head to throbbing. I hit the intercom, and when Mary answered, I asked her to bring me a doughnut.

The deans' and directors' meeting blew my whole morning, as they always did. My report went down well, however, and just about everyone liked the fact that the university was now a part of the federal human trafficking task force through the campus police, surprising me. Usually, in the university, no one's in favor of anything that doesn't funnel money or prestige to their department or school. I finally understood when I had several deans grab me afterward to volunteer to have their professors do research studies for the task force. They thought there might be federal grant funding for such studies. I told them I'd take their offers to my next meeting at the federal courthouse in KC.

I'd set up a lunch with Karen Wise, my dearest friend, so my day picked up as I headed to the Herbal Coffee Shop to meet her. We hadn't seen each other as often as usual since her shepherd, Ignacio Valenzuela, had been badly wounded trying to protect her from a killer three months earlier. Lucky to survive, Ignacio was still recovering from several surgeries, and Karen was taking care of him out on her farm while relying heavily on her student employees to help run her fiber arts shop. So today's lunch was a real treat for both of us.

Dolores Ramirez, owner of the Herbal and on-and-off girlfriend of Gil Mendez, showed me to the booth in back she knew we favored.

"I haven't seen Karen in weeks," she said. "Does she need anything? She always tells me she doesn't, but you know how she is."

I nodded as I sat down. "Karen's the first to tell me or anyone else to ask for and accept help, but she's not real good at it herself. Miryam, Annette, and Gran and I practically had to force meals and other help on her when Ignacio first came home, so she wouldn't run herself ragged, but he's getting around now, and things are much better. He told Karen he'd leave the farm and go back wherever he came from if she didn't start having a life of her own again. That's how we're having this lunch date."

Dolores laughed. "Good for him. I suppose you'll want coffee, even though it's almost like summer out there."

I rolled my eyes. "What else?"

She shook her head and went to greet Peter Hume and Dante Marcus at the door and show them to the table near my booth. Taking a deep breath of the peppermint-and-lemon-balm-scented air, I pulled out the specials card from the menu to see what I would order once Karen arrived.

"I just don't understand why you've got to keep creating scenes in public," Dante complained in the rich rolling voice of a radio or TV announcer. As far as I knew, he'd never worked as one, but he sure had the voice for it. Didn't seem fair since he was so gorgeous.

"I won't let Ash Mowbray and the rest of them get away with this. That's why." Peter's voice was even more husky and gravelly than usual, as if he'd screamed himself hoarse. "I won't just roll over and play dead. They know that now."

"Sweetie, no one wants you to just roll over and play dead or let them get away with this. But don't you think there are more civil ways to handle it?" Dante sounded so patient and caring that I had to revise my opinion of him.

I'd had little direct contact with Dante, so, like most of the town, I'd just assumed the movie-star-handsome young African American who'd moved in with Peter six months ago was primarily interested in the comfortable life Peter had to offer. After all, Peter was much older, potbellied, and balding. But there was so much affection and concern in Dante's voice that I knew common knowledge was wrong and he was with Peter for a lot more than Peter's money. This made me happy for Peter and disgusted with myself because I'd just bought into the stereotype the town had of Dante without bothering to find out anything about the real man.

"He's trying to destroy my—our livelihood, Dante. How civil is that?" Peter's voice was so querulous that he sounded even older than he was. He slammed his fist carefully against the table.

"Well, but all this anger—it's scary sometimes, sugar. I feel like I don't know this Peter who's ready to beat the hell out of all these people." Dante sounded and looked troubled.

Peter laughed unpleasantly. "Not all of them, but I'd sure like to kick the shit out of that Mowbray. Just kick his teeth out."

"See, that's what bothers me." Dante leaned over the table to place his hand on top of Peter's and stared at him with puppy-dog eyes. "I don't like that kind of talk. I don't like that kind of thinking. You've got to stop this, love. You need to stop now. It's not healthy for you. I'm afraid of what will happen if you keep stressing yourself this way."

I eavesdropped shamelessly, not that I could have avoided it. Some people, especially men, seem totally unaware of how well and how far their voices carry. I was as startled as Dante was at the violence of Peter's speech. Could he have swung that golf club at Ash's head? Though he seemed unaware that Ash was dead. Still, how likely was that when the whole town probably already knew?

One of Dolores's waitresses showed up with a cup of coffee for me and two glasses of herbal iced teas for Peter and Dante. She took their order for lunch as I went back to checking the specials card.

"Try the quinoa, avocado, and cheese salad. It's got a great lime-cilantro vinaigrette." Terry Heldrich suddenly stood next to my booth. I didn't know how that man moved so silently. "It's got corn and black beans in it, too. Tasty. I just had it." He stared down at me with those intense dark eyes until I found my hand checking to make sure my shirt hadn't come unbuttoned or something.

"Thanks for the tip. I'd have figured that, though, since all of Dolores's dishes are pretty delicious. I think I'll go for the turkey, apple, and cranberry salad instead, but thanks anyway." I turned back to the menu, hoping if I ignored him he'd go away.

From behind him, Peter's voice rang out. "Someone needs to teach that damn Mowbray a lesson, that's for sure."

As Dante tried to hush him, Terry's left eyebrow rose. "Another who'd like the world to be rid of Ash Mowbray. That seems to be my lunchtime theme."

"Who else?" I asked, thinking of Ash sprawled on the lush green of the golf course.

Terry gave a little grimace. "My boss feels he's a public relations nightmare." He shrugged slightly. "It's apparent the guy had an agenda in coming back here, and it wasn't just to build a shopping center. Walker's not happy about that."

"So does he want you to take care of it for him?" I asked, trying to sound careless.

Terry's bronze face darkened, and he leaned over me, reminding me of all the reasons I shouldn't make this dangerous man angry.

"I've told you before, Skeet. I don't *take care* of those kinds of problems for Walker Lynch. And I'm not responsible for what he hires some goon to do." He stared directly into my eyes, and I had to fight not to lower my gaze in submission or look elsewhere to escape his stare. I wasn't about to let him believe he'd intimidated me, however, so I met his gaze.

"Please, Peter, could we have one meal in peace without you ranting about that muscle-bound idiot? You're obsessed with him." Dante's voice had risen and rang with exasperation. "One nice, peaceful meal. Is that too much to ask?"

"All right!" Something slammed against the table, and I

thought it was probably Peter's fist again—not so carefully this time. "Fine. I'll shut up if that's what you want."

Terry had pulled back as the conversation behind him heated up, and I pulled my eyes away from his. Dante began a softer, conciliatory murmuring.

"Sorry," Terry said. "I just get tired of people thinking I'm Walker's hired thug or assassin." He laughed, and I couldn't stop myself from looking back at his face for the smile I knew would be there, placing those high cheekbones in relief. The man had an incredible smile that brought his whole face alive under the gray hat he so often wore. "I'm really quite white-collar now, you know."

I had to smile at the deck shoes, jeans, and T-shirt that were his version of formal business attire. "I won't tell anyone and spoil your street cred."

This brought heartier, even more infectious laughter. I couldn't help but like Terry, even though I didn't trust him.

"No chance of my ego getting out of control with you around to skewer it, is there?" He shook his head ruefully. "I've got to go, but tell me you haven't lost my new address."

I sighed. "I haven't lost it, but you need to stop waiting for me to come by. It's not going to happen. I've told you that before."

"Who knows? You might get lonely and want a friend." He gave me a serious look. "That's all I'm asking, Skeet. A chance to get to know you and become friends."

I waved him off and returned to the menu. I was determined not to look up and see him tip his hat to me, with a crook of his mouth the way he always did. Friends. Oh, yeah. Not likely.

Suddenly Karen gave me a hug and slid into the booth opposite me. "You're really studying that menu, Skeet. Trying to memorize it?"

I laughed. "Just trying to ignore someone irritating. How are you? And how's Ignacio doing?"

"He must be getting better. He's growing as stubborn as he ever was." She laughed happily.

"That's great to hear." I knew how she'd feared that Ignacio wouldn't live through the first surgery that saved his life and later that he might never again be the strong, capable man he'd been when she first hired him as her shepherd.

"At least when he's giving me a hard time, I know the pain is finally under control and he's getting his strength back." She shook her head. "He's talking about going back to the fields. I've told him that's not necessary. I've had the Alleshir boy taking care of the animals. He's hardly Ignacio, but he'll manage till Nacio's all healed."

"I know what that's like. Wanting to get back on the job after being shot. Wanting to bring your life back to normal. That's a good sign."

The waitress showed up to take our orders. Karen ordered the grilled salmon sandwich with baked sweet potato fries, and I ordered the quinoa, avocado, and cheese salad with lime-cilantro vinaigrette, saying I'd heard somewhere it was absolutely delicious.

"So, tell me about this body you found this morning, Skeet?" Karen asked as we settled in. "Was it really that dreadful Ash Mowbray?"

It seemed Peter, Dante, and Terry were the only ones in town who'd not heard about that morning's discovery. Once more I wondered how likely it was that any of them really didn't know Ash had been killed.

As Karen and I finished our meal and our conversation wound down, Miryam showed up at our booth.

"Have you heard? Joe's taken in Noah Steen for questioning. They found his fingerprints on the golf club that killed Ash Mowbray. Well, they would since it was his club, wouldn't they? And they also found a charm that was his mother's. Wonder why they didn't pull in Chelsea, too?"

Karen reached up and pulled Miryam's blond head down to kiss her cheek and hug her. "Hello to you, too, Miryam. Why yes, I'm doing well, thank you."

Miryam blushed slightly. "Sorry. I guess I got too distracted." Her face returned to the eager state it had been in when she arrived. "I think we have another mystery on our hands. Isn't that terrific?"

"No," I said firmly. "No, it's not terrific, and no, it's not on our hands. It's a city problem, and Joe will handle it."

"It's a tragedy, Miryam." Karen gave her a stern look. "Someone's life has been snuffed out. That's not the stuff of excitement and entertainment."

"Well, you can't tell me anyone's going to cry over Ash being dead. He was one mean, greedy man. We all hated him and wanted him gone. They'll arrest Noah, and because he's a kid, he won't have to go to prison, so it all works out great."

"They're not arresting Noah, Miryam." I sighed in exasperation. What was Joe thinking?

"But they have to arrest him," Miryam said, her face showing disappointment. "It was his club used to kill Ash, and his fingerprints are on it and everything. Of course, they're arresting him."

"You sound like you're happy that poor boy's in trouble," Karen scolded. "Don't you understand what this could mean to his life?"

My phone rang, and I answered as the argument continued.

"Skeet, Joe's arrested Noah. You've got to help him." Brian's voice was distressed, and in the background behind, I could hear Angie coaching him.

"Tell her that Pearl says we need a good detective investigating this who can find the real killer—that they're going to make Noah a scapegoat because it's easiest and they're just frigging lazy."

"Calm down, Brian. And tell Angie to cool it, as well. Noah's not been arrested. They're just questioning him. After all, he had a huge public run-in with Ash just before the murder. It's standard operating procedure. They'll pull in others who were mad at Ash, like Bea and Peter, too."

I was a little surprised that Joe had taken in Noah to question rather than just asking him what he wanted at home. Usually, you didn't take someone in to the station for questioning unless you thought they'd done it and wanted to put pressure on them, but it was way too early for that in this investigation.

"They're going to railroad him!' Angie shrieked, and I wondered if Brian would have any hearing left.

"Angie's afraid—" Brian started to say.

"I can hear Angie. I imagine the whole coffee shop can hear Angie. Joe's not going to railroad anyone. Certainly not Noah Steen."

"But can't you—"

I interrupted him again. "Brian, I'm not going to investigate this. Noah has not been arrested. You watch. He'll be sent home soon. I have to go now."

He hesitated. "Okay, I'll see you after my class with Professor Garton. But just think about it, Skeet. Please."

"I'll pick you up at the usual time then. You two stop worrying. You'll make yourselves sick for nothing."

I hung up and counted out cash for my check and tip. Miryam and Karen were still arguing over Ash's murder, Miryam trying to convince Karen that whoever had killed him had done a good thing.

I stood up. "I've got to get back to work. You two try to keep from coming to blows, okay?"

I left before they could say anything and headed back to the university. In the back of my mind, a question was nagging at me. Why had Joe taken Noah in for questioning? Surely, he wouldn't try to nail the kid for this because it was easier. Surely, Angie was wrong. Wasn't she?

CHAPTER 5

The mild, sunny weather still held, but even that was screwy for this time of year in this part of the country, and had started to take on a sinister feel, especially with Gran swearing there'd be a blizzard soon (which would also be screwy for this time of year in this part of the country). I tried not to think about it, just the way I tried not to think about why Joe had brought in Noah for questioning.

But I found myself faced squarely with one of those questions when I drove up to Ormond Hall to pick up Brian from his music theory class. A train clattered through the center of town, visible below us like a child's toy clanking its way north, past the courthouse square with its picturesque shops. Angie sat on the concrete steps out front with Brian, looking despondent. I sighed, realizing I was about to face another attempt to make me rescue her boyfriend from Joe's clutches.

Brian and Angie piled into the backseat. "I told Angie we could give her a ride home, okay?" asked Brian.

I nodded. "Sure."

We drove in silence for a few seconds before she started on

me. "Skeet, I wish you'd find the real killer so Noah could go free. Pearl Brewster thinks you should, too."

I glanced at her for a second. "Why were you and Pearl discussing this and me?"

Angie's face colored a little under all the makeup. She shrugged. "Sometimes I go talk to her when I'm worried about something. For an old lady, she's pretty cool."

Brian nodded. "Kids at school know Pearl's someone you can talk to who won't yell or lecture, and sometimes she can actually help you with some problem."

"Do you go to Pearl with your problems, Brian?" I asked, afraid to hear that he did, that somehow I was failing him as a mother.

"Nah," he said, as if amused at my silliness. "I've got you. And Gran. It's kids like Angie who don't have someone good at home who go to Pearl."

"Anyway," Angie said impatiently, "Pearl agrees that you should find the real killer so Noah doesn't get framed for something he didn't do. We need your help to set him free."

"Angie, I imagine Noah is already at home. He always was free. Joe never arrested him." I tried to keep my voice calm and matter-of-fact.

"But he's under suspicion," she cried. "And while he's under suspicion, Joe won't look at anyone else."

"Come on, Angie." My tone was sharper now. "That's not really fair to Joe. He's not going to treat Noah or anyone else unfairly."

"I like Joe, too, Skeet," Brian said in an unhappy voice. "You know that. But I think Angie's right. He's not going to give Noah a fair chance. He's not going to be allowed to by the political powers in town."

"Noah's family is prominent in this town," I protested. "He's not likely to be scapegoated."

"When they haven't got anyone else?" Angie asked, voice dripping with skepticism. "Noah's folks don't have big political power, and the ones with political power want this all swept under the rug."

I sighed, exasperated by her naïveté. "Angie, if they're going to railroad someone, it will be someone poor and probably someone nonwhite, preferably a vagrant just passing through."

"But what if it's Walker Lynch behind it? He can get any investigation stopped dead." Angie sounded as if she might start crying. "He was Ash's partner, and Ash was causing him trouble with all this mess. I heard him bitching about Ash to Liz. He wanted the bad publicity stopped. He's got more money than God—and more power, too. I'm afraid he wants Joe to just stop at Noah and not look any further, and I don't think Joe can stand up to Walker."

I inhaled deeply. I hated to admit it, but the kid might actually have a point there. Walker had so much money and power that few would or could stand up to him. I'd already seen that. I believed he was involved in major crimes like human trafficking, but I couldn't prove it—yet.

Terry said he didn't—wouldn't—commit violence or any other illegal act for Walker, and I believed him. Well, maybe I wanted to believe him. Still, that didn't mean Walker couldn't hire some muscle to get rid of someone. That would explain Noah's golf club and Chelsea's charm tossed at the murder scene. And Liz Richar, Angie's stepmother, was one of Walker's confidants, so she might well have heard him discuss the need to stop Ash's troublemaking.

We arrived outside Angie's house where she lived with the

wealthy stepmother who hated her. I disliked having to leave her there, but I thought she'd be safe since I made regular comments to Liz, reminding her I was watching, in case she did anything to harm Angie.

"I'm sorry, kids. There's really nothing I can do. This case isn't in my jurisdiction. I think Joe will do a good job, though. I know you're worried about Noah. He'd threatened Ash, and Ash was killed with Noah's golf club. But others also threatened Ash. I think you'll see Joe pulling in some of them for questioning, as well."

Tears were streaming down Angie's cheeks when she got out of the car in silence and ran up to the house. It was hard to see her having to deal with all this stress and fear. She'd been through enough recently.

Brian didn't take up the badgering as we drove off. That surprised me, and it was a relief. I was still rolling around in my head what Angie'd said about Walker and getting a bad feeling from it. My one relief was that Joe was in charge. He was a good guy, and I thought he'd stand as tough as I would if Walker started pulling political strings to try to have Noah arrested without a solid investigation.

After we arrived home, I changed into jeans and settled on the couch with Wilma Mankiller curled up beside me. I picked up my knitting—a pink mohair lace scarf for Miryam's birthday next month—while Brian practiced his flute, Lady's feathery tail thumping happily on the floor between us in time to Brian's music. It wasn't until Gran came back from settling Charlie down for the night in Kansas City that Brian finally brought it up again as we sat down to a late dinner of chicken and dumplings with honey-baked squash that I'd heated up while Gran made some quick biscuits.

"Skeet, I wish you'd rethink things and help Noah." He stopped shoveling the chicken and dumplings into his mouth to watch me.

I had to swallow a bite of squash before I could answer. "Why do you want me to do this, Brian? You hated Noah not very long ago because of Angie. What's changed that?"

He blushed a little and stared down at his plate, mixing honey and squash with his fork, as if that needed all his attention. Finally, he looked up at me. "I'm not happy about the whole Angie-Noah thing. That hasn't changed. But I want you to help him anyway because it's the right thing to do. You've always taught me that I should do the right thing, even if it's hard. And making sure Noah doesn't get arrested for something he didn't do is the right thing."

He turned his gaze back to his plate, as if buttering his biscuit was the most important thing in the world.

I hardly knew what to say to that. He'd basically thrown all my platitudes right back in my face, and I knew how hard it must be when he really wanted Noah out of his way.

We finished off our meal in silence punctuated by bits of small talk. When we'd finished and were clearing the table, Brian asked me again. "Skeet, at least talk to Joe. Please?"

"Go get your homework done. I'll think about it. Now, go on." I shoved him slightly to get him moving out of the room.

"He's right, you know," Gran said after we silently cleared the table and filled the dishwasher. "It is the right thing to do, and you need to talk to Joe and see if you can't help find the real killer."

"Gran, that nice boy, Noah, may well be the real killer." I rubbed my temples and made myself a cup of cocoa. I tried to avoid coffee in the evenings so I'd have at least a chance at sleep.

She nodded. "He might, but I don't think so, and neither do you."

"I don't know what to think because I haven't seen any of the evidence or the coroner's report or anything. But I saw the body, and someone hit that man with tremendous force several times. I'd bet those blows were driven by anger or hate. And Noah was certainly furious with Ash." I turned around and leaned back against the counter on my elbows.

"I can tell you're not happy about the way Joe's handling this," Gran said, measuring detergent into the dishwasher.

I shrugged. "I'm just a little puzzled at his taking Noah in for questioning. That's not the way it's done unless you're pretty sure you've got your guy because people, especially the press, get that word out right away and always interpret it as an arrest. And I don't think he can be close to making an arrest and closing the case yet. There's probably not been enough time to get a coroner's report from Sid or anything."

"Maybe Joe's under pressure." Gran turned on the dishwasher.

"That's what the kids think." I had to speak louder to be heard over the dishwasher's rumble. "They think Joe's getting political pressure. Maybe from Walker Lynch."

Gran shook her head. "You know I don't like that man. He's a bad one."

It was one of the things Gran and I saw eye-to-eye on instantly. The first time she met Walker, her eyes had widened slightly, and she'd quietly slipped back away from him in the crowded room. She'd sought me out a little later and warned me to watch out for him. I'd told her not to worry, that I knew Walker was a snake and watched out for him all the time.

"I think you should talk to Joe, at least. And if you don't like the answers, you'll know what to do." She nodded her head decisively, lifting her short white hair with the movement. As far as she was concerned, it was settled.

I could feel myself being dragged, kicking and screaming, into this messy investigation that was really none of my business. And, of course, there was the problem of Walker Lynch.

Next morning, bright and early, before I hit work, I stopped by Joe's office. To the whistle of a train on its way into town, I carried in good coffee from the Herbal as a goodwill offering. I knew how bad the coffee at the Brewster PD was.

The department secretary waved me on into his office, accustomed to our visits back and forth in the past. What I saw as I entered his office alarmed me. Almost overnight, Joe had developed new creases between his eyebrows and lines at the corners of his mouth. I immediately thought of Gran's and the kids' fears that he was being politically pressured.

His whole face brightened when he saw me, though. "Hey, Skeet. What or who do I owe for this visit?"

I handed him a cup of coffee and watched him pull off the cover with a greedy smile. "Gran. She wanted me to come find out what's going on with you bringing in Noah for questioning."

The smile left his face. "You know, another woman would at least have let me pretend it was because you wanted to see me." He set down the coffee.

I just looked at him, not knowing what to say to that. I wasn't another woman, after all. I was just me. That was the problem with our friendship. Joe had always acted like he was happy with me just as I was until recently, so I'd been happy with what I thought was his accepting friendship until recently. I'd begun to think that neither of us really knew the other.

He shook his head. "I guess it's not likely you'd pretend about much of anything." He gave a little sigh. "It would be nice once in a while, though."

"If you were a crook, and I had to pretend something to catch you . . ." I offered.

He laughed. "Yeah, I know." He shook his head with a bit of a sad smile. "So what is it you want to know?"

I sat down and took a drink of my coffee. "Why'd you bring the kid in for questioning? Right at the start? You couldn't even have had the coroner's report yet."

He shrugged. "You know the drill. Try to shake him up. Work him until he makes a misstep." He took a big gulp of coffee.

"Yeah, but you only do that when you're sure you've got the guy." Could Gran and the kids be right? Was Joe willing to just toss Noah to the sharks?

"Skeet, Ash was killed with the kid's golf club," he said impatiently, "and his were the only prints on it. His mother's good luck charm was dropped at the scene. He threatened to kill Ash twice in front of witnesses."

"Hell, Joe, you know that was just an angry teenager mouthing off after being blindsided with shocking news." I slammed my cup against his desk and coffee splashed out.

His jaw tightened and his voice rose. "It's more than that when there's evidence like fingerprints on the murder weapon."

I rolled my eyes. "It was his club, Joe. For God's sake, you know whoever did it could grab it with gloves and leave it as a ready-made distraction. Why are you falling for this? I could name you at least seven people off the top of my head who had a motive to kill Ash. And I'm sure there were more."

He threw his head back with an exasperated sigh. "You women! That's like Chelsea saying there was no way Noah could have taken the charm from her purse. If you don't think that woman would lie to protect her son, you don't know anything, Skeet. She'd probably do anything to protect that boy, even kill. You just don't want it to be the kid because he's one of Brian's friends."

He wasn't the only one growing angry. *You women?* What was that all about?

I tried to calm down and keep my voice under control. "Wrong. I just want to see you investigating this murder and looking at all the possible suspects, following the trail of real evidence and questioning people other than a scared high school senior."

I stared right into his eyes, something I don't often do except with suspects when I'm grilling them. He dropped his gaze to the floor.

"Joe, are you under political pressure to get a quick arrest of this kid? I had someone tell me that was the case, and I didn't want to believe it. I said, no, Joe would never do anything like that—he's a good cop."

His jaw clenched in indignation, and his lower lip jutted out. "Who the hell are you to sit in judgment on me, Skeet? I've got a kid, and my job's on the line. I can be fired in a flash with no real way to fight it unless I've got the money for a lawsuit, and I don't. So I have to go along to get along. You've got a kid now, and you might find you'd have to do the same thing in the same circumstances."

"No way." I pushed back from the desk. "I wouldn't, Joe. I can always get another job."

He nodded with a sneer. "Sure you can. But I'm not a woman—and a minority hire at that—who gets opportunity handed to her."

I shot out of my chair. "If you think I've had my career handed to me, you are stupider than I'm even now starting to think you are."

I slapped my hands on the desk and leaned over it into his face. "For your information, I've had to work twice as hard for everything I've achieved. I've had to watch white guys that I trained get the promotions I should have had—with less education and less experience and less damn ability. The only way I got the opportunities I got was because I'd work so damn hard and do so well that they were embarrassed not to give them to me. Meanwhile, guys like you just go along to get along. That shit sucks, Joe."

I whirled around and marched out of his office. I had a full-time job to go to—and now it looked as if I'd have a damn murder to solve, as well, since the police weren't going to bother.

CHAPTER 6

I was still steaming when I got to the university, but I knew that a good leader has to compartmentalize emotion to a certain extent. You can't take out your anger on your staff just because you're mad at someone somewhere else. So I shoved it down deep inside and spent some time talking and joking with the officers at shift change. By the time I made it into my office, I was in a better mood.

So Joe was tossing out sexist bull. He was hardly the first guy in police work or elsewhere to do that. I'd encountered plenty of it. This hurt a little more because I'd thought Joe was different. He wasn't. I'd thought he was my friend. He wasn't. Nothing to do about that but suck it up and move on.

My second-in-command, Frank Booth, and Gil Mendez, lead investigator, joined me for a meeting about a rash of thefts in student housing. Gil thought he had a couple of suspects he wanted to put surveillance on, and Frank wanted extra security at the dorms. I approved both requests, and our meeting ended on an optimistic note. I thought Gil would probably have the thieves arrested in a week or so. I thought again of the

KCPD guys and feds on the human trafficking task force who were probably even now plotting to hire him away, now that they were getting a taste of his dual skills in finance and investigation.

That little waking nightmare was interrupted by a phone call from Elliott Steen.

"Skeet, would it be possible for you to meet with me today?" he asked abruptly when I answered.

My voice probably sounded surprised. I certainly was. I'd not exchanged more than casual greetings with Elliott since coming to Brewster two years earlier. "I guess so, Elliott. When do you want to meet?"

"At your earliest convenience. As soon as possible." It felt like he was spouting random business correspondence phrases, and I wondered if Elliott could actually carry on a conversation outside of the business realm.

I looked at my calendar. "Well, I've got some time open before lunch. I could stop by at about eleven. Would that work?"

"Excellent. I'll look forward to seeing you then. Thanks, Skeet." His voice grew so enthusiastic it made me wonder what I was getting into, but before I could ask questions, he'd hung up.

As I penciled the meeting with him into my calendar, I wondered if this was about Joe pulling in Noah for questioning. It wasn't likely I'd forget it since it wasn't far off, but I tried to put everything in my calendar, so Mary would know where I was in case of emergencies.

I arrived at his office, in an old restored Victorian house half a block off the courthouse square, a few minutes early because my curiosity got the best of me. I'd walked rather than driven in order to take advantage of the mild, sunny weather and enjoy the landscape. With so many old, established trees in the heart of Brewster and the unseasonable weather, this fall's foliage display had been incredible. It was rare to find any extended periods of time when it was pleasant to wander around outside in this part of the country. Usually spring lasted for a few minutes, and autumn was a matter of weeks, with summer blazing and winter icy. So I wanted to take advantage of this weather while we had it.

The whole way I wondered why exactly Elliott had called me. This meeting had to have something to do with Ash's death and Joe's treatment of Noah, I was sure. I wondered if Elliott was going to try to sue Joe or something. I didn't like what Joe was doing, but I couldn't believe that he'd be able to go through with it in the long run and railroad Noah into jail or a psych facility without even trying to find out who really killed Ash. I didn't want to end up in court testifying against him. At the same time, I couldn't let Noah be arrested and go to trial unless there was real evidence that he was definitely the killer. Not when there were so many with such hate of Ash and such good motives and opportunities for killing him. That was for sure.

"Skeet, come in. Sit down. Would you like some coffee?"

I never turn down caffeine, so I took the cup of good, strong coffee Elliott offered. "What's going on, Elliott? Why did you want to see me?"

He looked a little startled. I encounter that sometimes. I can do the whole social conversational dance thing. I'd never have made it to the upper levels of KCPD or my present job if I couldn't. But it's not my natural way of doing things. I like to get to the point and get things done. I didn't think there was any reason to adjust that for Elliott.

"Last night, Angie came by the house and told us all that you would investigate Ash's murder and come up with the real killer." He beamed at me. "We're so grateful, and we want to help in any way we can."

I opened my mouth to refuse, only to realize that I had decided sometime after the conversation with Joe that I had to investigate to make sure a real investigation was done. "Angie had no right to tell you that. When she did that, I hadn't decided what I'd do. But I have now decided to investigate Ash's murder."

Elliott smiled happily and started to thank me again, but I stopped him. "Just realize that you may be sorry I did. I won't promise who I'll find. I'm going wherever the evidence takes me, and so far, the top suspects are all members of your family. Including you, Elliott."

His enthusiasm dampened, he looked a little strained. "I know it had to be someone else. I know I didn't do it, and I'll never believe that Noah or Chelsea could."

"That's interesting. You don't say you couldn't kill him."

He sighed and looked at the ground for a second before looking back at me. "I could have, but I didn't. Noah and Chelsea never could have done such a thing."

I almost smiled and I took out my notebook. "Tell me about when Ash left Chelsea pregnant. How did you two marry? How did the town—and Noah—come to think Noah was your child?"

"He is mine, you know. In every way that matters, that boy is my son." He looked away from me, past me, as if into that distant time. "She was just a kid, you know, just a sweet kid. I wasn't really much more than that myself. Just out of college and a couple of years selling insurance for another agency."

"How did you know Chelsea then?"

"She was working for me that summer, filling in for my regular secretary who was having surgery. I was just starting out with my own agency, and it was just me, two part-time green agents in their first jobs, and the secretary." He smiled at a memory. "Chelsea was a hard worker, though, and she kept us all straight."

"Did everyone know she was dating Ash?"

He shook his head. "They kept it secret because Ash and his family had such a bad reputation. Her dad would have had a fit. Ash would never have been good enough for her. I wouldn't have been good enough for her. He was mayor and the town's most prominent businessman."

"And it sounds as if Ash's family was pretty bottom of the barrel."

He glared at me. "They were the dregs of the town. Ash just played on her sympathies. He was handsome and charming and a con man of the first order. She was the prettiest, smartest, most popular girl in high school—and she had a big heart. He just wanted another conquest."

I looked up from scribbling in my notebook. "Elliott, I suspect Chelsea had more to do with this than you want to think. Unless Ash raped her—and it doesn't sound like that happened—she was an active partner in what happened to her."

He shrugged off my words. "Then he got money somehow to leave, and he was gone. Chelsea told him she was pregnant, but that didn't make any difference to that scumball. He was out of there so fast he seemed to have just disappeared."

I made a note to find out where Ash got the money to leave. Pearl said she'd given to some fund for Ash when he left. Who organized it? Where did he get the rest of the money he needed?

If he'd stolen or conned it from someone, they might have a motive still for killing him.

"She was sick to her stomach a lot, said the heat was bothering her," Elliott went on. "Then I came back early from a meeting and found her sobbing hysterically. I got the truth out of her. I was already in love with her—who wouldn't be?—so I offered to marry her and raise the kid as my own. I didn't think she'd accept, but she was desperate."

I wondered how that made Elliott really feel, to know that she only came to him because she was desperate and didn't have any other choice. That would bother the hell out of me, and I thought it would have to do the same to Elliott.

He locked his eyes back on me. "I made sure she got to finish school the next year and graduate. I was there with little Noah cheering her on." He smiled at the memory. "He was just a baby, but I held him up to see his mama up there getting her diploma. I never wanted her to have any regrets. I offered to send her to college. Didn't know how I'd do it. But I'd have found a way. I never wanted her to feel she'd had to give up anything to marry me. She didn't want to, though. She wanted to stay home with Noah, and she did."

I wondered if Chelsea had realized that Elliott couldn't really afford to send her to college and made that choice to spare him. "How did her parents take it? You said you wouldn't have met her father's criteria as someone to date."

He laughed bitterly. "And I wouldn't. But Chelsea told them the whole story. They were the only ones who knew the truth besides Chelsea and me—and Ash. Suddenly, I was good enough. Although I think her mother offered to take her somewhere for an abortion behind her father's back. But Chelsea said no, and we had our wedding. And I was suddenly a member of the family." He shook his head at the memory. "I will say, they were good to me, and I think when Chelsea's dad died a couple of years later, her mother came to really appreciate me in the years before her death."

I thought what that might have been like for him. "That must have been hard for you, knowing that you were just the least of bad options."

"You could say so, I guess. I never looked at it that way. I was so in love with Chelsea—and then with Noah. You should have seen that boy as a baby and toddler and little kid. He was such a joy. Still is. I couldn't love Noah any more if he was my genetic son. In every way that counts, he's mine. I've worked hard to try to make sure Chelsea never has too many regrets about her decision, and she's been all the wife and mother I could have asked for. I think we were pretty happy until Ash came on the scene."

"And once he did? What happened then?"

He pulled his jacket tight around his body and looked away from me. "After we first heard that he was back in town, Chelsea and I agreed that he'd have no reason to think Noah was his or acknowledge him if he did suspect. He had as much to lose as we did, we thought. But shortly after that, Chelsea grew secretive and moody, so I knew it was upsetting her. When she's hurt or sick, she pulls into herself and shuts everyone else out while she deals with it. I wanted to help her, but I knew there wasn't anything I could do until she worked it through and let me in to help her deal with it."

I thought of what his wife had told me and knew this withdrawal was probably triggered by Ash's extorting sex from her with the threat to tell her son the truth of his paternity.

His face turned grim. "Who would have thought he would

come back all these years later, wanting the child he tossed aside? If I'd known what he had in mind, I'd have bought a gun and learned to shoot it so I could shoot him when he first showed his face around here."

I remembered that serious businesslike threat Elliott had made to Ash in the city council chambers. Had Elliott picked up a golf club when Ash was turning away from him and beaten him to death?

He shook his head, as if to clear his thoughts of the violence he'd just expressed. "Well, fortunately or unfortunately, I didn't know what he had in mind, so the damage is done."

My eyes caught my earlier note to myself, and I asked, "Where do you think Ash got the money to leave town originally?"

He shrugged. "I don't know, but Pearl might. She's always been there for teens, doling out advice, listening to their troubles, helping with their problems—probably because she never had any of her own. If Chelsea hadn't told me she was pregnant when she did, she'd probably have gone to Pearl, and Pearl would probably have found Ash and made him come back, so I'm glad that didn't happen. I sort of remember that Ash was one of her kids. He was troubled enough to be. Maybe he confided in her."

I nodded and noted that. "I might go see if I can speak with her next. But I will need to talk to Noah, as well. When would be best for that? This evening?"

"Any time you want to come by. He's not going anywhere. Everyone's talking about him, and he doesn't want to face all that gossip. Plus he's terrified that Joe's going to arrest him and he'll go to jail for a murder he didn't commit. We've told him that won't happen, but he doesn't believe us."

We made our good-byes, and I left, intending to call Pearl and see if I could take her to lunch. As I walked out, I thought of Noah, afraid of being arrested for his biological father's murder. Smart kid. Smarter than his parents.

Pearl Brewster's old Victorian house was less than a block from Elliott's office just off the courthouse square. At my call, she'd told me to come on over and join her for lunch at the house, so I walked to the huge old mansion, full of scrolls and fancywork above the porch and a first floor overhang.

Of course, when originally built, Pearl's house sat on a huge estate, which had been sold off in pieces to developers over the years as her grandparents and parents tried to re-coup some of the fortune old Dolph Brewster, town founder, had left and they had lost. Now, Pearl had only one and a half lots, which still allowed her an enormous garden behind the house.

Pearl greeted me with a laugh and a hug. She had a great laugh, almost as though the earth itself laughed happily and outrageously at the silliness of humans. I'd missed that laugh at the last two angry occasions where I'd seen her.

"Come in, Skeet. Have some iced tea with fresh mint and lemon balm from the herb garden."

I didn't suppose I could ask for coffee without being impo-lite so I took the tea, which was surprisingly strong and good with nice hints of minty lemon flavor. My problem with most of the iced tea in town was that it was either non-caffeinated herbal tea or too weak. "This is good." Even I could hear the surprise in my voice, but she just laughed again.

"Come over here and have a seat." She gestured as she walked from the hall into a large living room. "I'll be right back with a tray for us. At my age, I believe in being comfortable when I eat." She headed to a doorway at the back of the room.

"I can carry the tray," I offered.

She turned and rolled her eyes at me. "Don't be ridiculous. The day I can't handle a tray of light sandwiches, just stick me out on an ice floe the way the Eskimos do and leave me to starve to death."

I didn't tell her that the Inuit would rather not be called Eskimo or that in the distant past their elders usually chose voluntarily to go away and die during times of famine when they felt they were an unproductive burden on their families. I'd learned the hard way when I was a kid that most people didn't want to be corrected in their stereotypes of Native peoples. They liked those caricatures the anthropologists had created of us.

I wandered around the room, which to my pleasant surprise, was not furnished in Victorian antique furniture. A large linen-covered sofa stretched down the center of the room, and substantial armchairs were scattered around the perimeter of the room. The huge Oriental rug that covered the middle of the wood floor might well have dated back to the last part of Victoria's reign, however.

From the table between the two Queen Anne chairs facing the fire, I picked up a hinged silver photo frame. It held a photo of a handsome young soldier in uniform, probably during World War II or right afterward. The other side of the frame held a candid snapshot of the same young man in casual civilian clothes with his arm around a stunningly beautiful teenage girl. Both were happy and laughing, and something about the way the girl threw back her head reminded me of my hostess.

"Yes, we'll sit in those chairs. They're quite comfortable

and with the table between us, it'll be just like sitting in a very nice teahouse."

Pearl carried in a silver tray with a dinner plate of sandwiches, one with turnovers, and a stack of green glass luncheon plates just like my aunt Agnes had. She gestured back toward the kitchen. "I should have taken you up on your offer. There wasn't room for the pitcher on the tray. Would you bring it out? And those napkins right beside it."

I set down the frame and headed for the kitchen. "Is that you in that photo?"

I snatched up the linen napkins and the glass pitcher with pink and green flowers etched on it. Next to it on the kitchen counter lay two bunches of the recently harvested herbs with the sharp garden knife that had just been used to cut them. No wonder they tasted so fresh.

By the time I returned to the living room, Pearl had the table between the chairs all set for us and the tray and plate of turnovers on another table within reach. She was holding the hinged frame and looking at the photos.

"Just set the pitcher over there with the tray," she said, "and bring the napkins here. Yes, that's me. Though you'd hardly know it now. Enjoy your youth and beauty, Skeet. It's so fleeting." She set the frame up on the mantel and took her chair as I took mine.

"I'm not that young or beautiful." I laughed.

She smiled and shook her head. "You'll look back at a picture from now when you're sixty or seventy and know how beautiful and young you were and how dumb not to know it at the time."

I looked for a way to change the subject. "Who's the man?"

Her smile dimmed without quite leaving her face. She

looked up at the photos sitting on the mantel. "That was my husband, Darrell."

I'd assumed from her last name that Pearl had never married.

"He died in Korea," she said matter-of-factly, still looking up at the photos. I was relieved to realize that it was so long ago that the grief was no longer fresh and sharp. "Although I always have believed that my father killed him."

Caught by surprise, I was silent for a second before asking, "Why do you believe that?"

She looked back at me. "It's a long story. Let's eat while I tell it. I was a wild thing when I was young, gave my family fits. I guess I was spoiled silly."

I looked at my sandwich, chicken salad with grapes, almonds, and more of the fresh lemon balm leaves, and took a bite. It was delicious.

After swallowing a bite herself, Pearl continued. "Then, at sixteen, I fell in love with Darrell. He was my father's gardener, son of a local farmer, but smart as a whip and sweet as anything. He told me my father would stop us, but I didn't think anything could stop me. Hell, I was sixteen, Skeet. We all think we're indestructible and unstoppable at that age." She gave a rueful laugh.

I washed down chicken salad with my tea and listened.

"He wasn't poor, you know. His father's farm was successful, and he'd inherit. He had such plans to save up and buy more land, put all the new methods of farming he'd been reading about into play. I became a gardener for him and came to see why he loved growing things and working with the earth. Just one of many things he gave me."

She took a sip of tea while I ate my sandwich.

"I insisted we elope and get married in Oklahoma. You didn't have to wait there, and I was old enough by their state laws. Father sent the police after us, claiming I was kidnapped and threw Darrell in jail while I was dragged home, kicking and screaming. Mother threatened to have me committed to the state hospital or Menninger's. They could do that in those days, you know. No court hearing. Just sign you in. Then you were imprisoned until they said you could get out. Some people spent their whole lives there."

I shivered. "We forget how barbaric the good old days were."

Pearl nodded with a sad smile. "My father told Darrell he had a choice of going to prison or going to the Korean War. Darrell chose the army, saying we could be together when he came back. He kept getting transferred to units right before they went into the thick of the worst fighting. I'm sure my father was responsible for that. Darrell never came back. He was killed at Heartbreak Ridge."

She shook her head, as if coming out of a nightmare. "Sad story for such a beautiful day, I'm afraid. Grab that plate of turnovers and bring them over, will you? They're made with apples from my own trees."

I brought the plate over to her and held it out so she could serve herself. "They look delicious."

"The funny thing is," she said as she took one and put it on her plate, "that I did end up in Menninger's. For eighteen months. They sent me to boarding school in New England, but I ran off and tried to enlist as a WAC so I could follow Darrell to Korea. Father's detective caught me before I could and brought me home. The next day while we were screaming at each other, I learned Darrell had been killed and had a nervous breakdown."

"Oh, Pearl." I was horrified at what that young girl had experienced.

She gave me a rueful smile. "I don't know why I'm revisiting the past today. I had my revenge on my father. I never married again, never had a child. I'm the last of the Brewsters, and he died, knowing his line—of which he was so inordinately proud—would die with me."

My eyes widened at that. Revenge, indeed. I finished off my apple turnover, which was truly delicious. "But you've gone on to have a full life. You haven't let it destroy you. I admire that. So many women just can't believe they can go through life without a man."

"Well, I'd rather have gone through life with Darrell by my side," she retorted. "I'm not someone who chose a single life for political reasons. But I wasn't going to take some paltry substitute. Better alone than with some lesser man."

She handed me the plate of apple turnovers with a wicked grin. "There's another for each of us."

"I probably shouldn't," I demurred.

"Listen to this old woman, Skeet. Take all the pleasure you can in life and store it up. Because there'll be a hell of a lot of pain and irritation. You have to keep that balance in your favor." She winked and shoved the plate at me, and I took the turnover. "Now, what did you come here for? I know it wasn't to listen to some maudlin old woman tell of her long-lost love."

"No, it wasn't. I had no idea you had such a dramatic history. Actually, I'd hoped you could fill me in on some more recent history. Ash Mowbray. You said you knew him when he was growing up here."

She frowned. "Everyone knew him. He sometimes talked to me about his troubles with his parents. He had a lot of them.

He did yard work for about five or six single or widowed women in town—not me, of course. I do all of my own gardening and yard work still." She smiled with pride in her independence. "It's a way to feel close to Darrell again."

Her smile faded and she sighed. "Those odd jobs Ash picked up were probably the only way he ate, other than the groceries that I got the Episcopal Church to give to him. His parents were real degenerates. I guess I should have realized that he would turn out as bad. Blood or upbringing, one or the other certainly played out true with him. Joe doesn't really think Noah killed him, surely?"

I sighed. "He's under a lot of pressure, and things look bad for Noah."

"No, we can't let that happen. You won't, will you, Skeet?" She stared directly into my eyes. "You mustn't. Angie's in a real panic over it. She thinks that big developer, Walker Lynch, is going to force Joe to arrest Noah for it without looking elsewhere. I agreed with her that she needed to get you to agree to investigate. You can't let Joe arrest Noah just because that's the easiest thing for him to do. There were so many others with reasons to harm Ash."

I nodded. There truly were a lot of folks who hated that man.

She frowned slightly, as if trying to remember something. "There was that charm found at the murder scene and that flash drive. Bea Roberts told me about them. I heard the charm was Chelsea's. Does Joe know who the flash drive belonged to? I imagine that should be pretty easy to learn."

"I hadn't heard about the flash drive. What about it?" My tone had become sharp. Joe did not mention the damn thing to me. A major piece of evidence. Even though the whole town seemed to know about it.

Pearl looked a little nervous at that hint of anger in my voice. "Well, I don't know. Bea just told me a flash drive was dropped at the scene of the murder. I didn't hear anything more. Wouldn't Joe know?"

I nodded. "I will definitely have to talk to him about that." I took a deep breath to calm myself. "Did you know that Ash and Chelsea were dating during his last year in high school?"

Pearl's mouth hardened. "I did not, and I'd have given him an earful if I'd realized he was seducing that girl. I was part of the group in town that helped him get away from his awful parents so he could try to make something of himself. If I'd known he was leaving that girl behind in trouble, I never would have, I swear."

She shook her head. "I'd have sworn that Chelsea would have been the last one to mess around with Ash. He was a little rough around the edges and wilder. She was the quintessential good girl. Honor roll. Class vice-president. All of that."

I shrugged. "Wouldn't be the first time a good girl went for a bad boy."

"You're right. Girls can be so stupid at that age." Pearl's expression turned sad. "After some people here tried to help him, he seems to want to make trouble for the whole town. I just wish he'd never come back."

"Yeah. So do I."

I rose from my chair. "This has been lovely—and help-ful. But I have to head back to work before the troops get restless. Can I take these things back to the kitchen and help you clean up?"

"No, don't worry about them, Skeet. That will only take a matter of minutes." She stood and walked beside me to the door.

I turned and fumbled for the right thing to say. "Thank you so much for the delightful lunch."

A smile erased the sadness from her face. "Thank you for listening to an old woman reliving her life's trauma. Not the happiest of lunchtime discussions, I'm afraid. I don't know what happened to my manners."

"Your manners are impeccable as always, Pearl. Take care now."

We hugged briefly, and I started down the steps.

"Skeet," Pearl called after me. I stopped and turned back to face her.

"Don't let Joe take the easy way out and use Noah as a scapegoat. He's been hurt enough already, and that will leave us with a killer running loose in our town."

CHAPTER 7

I spent that afternoon working on budget figures with Frank and Mary at the office until my cell phone alarm told me it was time to head home. It was the day for Brian's appointment with Karen, who was his therapist to help him deal with his earlier involvement with violence that left him an orphan. So I knew he'd have already walked on home. It was Sam's night with my dad, and I was grateful he hadn't had to call me during the day to say the dreadful Marie had shown up to spirit Charlie away again.

I'd arranged with Elliott to visit the Steens after supper to question Noah, and I didn't want to be late. I needed to find out not only what Noah would tell me but what Joe had asked him and what he'd answered. I was upset that Joe hadn't told me about the flash drive that had been found at the crime scene. If he'd hold out on that, what else was he not telling me?

So after a quick stop at home to eat dinner, I left Gran and Brian playing cutthroat poker at the kitchen table. She'd make him as good a poker player as she'd made me, I supposed. I hoped he'd find it as useful as I had. I reminded Brian he needed to walk Lady since I wouldn't be around, and I knew he'd do that when they finished and Gran hauled out her knitting—socks, always socks, unless someone had a baby coming that needed a blanket.

It was four blocks to the Steen house, and I walked them, enjoying the slight chill of evening and the quiet of the town at night with only the sound of crickets and the occasional whoosh of a car a few blocks away on the square. Brewster had some night life, but it was all on the other side of the square down in Girlville, the section which catered to students with fast food, theaters, and bars. I could hear a train's faint wail in the distance and knew it would soon be hooting and rattling through town.

All the lights were on when I arrived at the Steen house, which I'd have wondered at, except that was the case with most of the houses I passed, including Pearl's big, old mansion across the street from the Steens. A murder in town left everyone uneasy with too much darkness.

Chelsea answered the door and ushered me inside. I'd never been in their home before, and I was impressed. If I'd thought about it, I'd have expected icy elegance, given Chelsea's sense of style in clothes, but it was a relaxed, colorful home with lots of texture—pottery, baskets, and blooming plants—and homey touches, like an Amish quilt and two granny-square afghans, that I'd never have expected from Chelsea.

Noah sat on the edge of the denim-slipcovered couch, and in the leather easy chair next to it, Elliott put down the newspaper he was reading.

"Skeet, thank you for tackling this," Chelsea said. "We appreciate it so much."

I shook my head. "Don't get too happy about it. I'm going to find the killer, whoever it is, and you three currently have the best motives of anyone in town."

"But none of us killed Ash," Elliott said calmly. "And you'll prove that because you're not just trying to toss the easiest person in jail to keep the wolves away."

I tried not to roll my eyes. His faith in me was touching, his faith in his family's innocence even more so, and both could be so misplaced.

I turned to address his wife. "Chelsea, a charm was found at the murder scene. Joe says it was yours."

"Yes, I identified it. It's a silver shamrock, my lucky charm." A hint of sheepishness crept over her features. "My grandfather gave it to me when I was a girl. I've always carried it with me. We were close, he and I." Her eyes took on a faraway look, as if remembering. "My grandfather's dad was from Ireland."

"When did you first realize it was gone?" I wondered what she'd felt like when she realized it was missing. Had she just worried about losing her grandfather's gift, or had she been in a panic because she knew it must have happened while she killed Ash?

She gave me a puzzled look. "That's just it. I didn't realize it was gone until it showed up . . . out there."

"How did they know to show it to you to identify?" Had someone tipped Joe off to the fact that one of the items found at the crime scene belonged to Chelsea?

"They didn't. They showed it to Noah first, and he told them it looked like my charm." She gave a nervous laugh. "Later, Joe asked me to look at it and I identified it."

I wondered how it had come off its bracelet and then realized I'd never seen her wear any kind of charm bracelet. "And you didn't realize it was gone?"

"No. I had to look in my purse—that's where I always kept it—to see if it wasn't really still there when Joe showed it to me. I always kept it in with my change zipped into my wallet. Sometimes, I'd be in a hurry and dig it out for a dime." She laughed again without the nervousness of the earlier one. "When I first saw it, I thought, 'How odd. That looks like mine.' It was only when I dug in my change and couldn't find it that I realized it was mine."

I frowned at that. Who would have known about it and where she carried it? Who would have had access to it? "Who could have taken it from your purse?"

She shook her head. "I can't begin to think. I mean, why would someone steal only a charm like that from my purse—and then throw it away at a murder scene? Makes no sense to me."

"Perhaps someone wanted to incriminate you in Ash's murder." I stared straight into her eyes.

Creases formed between her perfect brows, and she narrowed her eyes. "Why?"

"Well, you have quite a motive. He made a real mess of your life when he came back and decided to go public about your past and Noah."

She shook her head in disbelief. "But why would someone hate me enough to want to incriminate me?"

I raised my eyebrows in disbelief. Surely, she wasn't that naïve. "They don't have to hate you, Chelsea. They just have to be afraid of being caught and punished for murder themselves. They might see throwing suspicion on you as an easy out."

"Oh." She nodded slightly. "Well, that makes sense, at least. Damn little else does."

I kept my tone casual and matter-of-fact as I completed my answer to her. "And then, of course, it could have accidentally fallen out of your purse when you killed Ash."

"Now, wait a minute!" Elliott cried, half-standing.

"No, Mom wouldn't do that!" Noah also shot to his feet.

Chelsea's expression turned brittle as she nodded her head in acknowledgment of what I'd said. "It's all right, Elliott, Noah. Sit back down." She turned her steely blue eyes on me. "This is what you mean about having to look at everything and everyone, right?"

"Exactly." I couldn't see that charm accidentally falling out of a zippered change compartment in a wallet inside her closed purse, no matter how hard she swung that golf club. Someone had to have deliberately placed it there after stealing it from her purse.

"You go right ahead," she said. "That's what we want. Someone to really investigate. That's the only way the real killer can be caught and Noah exonerated."

"I'm sorry I yelled at you, Skeet," Elliott said with a shame-faced look.

I cleared my throat. "Well, I've talked to you, Elliott. To-night I'm here to question Noah."

I looked at the kid, and he nodded his head in resignation. He hardly resembled the confident, successful high school heartthrob he'd been a few days earlier. His clothes looked like he'd slept in them. He hadn't shaved, and his eyes were like pits in his young face.

Elliott stood and walked over to Chelsea. Taking her arm, he said, "Let's leave Skeet and Noah to it then, dear. Is there any coffee made?" He started to move her toward the kitchen.

"I'd love some coffee," I said, "but you two shouldn't leave. One of you should always be with Noah when he's questioned. Didn't your lawyer or Joe tell you that when Noah was taken in for questioning the first time?"

Chelsea wheeled around to face me. "No! We didn't have our lawyer here when Joe took him, and Joe said we couldn't come with him."

I frowned. "You always have to have a parent or lawyer with a minor when you question them. It's required. Noah's not eighteen yet, is he?"

"No, I'm not," he said in a rusty voice, as if he hadn't spoken all day. "Not for two more months."

Joe must have thought he was already eighteen, but it was sloppy not to check. Anything he'd found out from that interrogation was inadmissible now.

Chelsea's face hardened with outrage. "He deliberately did that to try to trap Noah without us there to help him." She turned to Elliott. "I told you. He wants to steamroll Noah into jail, so he can say this is solved and over with."

Elliott patted her shoulder. "That's why we've asked Skeet to investigate. She doesn't have the pressure Joe has to come up fast with just anyone convenient. She's looking to find out who really killed Ash and stop him."

I sat down in a side chair directly across the coffee table from Noah's spot on the couch and pulled out my notebook. Elliott ushered Chelsea over to sit beside Noah and returned to his chair.

I decided to start out being very direct with no warm-up chatter and easy questions. "Noah, how did your golf club end up the murder weapon? Who had access to your clubs?"

He raised both hands, palms up, in a helpless gesture. "Anyone who had the keys to get into the clubhouse after closing could grab my clubs or those of anyone else who keeps theirs there. And someone—that damn Ash or whoever killed him— had those keys, or he wouldn't have been there with a golf cart that night. The golf carts are locked up, too. I can't get my own clubs once they've locked up the building. I told Joe that."

I found myself nodding. "Good point. But how did your mother's good luck charm get there?"

Noah shook his head wildly. "I don't know. But I didn't put it there, and neither did she. We were here that night, all of us."

I quirked an eyebrow in question at Elliott, and he nodded. "I told Joe. We were all home here together. We went to bed early, and no one left the house all night."

"How can you be sure of that?" I asked, remembering my own escapades, climbing down trellises and such, when I was a teen in Oklahoma. "Did you wake periodically and check beds?"

"No," he said sadly. "I can't swear to it that way. Though I'd know if either of them woke in the night, I'm sure."

"I would definitely know if my son left the house in the middle of the night," Chelsea said firmly. "And Noah's never been one of those kinds of kids, anyway. He doesn't stay out after his curfew. He doesn't get in trouble. He's a good kid."

I smiled at Noah. "I sure wish I could say I never get in trouble. That must be pretty great."

He shrugged. "I've just never thought it was worth all the hassle for the silly reasons most of the guys do it. It's just easier if you play the game by the rules. Works out better for everyone."

I sighed and scribbled in the notebook. "So, none of you has an alibi for the murder then? Any one of you could have snuck out in the middle of the night to meet Ash and kill him, right?"

"But if it was one of us, Skeet," Elliott asked, "why would

we use Noah's club and drop Chelsea's good luck charm? Why incriminate our own family?"

Chelsea nodded eagerly. "Can't you see we're being framed? And anyway, Ash had done his damage to us. He couldn't hurt us any longer after what he'd already done. But there were plenty of people who still feared what he was going to do to their livelihood."

I thought of what Chelsea had admitted to me that Ash had done to her since coming back to town and wondered if he'd done all the damage he could do. What would she have done to keep her husband and her son from finding out that she'd been having sex with Ash? And what would they have done if they'd learned he'd been forcing her to do it?

Noah still sat, silent and glum, looking at the floor.

"Noah," I said gently, looking straight at him. He looked up and met my eyes. "Did you meet Ash that night and have an argument with him? Maybe take a swing at him with that club without really meaning to harm him?"

"Now, wait a minute!" "You can't think——" Ellott and Chelsea erupted at the same time but were silenced when Noah answered me.

"No, Skeet. I hated him, and I was so angry with him. But I didn't take my golf club and hit him and kill him. I couldn't do something like that. I wouldn't. I might have belted him in the face back at the city council meeting if Dad hadn't held me back. But I didn't kill him."

The kid's face and tone were earnest. But there was something about the deliberate way he answered my question that seemed a little off. I had the sense he wasn't telling me everything. And, of course, he wasn't. People lie or hold back information in murder investigations. Often they're innocent, but they have something they don't want anyone to know, so they lie and evade. It always muddies the water. Noah had something he wanted to hide. I didn't believe it was murder, but it was something.

The next morning I headed for Joe's office early, walking in to the sound of a train hollering its protest in the distance. No offerings of coffee from the Herbal to sweeten the conversation, either. Joe had held back information from me that the whole town had. Now, that was his right, though it was a crappy thing to do to a friend. But interrogating a minor without a parent or guardian present was a flat-out violation of the law. And it wasn't like Joe. What in the hell was going on? I wanted answers, and I wasn't going away without them.

The department secretary hadn't received the word that I was persona non grata yet, so she waved me right in to her boss's office. She'd hear about it later, I knew. I figured I'd owe her some candy or a nice gift card of some kind after this.

"Good morning, Joe," I said as I breezed in and sat in front of him. "Time to talk, don't you think?"

He was starting to look as bad as Noah. His shirt was rumpled, and he'd missed some whiskers when shaving. His eyes didn't look like they were closing at night, at all. He groaned at the sight of me. I have that kind of effect on men sometimes.

"Skeet, what now?"

I leaned forward in a conversational manner with my elbows on the desk. "Oh, just two little things. First, a flash drive was found at the crime scene. Everyone in town seems to know about it. Except me. Why didn't you mention it, Joe? And what have you learned from it?"

He closed his eyes for a second. "I should have figured you'd hear about it." He took a deep breath. "I don't have to tell you anything, Skeet. You have no official standing in this investigation."

I stared at him. We were supposed to be friends. I could see how much that was worth after our last meeting and this one—just about spit.

He sighed and his voice softened a little. "Listen, Skeet. I don't know anything yet. I sent the flash drive off to the computer expert at the KCPD Crime Lab. We both went to that seminar where they talked about how ignorant police could mess up vital computer info on jump or flash drives and other hardware if they tried to work them themselves and how we should always send for the computer experts. So I did. Won't hear back for a few days, they said."

I nodded. "Okay, that makes sense. Though why you didn't mention it does not. But never mind about that." He'd started to protest but subsided at that. "Why on God's green earth did you interrogate Noah without his parents or guardian or lawyer present? You know better than that, Joe. He's a minor. Anything you got out of him will be thrown out of court."

He shrugged. "Well, then, it's a good thing I didn't get anything out of him, isn't it?"

I didn't know this Joe who could just blow off such unprofessional behavior as if it didn't matter. "But why do it? You know the procedure."

His nostrils flared. "Yes, I do, Skeet. I've been a cop all my adult life, a lot longer than you have, and I know the procedures backward and forward. I don't need you to teach me how to suck eggs."

I hadn't heard that term since I was a kid in Oklahoma, but I knew what it meant: You worthless greenhorn, don't come telling experienced me how to do things. I've forgotten more than you'll ever know.

I stiffened. "I thought we were friends, Joe. My mistake." I stood and leaned over the desk to face him. "But something's going on to make you do things that I'd have sworn you'd never do. I'm going to find out what it is. And I'm going to find out who the killer is and stop him, too. Since you don't seem to have any real interest in doing that."

I whirled and marched out of his office and past the surprised secretary as fast as my feet would take me. Before I said something worse. Before I really blew up. Who says I have anger management problems? I thought that was pretty good anger management right there.

The train had reached the heart of town now, and its clattering and clanking and blowing off steam mirrored my own mood.

Something was wrong with Joe. He might not consider me a friend any longer, and I wasn't sure I'd ever consider him one again, but he had been my friend and I was going to find out what or who had him doing things he'd normally never do. I'd help the stupid son of a gun, whether he wanted it or not.

The morning brought me a series of frustrating meetings on the campus-parking-garage-that-refused-to-be-completed during which I was sharper spoken than usual, I suppose. At least, Frank Booth asked when I'd finally decided to quit being patient and get hardass with the contractors like he thought I should have been for months. I had to catch myself to keep from snapping at him when he was actually trying to compliment me. Frank and I are not a great fit, and I got the job he wanted, but, fortunately, being good cops together is more important to both of us than waging war on the other, so I didn't want to mess up that delicate balance.

I left early for lunch to get outside and walk myself calm. I thought I'd stop at Peter Hume's shop, Creative Home Design, to interview him on the way to the Herbal for a quiet lunch alone, where I couldn't bite off anyone's head. The walk down the hill from the university and then over to the courthouse square with its trains moaning in the distance and trees flaming around me helped to clear my head. I hated the fact that I'd inherited my dad's explosive temper. You'd think I was a redhead like him instead of dark-haired like my mom's family. I wanted to get that hot head under better control.

Fortunately, I was in a better frame of mind when I reached Creative Home Design and entered, making the bell over the door jingle. Inside the store, it didn't look like a place of business at all but rather a large, open living room divided into spaces with different styles and stuffed with furniture and decorative items. I faced, on the back wall, a lofty, elaborately carved walnut hall tree with its own covered bench and sizable gilded mirror surrounded by ornate brass coat hooks. I hoped Gran never entered this shop because I'd have to find room for this monstrosity in my house if she did, and I'd never be able to.

From the dark back of the store, Dante Marcus poked his head out of the velvet curtain hiding the office door. "May I help you? Oh, Skeet."

He continued on into the room, and I walked toward him. "Hi, Dante. Is Peter around? I was hoping to talk with him."

He raised his eyebrows. "Well, I'm sorry I won't do, but he's not here right now." He smiled to let me know he wasn't serious.

I returned his smile. "You'd certainly do if I planned to decorate my house, but I'm afraid I wanted to talk to Peter about Ash Mowbray."

His cheerful face darkened. "That man. Has he found some way to cause trouble from beyond the grave?"

I gave a little involuntary laugh. "No, but I'm afraid the fact that Ash is in the grave will cause trouble for a while yet. Too many questions. I've been talking to people who had to deal with him, trying to piece together some answers, so life can get back to normal in town."

Dante nodded, then grew thoughtful. "Skeet, could I ask you a question or two? They might have to do with Ash. Then again, they might not." His expression grew more troubled as he spoke.

"Sure. Fire away." Curiosity aroused, I smiled to encourage him.

He gestured toward the curtained door. "Let's go into the office."

I followed him into another room that was all sleek modern office. This was obviously where all the business transactions took place. I took the leather chair he indicated, and he took its mate.

"What do you know about anonymous letters?" he asked.

Confused about what that might have to do with Ash's death, I peered at him. "If it's just one letter to one person, it's usually someone in that person's closest circle—immediate family, spouse, close friend. If it's a series of letters to the same person, the circle expands. Each of these usually arises from a past argument or a situation in which the letter writer feels wronged, even if the letters seem to have nothing to do with that event or situation."

He nodded deliberately, as if he was giving serious consideration to everything I said.

"If it's a series of letters to multiple people," I continued, "that's a different kettle of fish. In that case, it may well be someone who doesn't know the recipients well, at all."

Dante frowned slightly, as if thinking over what I'd said. "All I know about is one letter." He looked up at me.

"Did you receive it?" I was curious as to who would send an anonymous letter to Dante, who'd only been in town for six months and kept a pretty low profile. Then, again, there are always those who have problems with anyone different from themselves, so perhaps it was a bit of homophobia popping up. I hated to think of that happening in my nice town, but I knew ugliness resided in Brewster just as much as in Kansas City.

"No, Peter did. I noticed the strange lettering when he opened it. Letters cut from some printed material. I asked him what it was, just curious. I thought it might be some kind of invitation to an artist's show or something. He bit my head off, then apologized and said it was just an upsetting anonymous letter. But he hid it away and wouldn't let me see it when I asked." He frowned heavily, making him look older. "He said he'd burn it because it was poisonous trash."

I had to sigh at the expected response. *Destroy the nasty letter.* It was the normal one, but it made any investigation much harder. "When did it arrive?"

"In Tuesday morning's mail. I wondered if that wasn't why he was so explosively angry at the council meeting that night." He tilted his head sideways and held open his hands. "Like he'd already been so infuriated at the letter that the stuff Ash said poured gas on an already burning fire."

I nodded and wished I could get my hands on that letter to

see what it said. Peter probably had burned it, though, or more likely ripped it up and thrown it in the trash. People did appalling things like that most of the time. Usually, anonymous letter writers were harmless, at least physically. But sometimes the hatred that caused a poison-pen letter grew inside the writer until it erupted in violence. In those cases, the letters were crucial bits of evidence, and all too often they'd been destroyed.

"Is Peter still upset about it?"

Dante looked puzzled. "He seems much calmer since he learned Ash was dead. I don't know if that's because one of the causes of his anger is gone and he can handle the anger at the letter writer better, or if the letter had something to do with the whole Ash Mowbray mall thing. But something's better."

I nodded. "But you're still concerned?"

"Yes. If someone is out there sending anonymous hate mail to Peter, I want to find a way to stop them. I don't want Peter hurt any more than he's already been." Dante's face settled into determined lines.

I frowned. "How has Peter already been hurt?"

Dante looked embarrassed. "I probably shouldn't have said anything. Peter doesn't know that I know. His ex-partner dumped him for a younger guy and stole the business in Kansas City that they'd both invested in and built. Took it right out from under him. That was why Peter moved here to open this shop. From what I've heard, it was a nasty, painful time for him, and he never wants to talk about his past because of it." He stared down at the floor, as if he regretted telling me.

I nodded. "Then what exactly did you want to ask me about anonymous letters, Dante?"

He locked his eyes back on me. "How do we find out who sent them? And how do we stop them?"

"Without Peter learning what you're trying to do?" Of course, that was what he wanted. No one ever wanted to do anything the direct, easy way.

He hesitated for a fraction of a second. "Yes. I don't want him to find out that I know about what happened to him." His voice filled with intensity. "I want him to finally feel safe enough to tell me about it himself."

"Did the letter come through the mail?" I took out my notebook and pen.

His forehead wrinkled in concentration as he tried to remember. "I don't think so. It didn't look like there was a stamp on the envelope. I think it was dropped through the mail slot in the front door of the shop. We have that because the shop's not open every day that the mail comes, and some days it's only open in the afternoon while the mail comes in the morning. It just makes it easier."

"Makes it easier for anonymous letter writers, too," I muttered.

At that moment, my cell phone rang and I answered it to find Pearl on the line.

"Skeet, I hate to bother you, but I remember how upset you were to learn that Joe hadn't told you about that flash drive found at the murder scene. Bea's here with me. Her cousin is with the county and just told her there was something else found at the scene of the crime. I thought you'd want to know about it."

I sighed. "You're absolutely right. What was it?"

"That ridiculous huge tie pin that Harvey's always wearing!" Bea yelled in the background. "Left near Ash's hand, they say. Like he might have pulled it from Harvey's tie."

"Hush, Bea!" Pearl said. "No need to speculate and feed the rumors. Skeet, dear, I can't imagine what that was doing there because we all know Harvey couldn't have had anything to do with Ash's death—"

"Yes, he could!" shouted Bea in the background.

"But I thought you'd want to know," Pearl continued over her exclamations.

I sighed, a little mystified myself, both at the variety of clues and at Joe's uncharacteristic behavior. "Thanks, Pearl. It might be important and it might not. But we have to know about it first before we can determine that. And thank Bea for me, as well."

We hung up, and I could feel anger toward Joe rising in me. My first impulse was to storm out to his office and confront him, but I stifled it. I knew it wouldn't help the situation any. I had contacts with the county crime scene techs and KCPD's crime lab. I'd find out what I needed to know from them and just bypass old Joe altogether.

"What was that?" Dante asked anxiously.

"Nothing concerning you or Peter," I reassured him. "Just another troubling question about Mr. Ashton Mowbray."

I rose from the comfortable leather chair. "I've got to go, Dante, but I'll do what I can on this anonymous letter thing. It might not have anything to do with Ash and his death." I suspected my voice didn't sound convinced. "I'll be in touch."

He thanked me and saw me to the door of the shop. The whole time I was thinking that this letter had to tie in with Ash's murder somehow. Everything else seemed to. That death was like a tornado sucking everything and everyone into it and carrying them off to somewhere strange.

CHAPTER 8

After walking the short distance from Creative Home Design to the Herbal Coffee Shop, I entered its mint-scented air to settle into a booth in back for a quiet lunch and some serious thinking. There were too many bits and pieces of different people's lives showing up at Ash's death scene. All of those people—Noah, Chelsea, Harvey, and whoever owned the jump drive—couldn't have killed Ash. This wasn't some *Murder on the Orient Express*–style crime. This had been a quickly executed, rather brutal murder. It wasn't some complex locked-room mystery. So why were all of these varied clues showing up?

Obviously, someone was doing it, trying to mislead investigators and incriminate other people. That seemed a bit sophisticated for a high schooler to me. I couldn't see Noah even obtaining all of these pieces of evidence to incriminate others, let alone conceiving the idea and executing it. So who was behind it? And what did Peter's anonymous letter have to do with it all, if anything?

Terry Heldrich interrupted my thought process by sliding

into the seat opposite mine. "You don't mind if I join you, Skeet, do you?"

"Yes——" I began to object.

"Since I've got something about Ash Mowbray's murder to tell you, and I've heard you're investigating it behind Joe's back," he continued smoothly, with a little smirk.

"I'm not going behind Joe's back," I objected. "I've told him what I'm doing and why."

"And he's thrilled, no doubt." Terry's tone was sarcastic.

As I was about to retort, I thought better of it and asked, "What do you have to tell me about the murder then?"

"Walker and that Peter Hume fellow got into a huge argument about Ash. You know Walker was funding the project. Ash was really just the front man. Of course, he had an investment in it, but most of the money was going to come from Walker's companies. Ash was involved because he was a local boy made good. He was supposed to be able to obtain good publicity and local approval." He laughed harshly.

"Well, Walker picked a real winner there, didn't he?" I asked in my own driest tones.

He nodded. "No one knew Ash was more fixated on coming back and taking vengeance on those who scorned him as a kid than on a successful project. Too bad. He'd have made a fortune and stayed alive if he'd stuck with the program."

I stared at him, considering what he'd said. "And how did Walker feel about being used for Ash's own agenda?"

He smiled with genuine happiness. "Oh, he was livid. You know Walker. He likes to be the manipulator, not the manipulated."

Walker had the brutality to pull off that murder and the smarts to scatter other people's belongings around as red herrings. Maybe this would be my chance to take Walker Lynch down and put him behind bars where he couldn't hurt anyone again.

"And where did you just disappear to?" Terry asked, bringing me out of my inner speculation. "Don't get interested in Walker. He's not safe for women. Not safe, at all."

I gave a little laugh. "Not interested in that way in your boss. Never. I can see what he really is. And if you can, why do you work for him?"

"He pays well." He looked uncomfortable. "Trust me."

At that, I laughed in earnest. "Trust you? Not likely, Mr. Secretive. That's like Coyote telling Rabbit to trust him to carry Rabbit across the stream in his jaws."

He joined in my laughter, but his eyes were pensive. "But Rabbit's a trickster, too. He always has some ploy to escape and make a fool out of anyone."

I was surprised that he knew about Rabbit. Quite a few people have heard of Coyote the Trickster, but very few outside of the Cherokee and other Southeastern tribes are aware of Rabbit the Trickster. Gran told me that our Rabbit was the prototype for the slave narratives of Bre'r Rabbit.

His eyes took on that hooded, intense air as he watched me. I could feel the heat of his gaze on my skin, and I didn't like it. Sometimes Terry had a kind of electrifying effect on me, but I'd long ago decided it was just because I hadn't had sex in a while, nothing important. The best thing to do was to stay away from him and ignore him when I couldn't.

I shifted in my seat. "So what was this argument that Walker and Peter had? You know, the excuse you used to invade my quiet lunch?"

He pulled his gaze away from me, and things returned to

normal between us, except for the fact that both of us were breathing a little faster than usual. He shook his head with a rueful laugh. "You never give an inch, do you?"

"Never. Tell me about this argument."

"Peter accosted Walker. Quite threateningly, so I had to step in and ask him to back off."

I rolled my eyes. "Middle-aged, potbellied Peter was a threat to Walker that required your hard-ass, military intervention? Since when? Walker's younger, taller, more fit. Why couldn't he back Peter down by himself?"

Terry shrugged gracefully. "I merely asked him politely to step back and let go of Walker's lapel, Skeet. I didn't pull a gun on him."

I could feel my lips purse in cynicism. "You politely threatened him with your own obviously dangerous self, right?"

He shook his head in distress. "Peter backed off physically but continued to yell at Walker because he blamed him for bringing Ash and this project to Brewster to ruin him and all the other shopkeepers on the square. Walker, of course, denied that it would harm them—much—and said he was only interested in progress and the continuing welfare of the town." With his last words, Terry's voice had taken on a singsong cadence as if reciting something he'd heard over and over again.

I shrugged. "There's nothing new there, Terry. Head on out. I vant to be alone." I turned back to my food, determined to ignore him until he left.

"You haven't heard it all, Skeet."

I refused to look up.

"Peter threatened physical harm to either Walker or 'his boy' Ash."

I looked up at that.

"He said, 'Maybe you've got this thug'—I believe that was a reference to me—'to protect you, but who's going to protect your boy, Ash, when someone decides the world will be a better place without him in it?' Walker said, 'Are you threatening to kill Ash or me?' And Peter said, 'Are you afraid? You and your boy really ought to be.'"

I stared at him. "When was this?"

"Early Tuesday afternoon. I'd not have paid much attention to it—as you noted, he's not an intimidating figure—but the next morning Ash was found dead."

I nodded, my mind flipping from the arrival of the anonymous letter at Peter's shop to this threat to Walker to the mini-riot at the city council meeting that evening, all leading to Ash's body on the golf course the next morning when Joe and I were running. Could Peter have lured Ash to the golf course Tuesday night and struck him with Noah's golf club when his back was turned? None of the personal articles strewn about that murder scene belonged to Peter. Could he have collected items that day as he planned to end his problem permanently that night?

I pulled out my notebook and wrote down the conversation Terry had quoted. "Thanks. I'll keep this in mind."

He reached across the table to lightly tap the back of my writing hand, sending a jolt through my nerves that I was sure was simply caused by surprise. I'd have pulled my hand away, but his finger was already gone and I didn't want to show that much reaction to his touch.

"Have dinner with me, Skeet. We could drive into Kansas City. Do you like Thai food? There's a wonderful Thai restaurant that I love to visit. Best panang curry I've had outside of Thailand."

I wondered how he knew I liked Thai food. Before I could refuse, his phone rang. He looked at it and cursed softly before answering. He listened and didn't say a word before hanging up.

"Sorry. That was work-related. I'm afraid I have to go. Do consider having dinner with me, though. I'll ask for your answer later."

He slid from the booth. "And don't lose the address to my apartment. I still expect you to come see it someday."

I threw up my hands in resignation and shook my head as he walked out. I couldn't help watching him all the way out the door and then through the big front window. He was an eye-catching man with a seductive aura of dangerous strength, though I'd be damned if I'd ever admit that to anyone. Didn't even want to admit it to myself. I had to smile a little at his eternal optimism when it came to me. When would he learn?

He stopped at a blue Jaguar parked out front with a blond woman behind the wheel. Terry opened the passenger door and got in, and the blond took off with a roar.

Work-related! Hah! It was a good thing I'd kept myself so armored against him, or I might have felt hurt or disappointed or angry. Asking me out just as he's about to go off with some beautiful bimbo who was obviously more his type than a drab female cop. I refused to waste my time thinking about him, though. I'd known from the beginning he was bad news, and that opinion had just been confirmed. I had plenty of other things to think about. Like Peter Hume and the questions that were mounting about his relationship to Ash's murder.

Just as I finished eating, Miryam slid into the seat across the table from me where Terry had sat earlier. I thought of the blond in that car. She and Miryam were the same type. They knew how to play men. They just expected men to run after them and do whatever they wanted. And men did. Witness Terry. Dropped a conversation with a woman he was trying to go out with to run off at a call. I wondered what it was like to have that kind of power over men.

"Hi, Skeet." Miryam looked around furtively, as if playing a glamorous movie spy who had to worry about being overheard. "Will Ash's murder end this mall project?"

I looked at her with curiosity. "I don't know. It might or it might not. Walker was really behind the project. He might just get a new front man."

She shuddered at the mention of Walker's name. I'd witnessed a strange interaction between the two of them a few months earlier, in which Walker seemed to bully Miryam because of some past connection they'd had, the memory of which seemed to horrify Miryam. I'd had to break up Walker's nasty harassment, and he'd never forgiven me for it. I'd never forgotten the sight I'd had of his true sociopathic nature.

"Miryam, what is it with you and Walker? What does he have to do with you?"

"Nothing!" Her head whipped back and forth in denial. "I won't have anything to do with that man. I know how evil he is."

I held up my hands to calm her. "How do you know he's evil?" I dropped my voice into its lowest, warmest register in the hope of making her feel safe enough to confide in me. "What happened? What did he do to you?"

Miryam held her face in her hands. "I can't tell anyone, Skeet. I just can't talk about it."

I sighed. "You know he's still got power over you. As long as you keep whatever it is secret, he's got a hold on you."

She stared at me, eyes wide in horror. "No, he can't . . . I can't let him have any hold on me." A tear ran from the inside corner of her right eye until it caught in the crease where her nose met her cheek.

I sat and waited in silence for her to open up. It was obvious to me that she wanted and needed to tell someone, but I wasn't sure she'd be able to do it.

She turned her head away from my face to stare off to the side. "Do you remember my sweet old guy I was engaged to marry? Harry?"

I nodded, but she couldn't see and continued anyway. "He died unexpectedly. Heart. Right before we were going to get married. We'd made all the arrangements, had the license, the hall for a reception, a judge to preside, everything."

More silent tears had joined the first. "I found him, you know. Dead. I couldn't believe he'd died and left me. Harry was like a rock. I was in shock for days, I think. Just going through the motions of the funeral and everything. I was kind of lost."

Her voice had softened and grown younger somehow, as if she was turning back the clock. "A friend took me to a party to try to bring me out of myself and get me back into the social whirl. I wasn't ready, though. It was all too much for me. I hid in the library, crying for Harry. Walker found me there."

I didn't like where I feared this was going, but I kept my peace and let her talk.

"He was very sweet and kind. Gave me a handkerchief. Said I didn't have to go mingle. Offered to go bring me a drink to settle my nerves. I was feeling a little better by the time he returned with it. I thought he was probably right. I'd steady my nerves and go out and ask my friend to take me home."

The tears stopped, and her voice grew more detached, as

if she described something she saw on a movie screen that had nothing to do with her. "He was very kind as he talked to me for a minute while I sipped my drink. I started to feel dizzy and funny, and I had trouble talking. I tried to stand, and he caught me before I fell. The next thing I knew he was half-carrying me out of the library."

She turned back to me and looked at me with despair in her eyes. "I couldn't talk to tell anyone there was trouble. He told people I wasn't feeling well and had asked him to take me home."

My jaw was locked with tension. I nodded. "He'd given you some kind of drug, a roofie, right?"

She nodded. "When I came to, I was naked on the floor of his living room. I hurt everywhere and could hardly stand up and walk to gather my clothes, which were scattered all over that floor. With other things I didn't like to look at."

She dropped her head into both hands, covering her face for a second, and spoke through her fingers to the table beneath her. "I can't think about what he might have done to me that night, Skeet. I'd go crazy if I did. I don't think anything's beyond him. I think I'm lucky I'm alive, actually. I remind myself of that when I get to feeling sick about what he must have done to me. I could so easily have just vanished. A grief-stricken woman under mental distress."

"That bastard!" I muttered through clenched teeth.

Miryam looked up, and her perpetually youthful and beautiful face seemed to have aged while in her hands. "You can't let him know I told you. I dressed and called a cab to get home that morning. But he called my condo later and told me what he'd do to me if I ever told anyone. And he made sure I understood that he could do everything he said he would."

I had no doubt that he could do whatever he'd threatened

her with. Walker had a lot of money and tremendous political clout. Lots of powerful people owed him. People like Walker didn't usually need to commit crimes because they could afford whatever they wanted, but sometimes there were things even they couldn't buy. Other people, for example. When people with that kind of wealth and influence turned criminal, it was a cop's nightmare because a lot of the time there was nothing you could do, even when you knew they were guilty.

Miryam made a visible effort to compose herself. "We just need to have him leave and go back to Kansas City. I-I want him out of my town."

I reached across to pat her small white hand. "I won't let him hurt you again, Miryam. I promise that. I may not be able to throw him in jail or make him leave town, but I will not allow him to hurt you ever again."

She stared deeply into my eyes for a second. Then she smiled a shadowy version of her usual brilliant smile. "Thanks, Skeet. But you be careful and stay away from that man. He's pure bad. So much worse than anyone would ever think from looking at him or hearing him talk." She wiped her face with a napkin. "And I've taken enough of your time here. I need to get back to the bookstore, and you probably need to get back to your office."

We both stood, an awkward silence between us.

"Thanks, sweetie." She pressed a quick kiss against my cheek and flitted off toward the door.

I watched her leave and added one more big black mark against Walker Lynch's account in my books. Someday I was going to have the chance to put that man behind bars. Surely, that would come to pass. If I could just be patient enough and work at it.

I decided to walk the long way around the courthouse square to go back to work at the university. My mind was awash in images from Miryam's story that I didn't want to carry around with me and certainly didn't want to carry back to work. I hoped fresh air, train whistles, and the scenic antique store-fronts would clear those images from my head. I also planned to put my mind to work untangling an unrelated problem, like Peter's anonymous letter or Terry's mysterious blond bimbo.

As I walked on past Tintagel Gallery, I heard shouting coming from next door in front of Art's Bar and Grill, where I found Bea Roberts screaming at Mayor Harvey Peebles.

"It's all your fault! You're the one who brought that trailer trash back to town!"

"Bea, that's absolutely no way to speak about someone who's passed away under unfortunate circumstances," Harvey sputtered. "And I did not bring him to town. It was Walker Lynch who brought him in. My initial conversation was with Walker."

I grimaced at that name. Walker Lynch was like some devil that I couldn't escape today, turning up everywhere I looked.

Bea ignored everything Harvey said. "It's absolutely your fault we've had this happen in Brewster. If you hadn't brought Ashton Mowbray back to terrorize this town—"

"But I didn't, Bea," Harvey bleated. "I didn't."

I could see that Bea was only getting wound up and decided this would be a good time to distract her before she gave poor old Harvey a stroke. "Bea, I'm so glad I ran into you."

Still swollen like a frigate bird with righteous anger, she turned to face me. "Why? What do you want with me, Skeet Bannion?"

I smiled and made my tone easy and confident. "I'd like to

ask you some questions about the things you said about Ash at the Clubhouse Restaurant and at the council meeting later."

"Why? They were all true." She threw back her head in a dramatically defiant gesture. "There's no law against saying true things about someone, even if it's about their filthy parents and criminal background."

I noticed Harvey creeping away. "So Ash had a criminal background when he lived here as a teenager?"

Bea lifted her chin high. "You bet he did. It was all juvenile stuff, of course, and I don't think they really charged him with it. Gave him a talking-to is more like it. But he was caught stealing more than once as a kid."

I pulled out my notebook. "Was this while he was in high school?"

She waved her hand airily. "Oh, no. By that time he'd grown too smart to get caught, and he'd discovered other ways to get what he wanted. He was a good-looking boy. Very much like Noah. I don't know why we didn't all see that before he pointed it out. Women—and some men—are vulnerable to good-looking, predatory young men." She gave me a knowing look and a slow nod.

"Really? That is interesting." Harvey vanished around the corner. "Could we move into your shop and sit while you tell me more?"

"Of course." She smoothed down the white waves of her hair and preened a little. "You've come to the right person if you want to know the truth."

She opened the door to Aunt Bea's Antiques and Collectibles and gestured me into her realm. The shop was stuffed with all kinds of kitschy items from my parents' and grandparents' days, but I saw hardly any real antiques—or at least, not what I'd call antiques. To me, it looked like a fancy, overpriced junk shop and smelled like that heavy kind of old woman's perfume. I had to keep from wrinkling my nose at the scent, which had been sprayed much too lavishly.

In the back of the shop, she had a small glass-topped table with three wrought-iron chairs around it. Uncomfortable, to be sure, but at least sturdy. I'd feared she'd seat me on some spindly, splintering ancient Victorian stool or horsehair fainting couch.

I set my notebook on the table. "About these women—and men—who were vulnerable to Ash. Could you tell me who they were?"

She giggled, as if only sixteen instead of sixty-eight or -nine. "I could, but I won't. I don't think they'd be too happy to have me spreading their shame all over the town."

I could tell she didn't really mean her refusal and just wanted me to give her an excuse to do that shame-spreading. "There can't have been any people of real importance, surely."

"Hah! That's what you think. Lots of women who should have known better, women with their noses up in the air all the time, got taken in by those smooth, strong muscles and the way the sweat stained the back of his T-shirt and stuck it to his skin until he finally peeled it right off."

It sounded to me like Bea hadn't been exactly immune to Ash's teenage charms herself. I wondered if there really were women who had used Ash as a gigolo, other than Bea, or if she just wanted to believe that it was all right for her to do it because everyone else surely did it, as well.

She gave a loud sigh. "He really was a sight out mowing the lawn or cutting back the shrubs. Tall and full of muscles. Just watching him move in those tight jeans was a real treat. And he was so good with his hands." She blushed slightly. "You know, fixing things." She closed her eyes for a second in remembrance.

I cleared my throat to bring her back to the point.

Her eyes flew open. "I never really noticed, you know, until Mrs. Morlock, the high school history teacher, told me about him, and I started having him do things for me. She had Ash working at her house twice a week." Her voice held scorn that clearly said no one needed yard work twice a week.

I wrote down that name. "I don't believe I know her. Is she retired from the high school now?"

"Oh no. She's dead. She died of breast cancer about four years after Ash left town."

I scribbled through Mrs. Morlock's name. "Was there someone else involved with Ash?"

"Well, there were several of us who used Ash for our yard work. Connie Selmore used to just rave about him. I think she was more depressed about leaving Ash behind when they moved to the city than anything else. Of course, Pearl Brewster didn't use him. I think she was the only single woman who didn't, but she's so hearty and athletic. She just did all her own work. Anyway, I doubt she ever saw Ash as anything but one of her troubled teens."

She gave me a knowing look. "Never been involved with a man, you know. After the big elopement. She had that nervous breakdown, and they gave her electric shock treatments. I always thought that was the great tragedy of her life, taking away her womanhood, you know. She might have had a husband after that and children like a normal woman, but I think those electric shocks took all that away from her."

I had to keep from rolling my eyes at that. "Who else hired Ash for the kind of work you did?"

She pursed her lips. "Well, there was the woman who lived down the block from me. They only lived there a year or two before they moved away." She shook her head. "I can't remember her name now. Nondescript little thing who used to stand at her screen door and watch him work, just aching to touch him. You could tell."

She squinted as she tried to remember. "And the top county judge's wife used him all the time—and had him in for lemonade in her parlor. For hours in the afternoon, you know." She tilted her head and looked out of the corner of her eyes at me with a wry nod. "So proper and above us all, she was. We were her social inferiors, she let us know. But she left the judge for another woman. Would you believe it? Mrs. High and Mighty Better Than You."

She stared into the distant past for a second, then sighed heavily. "To be fair, Ash pushed for it. Very seductive. More often than not, he was the one who initiated sex."

I frowned. It sounded to me like listening to one of the guys who liked to screw too-young girls, only gender-reversed. *It was all her/his fault.*

"And you, Bea? Were you involved sexually with Ash?" I stared directly into her eyes, and she flinched away from my gaze.

She laughed nervously. "You can't expect a girl to give away all her secrets, can you?" Winking at me, she stood. "I don't know about you police, but I've got to get back to work."

It was becoming pretty clear to me that Bea didn't know anything about any woman actually being involved sexually with Ash, other than herself, and she wasn't going to be pinned down on that. I stood and tucked my notebook away. "Thanks for taking time to answer my questions, Bea. I know a successful businesswoman like you must have lots of work to do, and I don't want to keep you from it any longer."

"Oh, yes. You have no idea." She waved a hand around the crowded shop. "All this didn't just happen. It took lots of hard work and tending to business."

"I'm sure it did. And I'd better let you get back to it now." I smiled and thanked her again for her time as I made my way through the crowded interior to the front door, hoping I wouldn't bump into some frumpy collectible and knock it down.

Once outside, I set off directly for the office. One thing Bea had done was take my mind off Walker and Miryam for a moment and focus it back on the question of who in my little town had murdered Ashton Mowbray. And I needed to add Bea herself to the list, not only for Ash's involvement with the mall project but because at the Clubhouse Restaurant earlier in the week he'd made a threat to expose "old ladies who liked a young boy's body in their beds after he mowed their lawns and got all hot and sweaty." I remembered Bea's gasp of horror at the time. Now I understood it. I wondered if she'd done something drastic to keep hidden the secrets that only Ash knew.

CHAPTER 9

Questions about Ash and all the people who had reasons to fear or hate him kept running through my mind as I worked the rest of the afternoon on budget and staffing increase proposals that Frank and I had been planning for months. Now that we were going to get a new permanent chancellor in January, we were trying to make sure we had everything ready.

Before I left my office for the week, I placed a phone call to a computer guy I knew at the KCPD Crime Lab, where Joe had sent the flash drive. I promised to buy him breakfast at Cascone's Grill in the River Market, so early Saturday morning found me sitting under an Italian flag at the window end of an eighteen-person table with an Italian sausage omelet, hash browns, and thick Italian bread toast across the table from Martín Cerda, forensic computer analyst and my personal go-to guy on all things computer.

Martín had saved my butt more than once when my PC or laptop had gone berserk on me. Currently, his head was shaved on one side with black hair flopping over his eye on the other. He was one of those young guys who were practically born with a computer in his hands and could make them sit up and dance for him. He also owed me big time for saving his younger brother from a prison sentence.

"This was a nothing job, Skeet." He slid a couple of sheets of paper across the table before digging into his Italian steak with scrambled eggs and potatoes. "This thumb drive belonged to someone named Peter Hume. At least, all the documents on here were created by his computer or downloaded from his Gmail account. And none of it was anything of interest, except that e-mail I printed out for you there. The rest was invoices, orders, basic business correspondence, stuff like that. This e-mail was different, though. It accuses him of theft and claims to have given info on that theft to Ashton Mowbray, which is the name of your victim, right? So I thought that was a little ah-ha you might find useful."

The e-mail, shorn of all the gibberish at the beginning and end that Martín called metadata, came from jd.sloan@aviz.com and was short and to the point.

> *Pete, a guy named Ashton Mowbray came looking for dirt on you. Seems you're up to old tricks, huh? I gave him all the documents showing how you stole money that belonged to me to start your shop in a fit of jealousy and pique. You've ignored all my requests that you repay me, so I'll get my pound of flesh another way. I understand this guy can make your situation very hot in that little backwater where you absconded. Hope he makes things really sticky for you, you nasty old dear. JD*

My eyes widened. Peter Hume, a thief? I'd never have guessed that one. That was not what Dante had told me.

And it certainly deepened his need to have Ash out of the picture. I thought of the anonymous letter Dante had witnessed him receive and wondered if it had been from J. D. himself or whether someone else had learned about the misdeed mentioned in this e-mail.

I looked up at Martín as he poured syrup on a plate of huge fluffy pancakes. I wondered where he was putting all that food in his skinny body. "Were there prints on the drive?"

"Sure. Three sets. None of them have given hits from IAFIS." IAFIS was the FBI's national fingerprint database. He shook his long bangs out of his face. "But they're probably good upstanding cits there in Brewster. I'd bet on it."

I nodded. "You're probably right. Peter, for sure. Maybe Dante, his partner. But the third might be the one who dumped it at the crime scene."

He shrugged. "Or it could have slipped from this guy, Pete's, pocket when he did the deed."

"Third set of fingerprints," I reminded him.

He looked at me with old, skeptical eyes. "A secretary, bookkeeper, or temp worker. Doesn't necessarily mean he didn't drop this at the scene."

The waitress interrupted us with more coffee, and Martín asked for a half-order of biscuits and gravy. I stared at him, slender and oh-so-hip.

"Where are you putting all that food, Marty?" I was a little annoyed that he could eat so much with no trace of potbelly or other flab, so I called him what I knew his mother and family did.

"Don't call me Marty, Skeet. You know better." He waved his hand at me in irritation. "You're just jealous because you have to go running to hold the line against fat, and I don't. I have a naturally high metabolism."

"I hate you, Martín. Eating a meal with you is depressing." I reread the e-mail.

He laughed. "It's good genes. You can't help it if you didn't get them."

I glared at him. "One day you're going to wake up older and find that you can't stuff your face like that with impunity any longer. One day."

"Hah! You wish!" Just then, his biscuits and sausage gravy arrived. I had to leave. I'd given up biscuits and gravy because of the fat years earlier. I wasn't about to sit and watch someone else stuff them into his mouth.

"Why do you always want to meet here so damn early for breakfast?" I asked as I gathered his files.

He shrugged. "How do you know it's early for me? It could be the end of my night. I could be eating supper before going home." His eyes twinkled at me. "I could be staying up all night and eating all that food and still be going strong."

I stuck out my tongue at him in my most mature manner. "Okay, thanks for this." I shook the e-mail pages slightly. "It gives me a few more little pieces of the puzzle."

As I got up to go pay, he stood and said in a trained thespian's voice. "Thank you for feeding me, fair lady. I live for a week on your single gift."

I snorted. "You eat enough for a week. Let me know if you find anything else. Okay?

"Sure," he said, settling back into his chair and gorging on his biscuits and gravy.

After paying, I walked out into the chaos of the original and still largest farmer's market in Kansas City. I wandered down the rows under the big peaked wooden roof, working my way through the crowd, grabbing vegetables and fruits for

Gran to use, trying to wrap my brain around this latest twist in the Ash Mowbray murder.

When I got back to my house, I found Gran and Sid Ambrose, our part-time county coroner, sitting at the kitchen table drinking coffee, Gran knitting a tan sock. They'd gone fishing earlier in the morning before I even left for my breakfast meeting in KC.

"You two are back early. Fish not biting?" I walked over to the counter to pour myself a cup of coffee and join them.

"It's your grandmother's fault," Sid growled. "She dragged me back here just when the fish started biting."

Gran dismissed his complaint with a flip of her hand. "You saved some fish for the next time you want to go out. It's a delay, not a loss."

Sid harrumphed and didn't look convinced.

I pulled out a chair and sat at the table with them. "Why'd you drag him back so early, Gran? What's up?"

She laid down her knitting and leaned toward me. "That's exactly why I told him we needed to get back here and talk with you. Something is up, Skeet. And I'm afraid Joe's mixed up in it somehow."

I closed my eyes, not wanting to hear any more about Joe pulling some unprofessional stunt. I hated what was happening to that man. He used to be my friend, and I couldn't stop caring when he seemed hell-bent on ruining his career and professional reputation.

"What now? I've seen enough to know that Joe's not acting like himself with this Ash Mowbray murder. I don't know why, but I suspect someone's putting some heavy pressure on him somehow. So what have you got?"

Sid looked at me unhappily. "I got the tox screens back on Mowbray. Wasn't expecting much, except alcohol from that bottle of Southern Comfort that he seemed to have been chugging that night."

"And . . ." I prompted him.

He sighed. "Ash Mowbray had an amount of ethylene glycol in his body that would have left him drunken, delirious or euphoric, wobbly, and uncoordinated. That probably made it easier for someone to catch him off guard and beat him over the head with that golf club."

"He was poisoned?" In surprise, I set my cup down on the table too fast, splashing coffee on my hand. "What's ethylene glycol, and where would you find it?"

Sid shrugged and held out his hands. "In just about any garage. It's the main ingredient in antifreeze. Stupid teens and winos have drunk it before for a high that usually kills them. Or comes close to it. We had a case here a couple of winters ago where two kids at the high school drank some to get high and were hospitalized. They were lucky and lived, but it was touch and go for a while there." Sid frowned, remembering.

"So, would Ash have died from antifreeze poisoning, even if no one had hit him over the head?" This murder was getting trickier and more complicated all the time. And that wasn't right. Most murders were very simple, actually. Impulsive. Opportunistic. This one was turning into a spider's web of complications.

"Maybe. Maybe not." Sid stopped to think about it. "It was a small amount of antifreeze. If he'd managed to get to the hospital in time, he might well have survived with proper care. Possibly. If he'd just passed out and not been found in time, he might well have died. It would have been very problematic at that point."

Gran frowned and picked up her needles. I knew that look. She was doing some serious thinking, and somebody was liable to be in deep trouble. "So some person poisoned him, but they might not have intended to kill him? Or they poisoned him, intending to kill him, and then someone else came along and killed him before the antifreeze took full effect? Or they gave him the antifreeze to make it easier to kill him and maybe make sure he would die?"

"One of those." Sid thought for a second. "If someone wanted to kill him with the antifreeze, though, I'm surprised they didn't use more and make sure of it."

It was a puzzle, for sure. Like too much else about this killing.

"I suppose it's not likely that Ash drank the antifreeze intentionally?" I asked.

"Anything's possible, Skeet. You and I have seen enough strangeness to know that. But I doubt it very much." Sid stood and walked over to the counter to refill his cup and stir in some sugar. "He was a wealthy man. He had expensive alcohol to drink. He could afford other drugs for a high. If he had wanted to commit suicide, he could have afforded a much easier, less painful way. I don't see any scenario where Ash intentionally, knowingly, drank antifreeze."

"Unless he wanted to kill himself or make himself sick and see someone get blamed for it." Gran looked into the distance, obviously thinking aloud. "Someone of the age group that usually uses antifreeze that way. Someone he'd pinned big hopes on who'd just publicly rejected him twice."

I stared at her. "You think he'd kill himself and try to blame it on Noah?"

She shrugged. "People have done odder things. And he might

have intended only to make himself very ill and get to a hospital for help. Then Noah would be blamed and worry about him dying. He could be magnanimous and refuse to blame Noah. And he might manipulate that relationship to become more what he'd wanted it to be."

"That's evil, Amelia. To do something like that to his own son. That would just be evil." Sid looked bleak as he returned to his chair.

Gran gave a little grimace. "He wasn't a nice man or a good one. He seemed to have lived his life by manipulating and bullying people. Why should his relationship with the son he'd deserted in the womb and never known be any different?"

I stood and shook my head in disbelief as I headed to the counter for more coffee. "You guys are making this simple case a lot more byzantine than I want it to be."

I leaned back on the counter and looked over at the pair of them. "What's the problem with Joe with this? I doubt seriously that he gave Ash that antifreeze."

Sid sighed. "He wanted me to leave it out of my report. Said it didn't cause his death so it wasn't relevant."

"What!" For a few seconds after my involuntary cry, I couldn't speak or think. How could Joe have told Sid to leave off an important test result from his report.

"When I wouldn't agree to leave it out, he told me to send it out for tox screen again, that there must be some mistake." Sid shook his head. "Skeet, I can't send that back to them, for no reason. They've done it already. We haven't the budget for it. And it will piss people off that I have to work with and whose cooperation I need."

"It muddies the waters," I finally said. "That's why he wants it gone. For some reason, Joe just wants to charge Noah for this when I don't think he even believes the kid did it. He just needs it over with quickly."

"And, of course, Noah's a juvenile," Gran pointed out.

I nodded glumly. "He'd probably get remanded for psych evaluation because of the mess with Ash suddenly telling him his parentage in public and the shock that created. He probably wouldn't have to go to jail. A psych ward for a while maybe. But it would wreck the kid's life. And let the real killer get away with it."

"I don't care what Joe's got going on," Sid grumbled. "I've never falsified a report, not even when I was a drunk. I'm not about to start now."

Sid had been dry for twenty-five years now, but he never let himself forget his days as an alcoholic. I hoped my father would get to where Sid was one day.

"Fortunately, Joe can't make you do that." Gran's voice was matter-of-fact, but her lips were tightened into a straight line. She was pissed about this whole situation, and that meant someone would have to suffer to put it straight. I hoped that person wasn't going to be me. "You write your report as you need to. And you." She looked straight into my eyes and aimed the double-pointed needle in her hand at my face. "You need to have a come-to-Jesus talk with your friend Joe and make him stop all this. Find out who's pressuring him and fix it. Find the real killer and stop him. That's what you need to do."

It wasn't my fault that Joe was acting like a stupid ass, but that didn't matter. When Gran got like that, there was nothing to do but obey. I thought it might be a lot easier to find the killer and stop him than to fix what was wrong with Joe, but I could see she wouldn't be happy or let me rest until I'd done both.

Brian had gone over to Angie's to do homework—though they were probably really playing computer games or working on one of Angie's attempts at edgy documentary. They were both so bright that homework didn't take them long. I knew Brian went over there just to be with Angie and to give her support as she dealt with her stepmother, Liz Richar. Right now, Brian had said with some satisfaction, Noah wanted to spend time with his family without anyone else around. I'm sure his decision had upset Angie, but, of course, there was always good old Brian to turn to.

Normally, since the weather was so unnaturally nice, with just the slightest chill in the air to hint that it was late fall, I'd have called over to have him walk home for lunch, which was always later on weekends around our house. I decided to drive over and pick him up instead because I wanted to ask some questions of both Brian and Angie. Questions about antifreeze.

The home Angie and Liz lived in was in the wealthy Wickbrook section with a gorgeous view of the wildlife preserve, marred only by the ugly concrete box Liz and Angie's father, George Melvin, had purchased and moved into. I suspect Liz would have packed up and moved back to Kansas City when Mel died, except Angie was still healing from the terrible accident that almost killed her. An accident that I believed Liz had caused, though I couldn't prove it. I've learned that when people with a lot of money decide to do bad things, it can be hard to find proof. Money works so well to erase evidence of criminal wrongdoing.

I parked and walked to the front door slowly, the faint whistle of a train in the background as it went through downtown Brewster. I wanted to take in all the colors of the trees in the wildlife refuge behind the house. Normally by this time of the year, the leaves, which are beautiful around here in the fall, are mostly gone from early winter storms of freezing rain and ice. The view was breathtaking, and I slowed so I could absorb it. And also to delay knocking on the door.

I avoided Liz as much as I could because to be around her for any length of time caused me to think increasingly murderous thoughts. My own boy had been endangered with Angie, and I had to keep my contact with Liz to a minimum so I didn't become too tempted to take the law into my own hands.

Finally, I pushed myself into a brisk walk up to the door and knocked. With any luck, the maid or Angie would open the door and I could avoid the Dragon Queen. As luck would have it, though, Liz herself opened the door. Walker Lynch stood behind her, a drink in each hand, and he lifted one in a silent salute. I nodded the tiniest bit without a hint of a smile.

"Skeet." Liz looked at me with the disdain of a woman who is turned out fit for a magazine cover surveying a woman in tennis shoes, jeans, and long-sleeved T-shirt. "I suppose you're here for Brian?"

"Yes," I said. I couldn't keep from frowning at Walker behind her, and it obviously amused him.

"Come in. I'll call them for you." She turned and walked away to pick up a cell phone and dial. When I said something like that, I meant *I'll yell up the stairs or out the back door for them.* Angie and I agreed on two things—Brian was wonderful and Liz was really from another planet.

"Are you lonely, Skeet? Need your little dependent to make you feel whole?" Walker asked with mocking solicitude.

"She can't get a real man," Liz said airily as she set down

the phone. "Though she seems to be trying for Terry." She laughed harshly. "Good luck there."

"Yes, you didn't have any with him, did you?" Walker chuckled at Liz's sudden glare. "That gorgeous Danielle has him all tied up."

So the blonde in the Jaguar was named Danielle. It would be one of those upper-class, feminine names.

"Dani!" Liz said the name like a curse and then turned to me with a sneer. "Perhaps if you went blond. And lost a lot of weight. And learned how to dress. And . . . Oh, you'd just have to be someone other than plain old Skeet Bannion, wouldn't you?"

Walker laughed and held out one of the drinks to her, like a reward for her venom.

I didn't care. I wasn't interested in Walker's hired gun anyway, and Liz had wasted her poison. I knew perfectly well that I was plain old Skeet Bannion and no match for the blonde in the Jag. I was happy with who I was.

Dani. Of course, she'd have a name like that.

I closed the heavy carved door behind me as Liz walked over to Walker and took a drink from him with a soulful stare into his cold gray eyes. I wondered why Liz had tried for Terry. It had been clear to me for some time that Liz was in love with Walker, although she kept pairing off with different political office seekers. I suspected that was because Walker wanted her to. Maybe he'd sicced her on Terry, too.

Walker infuriated me, but he scared the shit out of me even more. I was convinced he was a sociopath who could hurt or kill a person without the slightest feeling of empathy, guilt, or shame. He and Liz made a good pair.

Liz and Walker headed out of the room to the back of the

house. I made a face at their retreating backs like the fully functional adult I was. Then I walked over to sit on an over-stuffed leather chair and wait for the kids to show up.

Soon enough Brian and Angie walked out of the opposite side of the house from the one Liz had disappeared into. Angie and Liz lived as far from each other in that house as they could. They hated each other, but Liz was determined to hang onto Angie for political reasons. Politics was her life. I'd always wondered why she didn't run for office herself. She had looks, brains, and money, but she preferred to marry men and help them run.

Now that Melvin was dead, she was keeping company with Randy Thorrson, state senator. It was too soon after his divorce and her husband's death for them to marry, so she played the noble grieving widow, struggling alone to raise her beloved husband's troubled daughter. That image was why she wouldn't allow Angie to live with her mother, who was a mess, admittedly, or with Gran and me, which would cramp us and would have had its problems but would have been much better for Angie.

"Hey, Skeet," Brian said with a big smile.

Angie nodded to me. "Surely, it's not time for Bri to go yet?"

"It's past lunchtime, and Gran wants him home while her food is still hot."

"Yeah," Brian said. "Gran takes her cooking seriously. Which is great for me 'cause I take my eating seriously, too."

Angie looked disappointed. Until Noah came along, Brian had been her only lifeline, and now that Noah was unavailable, I could see Brian was cast back in that role.

"Found out something today that freaked me out," I said as casually as I could. "Teens drinking antifreeze to get high."

"Only the dumb ones," Angie said with scorn. "You've got to be already nearly brain-dead to drink something that's likely to leave you brain-dead if it doesn't kill you."

Brian frowned. "Two kids at the high school did that before we got to high school here. They're seniors now, and I don't think they ever really recovered. They can't really discuss things in class. They have problems staying on topic."

"They're going to the LD sessions now, but I heard they were pretty smart before they did that. Couldn't have been very smart to guzzle antifreeze." Angie obviously had no sympathy.

"They're seniors? Like Noah?" My ears pricked up.

"Yeah. He'd been friends with one of them, sort of. Before, you know. They don't really have any friends now." Angie's voice was careless and unembarrassed as she told of the pain inflicted on Noah's former friend.

My hand itched to bring out my notebook and write that Noah knew about antifreeze poisoning, but I wouldn't do that in front of the kids.

"Time to go home if you want some of Gran's pot roast with potatoes and carrots," I told Brian. "She made her fresh dinner rolls to go with and lemon bread pudding for dessert. You're not going to pass that up, are you?"

"That sounds so good." Angie looked at me hopefully. I knew she wanted me to invite her for dinner, and I couldn't blame her. Aside from the allure of Gran's great cooking, it must have been hell to live in that house with Liz every day. Angie took every chance she had to get away.

"Angie could come with us, couldn't she?" Brian asked.

"Of course, but you've got to ask Liz if it's okay first." I held up both hands when she started to object. "She's your legal guardian and has to approve your coming with me, Angie.

Doesn't matter whether any of us like it or not. It's the way things are."

"I hate the way things are," she muttered under her breath.

I couldn't blame her. "Go ask. She'll probably say yes. You know that."

"We all know she really doesn't want me around," she cried. "So why won't she let me go? To you and Bri, if not to Denise?"

I knew Angie didn't need to hear me explain that her mother, Denise Melvin, was a drug addict in a rehab center and not likely to ever get custody of Angie again unless she turned her life around drastically. The kid had been the one trying to take care of her mom as Denise slid further and further into addiction. She knew the score all too well.

"Well, when she decides she's had enough and wants to move on without you, you're always welcome with us. Though it'll be a tighter fit now that Gran's there." I looked her straight in the eyes. "And there are rules in my house. Not a lot, but the ones I have are strict."

We both knew Angie got off on breaking rules and seeing herself as a wild rebel. I knew it was because she'd had to deal with more really bad crap than lots of adults ever face. I wasn't looking forward to the battles I knew would ensue if she was ever allowed to take me up on my offer, but it was a genuine offer anyway.

She looked down at the fancy parquet floor for a minute. When she looked up, she shook her head sadly. "Not going to happen, though, is it? She's going to keep her claws in me. But at least I can get away for today. I'll go ask. Don't leave without me."

I nodded, and she trudged off in the direction Liz had vanished. I called Gran on my cell phone.

"Have we got enough for Angie, too?" I asked when she answered.

"When do I not have enough for a guest? I'll cook up some succotash to go with it real quick. There'll be plenty." Gran laughed. "You worry too much."

Angie returned with a much lighter tread as I hung up. "I can go. She's probably glad to get rid of me, so she can sneak Randy in."

I raised an eyebrow. "She's seeing both of them?"

"Not at the same time. You're so naïve." Her face grew thoughtful. "Though I don't think Walker would mind that. But Randy sure would. Let's go."

"Gran's adding succotash to the menu," I told them.

Brian gave a little moan of pleasure. "Wait till you taste Gran's succotash, Angie. It's so good."

We headed out with the two teens talking food. As I drove them back to the house, I wondered if Liz was the reason Walker was so determined to hook his corporate claws into little Brewster, Missouri. And what involvement he might have with Ash's death.

CHAPTER 10

That evening it was my turn to drive into Kansas City and see Big Charlie Bannion, my father, fed, bathed, and put safely to bed. Gran rode shotgun. I'd asked her along in the hopes that her presence would keep Charlie (who was afraid of his ex-mother-in-law) in line and keep us from hacking away verbally at each other in mutual anger and frustration.

Gran knit the pair of tan socks she'd been working on for a few days while I drove us on the highway alongside the Missouri River until we crossed it right after the Kansas or Kaw River joined it. Gran still enjoyed the sight of the Kansas City skyline growing as we crossed the Broadway Bridge. Tahlequah's pretty small in comparison.

When I pulled up at Charlie's house a little ahead of time and saw the cars of not only Erika, his caretaker, but that of my ex-husband, Sam, I knew we were facing more trouble. Sam and I alternated nights of caring for Charlie. Probably sounded weird to others, but Charlie was the only father Sam had ever known, and to Charlie, Sam was the son he'd always wanted but never had. Yeah, that last was a little sore spot with me, but I'd lived with it a long time now.

The front door opened and Sam and Erika hurried out, only to pull up short when they saw it was us getting out of my cruiser.

"Don't tell me," I said. "Charlie's off with Marie again."

"I tried to stop them," Erika said, her Spanish accent stronger than normal because she was obviously upset. "But Charlie wouldn't listen to me. I couldn't stop him."

Sam patted her shoulder gently. "Not hardly. They're both almost twice your size. You were outclassed in that fight. No one blames you, Erika."

Sam was exaggerating, but Erika was tiny compared to the two miscreants.

"Of course, you couldn't stop him," I reassured her. "I just wish that woman would stop coming around trying to kill my father."

Marie had been Charlie's nurse assistant for two days, in which she had started my newly dry alcoholic father drinking again, fed him everything the doctors warned would kill him as he recovered from a major stroke and severe coronary artery disease. We'd fired her. The home health agency had fired her. And she'd decided to get even by wooing Charlie for his pension and savings and, I feared, killing him off with alcohol, cigarettes, and greasy food as quickly as she could once she talked him into marrying her. Sam and I had given Charlie an ultimatum, threatening to have nothing to do with him any longer if he kept running off with Marie. It didn't seem to be working, though.

"What are we going to do, Skeet?" Sam asked. "I don't want to abandon Charlie, but I'm damned if I can just stand here and watch her marry him for his little bit of money and kill him."

"He is getting stronger," Erika offered tentatively. "I have increased the repetitions of the exercises he does and have added some advanced ones the doctors wanted. He uses his cane to get up from the chair and bed and walk around the house all the time now."

"That's wonderful, Erika. How have you managed to get him to do all that? No one else has been able to." I really wanted to know. Charlie wouldn't do those exercises for me or any of Erika's predecessors. It seemed like a small miracle.

She smiled and blushed. "I told him it would make him a better lover, give him more . . ."

"Stamina?" Sam hooted with laughter. "Damn, girl. That was a smart way to handle the old grouch." He patted her shoulder again. It would have made me mad—too patronizing—but Erika smiled up at him happily.

I sighed. "That's great, Erika. But I don't know what we're going to do with him. I don't want to abandon him, either, Sam, but I feel the way you do about watching someone con him and encourage him to kill himself."

We'd almost lost Charlie when he'd had a major stroke after being beaten so badly that the beating itself almost killed him. I think only his stubbornness kept the old delinquent alive. We were trying our damnedest to keep him healthy and active, and while he'd been good and scared, there'd been hope. Until Marie Doerr showed up.

Gran had listened to us all in silence. Now she spoke. "You're asking the wrong question, you and Sam. There's nothing you can do. Charlie's a grown man and allowed to make his own decisions, even bad ones."

Sam and I both turned to her to argue when a loud motor interrupted us, and Marie and Charlie drove up in her blue SUV. She kept the engine idling as Charlie got out of the car and turned to give her a big, sloppy kiss. As embarrassing and irritating as that was to witness between teenagers in public, it was ten times worse when it was my white-haired, stroke-crippled father.

I could feel the anger building up inside me. Charlie and I were too alike to be good together. We inevitably ended up in screaming matches. It was hard to believe sometimes that I'd idolized this man throughout my childhood and adolescence and hated my mother for his sake. Heck, I'd become a cop as a way of trying to be like my beloved father, Big Charlie Bannion. Our adult relationship had soon shown me the ugly side of his alcoholism and sexism, but it had taken me years to break free of his influence over me. Now, we could hardly be in the same room without fighting.

"Charlie, what in the hell do you think you're doing?" Sam barked. "You're lucky I didn't put out an APB on you."

Charlie turned away from blond, heavily made-up Marie and laughed. "Aw, hell, you know you can't do that, Sam. Don't forget I was a cop, too. I know what you can and can't do."

"We could put out a Silver Alert on you, though." I didn't usually defend Sam, but Charlie was just too smug with that answer. "Put you in western Missouri for a diagnosis since you're being self-destructive."

Charlie bristled at that, and Marie drove off. Sam and I glared back at him in unison for once.

Erika came up to Charlie and took his arm gently. "Come inside and let me check your blood pressure, Charlie. The last time that you went with her, it was very high when you came back. Have you been having any angina?" She steered him into the house past our frowning faces.

Gran walked casually behind her. She turned on reaching

the door behind them. "Well, are you two going to come in or not? You know your faces might freeze like that." She shook her head. "The little Mexican nurse is the only one with any brains, it looks like to me." She stood in the doorway, and Sam and I looked at each other in confusion. How had we become the bad guys?

Gran stepped back outside and shut the front door. "You can't tell a grown man who to love. Maybe after almost dying, Charlie's taken stock of his life and seen what a mess it's been. Maybe he's decided he doesn't want to live alone and without love any longer."

I protested. "But Gran, that woman—"

"Is probably a gold digger, yes. But Charlie wasn't living a healthy life before, was he? You can't treat him like a child. And even if he hasn't learned self-discipline, maybe he's found out something important that you haven't learned yet. Maybe he's found that shutting yourself off from love because you've been hurt is really a fool's choice. Maybe he's decided to take a chance on love and open himself up to really living." She turned her back on us and entered the house.

"What if she's right?" Sam asked. "What if he's really in love?"

I shook my head. "What if he is? That woman's likely to be the death of him."

Sam nodded. "I'm afraid she will be. But your grandmother's right. He's a grown man. We can't tell him who he can or can't love." He glanced toward the house with a faraway look in his eyes. "Hell, we can't even tell ourselves who we can or can't love."

That was getting into sticky territory. Sam maintained that he still loved me and was sorry for the angry jealousy and infidelity that had driven me to divorce him. He was always pushing me for more than I wanted to or could give emotionally. I decided that retreat was the best strategy.

"I can't deal with this tonight. Since you're here, Sam—"

"Sure," he interrupted. "Erika and I can get him ready for bed. You and your gran head on back. We'll talk about this later. No need to decide tonight."

Relieved that he was taking that attitude, I gathered up Gran, said a controlled good-bye to Charlie, and left him to Erika's ministrations—and Sam's. I imagined Sam would offer to pay Erika extra for staying late. He was always fair with employees and subordinates. I had to admit Sam had good qualities, and he'd done a lot to prove himself to me in the past year. But I didn't want to think about any of that. Especially not about how a person could fall in love with someone she didn't want to love and knew was probably bad for her. Especially not that.

Sunday dawned with some clouds after a night of thunder and rain, and there was a chill in the air. Chill or not, Gran and Sid headed out to fish and took Brian with them—and, for the first time, Angie, who'd shown only revulsion and snark at the idea of fishing before. I didn't envy Sid and Gran, but I knew it wasn't likely Angie would get the best of Gran.

I'd arranged with Karen to have brunch at the Clubhouse Restaurant with Ignacio and her. It was terrific to see how well Ignacio was doing when we arrived. I might have given him a hug from sheer pleasure at seeing him so recovered, but neither Ignacio nor I were hugging people.

He insisted on pulling out our chairs for us and sitting only after he'd seated us. Karen rolled her eyes at me and scolded him. "Nacio, you don't have to do that. Just take care of yourself. You're not a hundred percent yet."

We'd all been afraid the brave Chilean shepherd had taken one chance too many to protect Karen from a killer a few months back, but he'd lived through emergency surgery and made it through a long recovery period. He still looked paler and thinner than usual, and he walked a little stiffly and carefully even now. Getting shot in the gut will do that to you.

Now, though, we were laughing and celebrating because Karen was going to start back to work full time in her shop on the square, Forgotten Arts, on Monday for the first time since Ignacio had been shot. And he would return to taking care of her flocks of Romney sheep and Angora goats—with a bit of help from a local teenager until he'd completely recovered all his strength. Life was finally getting back to normal after what could have been such a tragedy. And no one was happier than I was.

"It's great to see you getting around so well, Ignacio." I smiled at him, and he let a brief smile flicker across his serious face.

"It is good to be able to move under my own power again," he replied. "It is not easy being dependent on others."

"Especially me," said Karen with a laugh. "I'm kind of a worrywart, and I tend to fuss over him a little too much."

"A lot too much," he said with a strong emphasis. He turned to me. "If it had been left to Karen, I would have remained an invalid because you can't regain your strength if you don't put forth effort and struggle."

I grinned at them both. "Well, between you two, it all worked out. Karen took good care of you, and you didn't let her turn you into a permanent invalid. So there's a lot to celebrate."

I owed Ignacio a huge debt of gratitude. He'd saved my best friend and surrogate mother when I hadn't been in time. Without him, I doubted Karen would have lived to see November with me.

So we ate and talked and laughed as friends do. Ignacio asked about the murder of Ash Mowbray, and I told them both what I could. Then our talk turned to Brian and Gran and how having them had changed my life.

When it was time to leave, I insisted it was my treat and paid, and we headed back to our separate daily lives. After a good-bye hug from Karen and a solemn handshake from Ignacio, we walked through the restaurant, but they exited ahead of me as I was caught by first one person and then another to say hello. I thought it odd that Karen, who had lived in Brewster much longer than I had, wasn't stopped by anyone, but I put it down to people being considerate of Ignacio's waning strength.

As I neared the front door myself finally, Peter Hume reached out and snagged my arm when I passed the table where he sat with Dante and Bea.

"Skeet!" cried Bea. "We were just talking about how Peter should go talk to you, and here you are."

"I wasn't saying that," Dante said with an uncharacteristically sour expression.

"I saw something that you need to know about." Peter's avid expression made me shrink away from him. His hand on my arm pulled me back. "You are investigating that man's murder, Mowbray's, aren't you? That's what Dante and Bea said."

"Yes," I admitted.

Dante laid his hand gently on Peter's arm. When he spoke, his expression and voice softened. "Let Skeet go. This isn't what you want to do. Not really. You're not this kind of man."

I'd become curious about what Peter wanted to tell me by this time. "What is it, Peter?"

"That's right. Skeet needs to know this." Bea's face shone, and her smile took up so much of her face it was frightening.

Dante gave Peter one more pleading look, then let his hand slide off Peter's arm.

Peter leaned forward eagerly. "It was the night of the murder. Dante and I were out for a little walk. It was late, quite a bit after midnight—"

"No, Peter, it was a little less than ten minutes before midnight. I'd just checked my watch." Dante shook his head with a sad look at his partner.

Peter flung his hands up in frustration. "Whatever. It was nearly midnight. We were walking past the Steens, and I noticed Noah climbing down the tree next to the house. I said that I bet the kid had climbed out his bedroom window and was going to find a girlfriend. Didn't I?"

Dante nodded and Peter continued with relish. "We laughed about it a little, both having been teenage boys at one time."

Dante gave a little smile.

"We watched him sneak off, and then we resumed our walk and didn't think any further of it—until now, when we know a man he hated was murdered that very night." Peter nodded with great force and conviction. "He must have been going off to murder Ash Mowbray."

Dante rolled his eyes before closing them and leaning back in his chair. "You don't have any idea where he was going or how long he was gone. He could have climbed back up the tree into his room five minutes after we passed by."

Peter gave a short, hard laugh. "That's not what teenage boys climb out the window and down trees at night for."

"Well, they certainly don't climb down to go murder people," Dante shot back, sitting up and opening his eyes.

I held up my hand. "Wait now. Peter's right to tell about seeing this. He's not necessarily right about his conclusions, but it's an important piece of information. Thanks, Peter."

He sat back with a look of pride on his face. "See, I was just doing my duty as a citizen."

Dante turned his now-shuttered face away from Peter's. Bea smiled at him and nodded.

"Peter," I continued, "I want to talk with you more about this and about a flash drive of yours that's been found."

He jumped to his feet. "Shit! Look at the time! I'm going to be late for this client meeting." He moved out from behind the table. "We'll have to talk another time, Skeet. Come by the office any time. I'm usually there."

Dante got up more slowly. "What client meeting? It's Sunday."

Peter frowned at him. "It's the Goltraubs. The only time they can both get away to meet and decide on some of these things is Sunday." He headed out of the restaurant at a fast clip.

Dante looked at me and shrugged. He followed Peter out at a slower pace, as did Bea.

I wasn't happy about Peter slipping away from me, especially when he'd just given damning evidence against Noah Steen, who was supposed to have been safely at home all night when Ash was killed.

I needed to collar Peter, quiz him on the accusation and threat his ex-partner had made, and ask him to explain that flash drive of his that was found at the murder scene.

We had too much evidence incriminating too many people. Someone was deliberately trying to make innocent others look guilty. I didn't like it, and I intended to find out who was doing it and who had killed Ash.

CHAPTER 11

Through the rest of Sunday and all the night, I wrestled with all the unanswered questions and anomalies that were confronting me. Finally, Monday morning after very little sleep, I rose earlier than usual for my morning run, leaving the smell of cars and concrete to race alongside the Missouri River next to the wildlife sanctuary in the brightening, chill darkness of pre-dawn. The silence, except for the hushed rippling of the river current against its banks and the distant keening of a train, helped heal the whir of questions and thoughts in my head, and the exertion created its own warmth in my body. As the earliest birds began to call into the fading dark and answer each other, I became only a body, breathing in the fresh scent of the constantly moving river.

Gran had always told me the Cherokee settled near rivers and creeks so they could take their illnesses and troubles to water. Once again, it worked and I was restored. I knew what I needed to do.

Before I turned back to the parking lot, I watched a golden eagle fly out from woods across the river to soar over me, immobile for one brief second in the brightening morning sky. An eagle sighting was always fortunate, a good sign.

Gran told me when I was small that the Cherokee didn't go on vision quests like some other tribes because we read the signs in the world around us every day and communicated with the spiritual world for guidance in that way. Maybe I was getting better at that. I took the eagle's behavior as a sign that my decision was the right one to make.

After showering at home, I headed for Joe's office and parked outside next to his official parking spot to waylay him before he got in. I'd make him tell me who was putting the pressure on him to make him forget everything he'd ever known about good policing. Then I'd find a way to make that pressure stop.

It was still early when Joe showed up ahead of his secretary or any of the day shift. I figured he wasn't sleeping well, either. I hadn't tried to hide my car, so he knew I was there. I got out at the same time he did. He walked around his car to face me.

"Skeet." His voice was even but weary. The circles under his eyes said he hadn't slept soundly for many nights. His whole appearance was more rumpled and disheveled than Joe ever displayed. Joe wasn't a charming hunk like my ex, Sam, and he wasn't intriguing and dangerous like Terry. He was older and heavier than either of them, but he had a comfortable presence and his own brand of understated confidence. That was gone in the man before me. He'd never been a particularly dapper dresser, but he was always neat and well groomed. Not today, though.

"Joe. We need to talk." I struggled to make my voice warm and friendly, hiding the anger I felt because Joe was being such a fool and allowing someone to push him into behavior so un-like his usual self.

"I suspect we've already done too much of that." He spoke without looking at me, head down, the brown hair he always kept neatly combed flopping in his eyes as he pushed the passenger door handle open and closed. "But I don't suppose there's any way to stop you, is there?" He looked up with a bleak smile.

I looked straight at him, dead serious. "Not really."

He tilted his head to one side as he considered me. His eyes narrowed as if measuring me. Then he pulled the door open. "Get in. I don't want to talk where anyone else can hear us argue."

I locked my own car before sliding into his passenger seat as he walked around to the driver's side, got in, and started the car.

"What are we talking about today?" He drove with his head held high, chin thrust forward, and his shoulders squared, as if he had to be ready for attack at any moment.

I gave a slight shrug. "Ash Mowbray's murder, of course."

He nodded abruptly. "Of course." He kept his eyes straight ahead on the road, never turning the slightest to look at me. "Go ahead. Fire away."

I took a breath and started. "Why aren't you looking at Peter or Bea or Walker as hard as you are at Noah, Joe? That's not like you."

"You don't know what is or isn't like me," he said curtly. "You don't know me. Not really."

I hissed under my breath. "Well, you certainly led me to believe I knew who you were, but I've begun to see that it was all a façade. I had thought you were different and liked me as I was. I'd thought we were friends." I turned to look out the window for a second before turning back to him. "Whatever. I know you're a good cop. Or at least, you used to be." He flinched. "You're right. I don't know you, at all, I guess."

He drove without replying, leaning forward as if it was difficult to see. But the sun had come up, and the morning was bright and clear before us. On his third turn, I realized he was taking us to Sid's and Gran's favorite fishing spot.

I kept silent until Joe pulled up beside Turtle Creek near the spot where it left the wildlife sanctuary. Turtle Creek ran through the heart of Brewster from the river at the old train station and on through the wildlife sanctuary. Its best fishing was on the stretch that left the sanctuary to run through what was now being turned into Wickbrook subdivision.

We both got out and walked over to the creek bank in silence. A pile of tree limbs and rocks created a small pool on the left side of the creek. A turtle had climbed up the side of the pile to bask in the growing sun. I wondered what kind of sign Gran would have seen in it that I was missing.

"Joe, let's cut through all this. I know Peter's flash drive was found at the death scene. I know there was an e-mail on it from his ex-partner telling him he'd given Ash proof of a crime Peter committed, so Ash could blackmail him into silence or publicize it and destroy Peter's reputation. Good motive for murder, along with his public rage against Ash. I know Bea—"

"How in the hell did you learn that?" he erupted. "Did someone in my department give out that information? I'll—"

I continued right over him. "I didn't get it from anyone in your department. But the point is that the information is accessible to anyone who wants to look for it. As is the fact that you told Sid not to put the results of the tox screen in his report."

He glared at me for a minute, anger palpable in his hazel eyes, then shook his head as his shoulders slumped. "Of course, you and Sid go way back when you were with KCPD and he was in the ME's office there. And you drew on your contacts with KCPD to get the flash drive contents. You fit in so well here that sometimes I forget you were a big shot in Kansas City police circles."

"Joe, you've got a strong suspect in Peter, and you haven't even questioned him. Bea was most likely sexually involved with Ash when he was a kid, and he'd publicly threatened to reveal women who slept with him when he was just a teen. Plus, she, like Peter, was almost crazed with fear and anger at the thought of his mall destroying the courthouse square shops and her livelihood. Walker was furious with Ash for causing all this trouble and messing up his mall project, and he wanted him gone."

His chin went up, and his jaw hardened. "So what? He told your admirer to kill him?"

I gritted my teeth to keep from cussing him out. "It was Terry who told me Walker was ready to explode over all the bad publicity Ash had caused, idiot!"

He lowered his eyes to the ground and shuffled his feet.

"Someone's sending anonymous letters, including to Peter," I continued. "Almost everyone in town knew that antifreeze could be given in booze and would increase intoxication and then kill because some local teens wound up in the papers over doing that a couple of years ago. You're trying to pin this on a teenager without checking into all these other people with excellent motives—who have belongings of one kind or another dropped at the crime scene. What the hell is going on, Joe? Since when do you railroad people into jail terms, especially possibly innocent kids?"

"He won't go to jail," he muttered. He glanced up at my eyes and then sent his own gaze elsewhere as fast as he could. "All the stuff Ash did will be taken into consideration and his shock at learning about his father that way and everything. They'll get him a psych eval, and he may have to do a short stint in a hospital, but then he'll be home again. He's a juvenile."

"It will ruin him nonetheless, Joe." I got right up in his face in outrage at his easy assumption of no harm in setting up a kid for murder. "He'll be branded a killer. And what if he's innocent? What then? And what about the real killer? Still out there free to kill again? What the hell is going on with you? Since when do you do something like this?"

He threw his head back and roared at me. "You don't know anything about it, so back off, Skeet. Back off!"

I hadn't realized I was shouting and crowding him until he shoved me back out of his personal space, and I landed on the ground on my butt.

"Oh, shit! I'm sorry. I didn't mean to do that. No, damn it." He hovered over me, as if afraid he'd hurt me. I reached a hand up to him, and he pulled me back to my feet.

I wasn't about to let up. "What the hell is going on here, Joe? Why would you be willing to be part of framing a kid for murder?"

He jerked back at my words, as if I'd hit him in the face. His face swelled and reddened with anger, then seemed to deflate all at once. He slumped and wouldn't look at me.

"I don't want to frame anyone. It could be Noah. He hated

Ash, and he wouldn't suffer a lot." He looked up at me with a pleading gesture. "No prison. Nothing like that."

"Listen to yourself," I exploded. "Why are you willing to sacrifice a kid who may well be completely innocent?"

He stared down at the creek bank for a long silence that I refused to break—until he finally looked up at me with torment in his eyes. "It's Julie, Skeet. Walker Lynch wants this swept under the rug as quickly and quietly as possible, so he can get his mall through. He said if Noah was convicted, it would just be a psych thing and no great deal connected with the mall because he's a teen and it's a family matter."

I couldn't believe I was hearing Joe say these things. "Why didn't you tell him to kiss your ass, Joe? Why in the hell did you even listen to him?"

His eyes sank deeper into his skull. "He's found Julie's mother. Probably bailed her out of jail for drugs or prostitution. Something like that. And he'll pay her to file for Julie's sole custody and bankroll the suit. I can't afford to fight against the kind of lawyers he can bring. I can't live without my daughter, Skeet, and I can't let that woman have her. She'll leave her somewhere awful the minute Walker doesn't care to pay any longer. Maybe even sell her. I don't know how far she's gone, but she was on a real downhill slope when I divorced her and got custody of Julie. Damn drugs had left her incapable of caring about anyone."

I stared at him in horror, then shook my head. "She could never get custody here, Joe. The first things I heard in this town were what a scuzz your ex was and how relieved everyone was that she couldn't have anything to do with Julie."

He gave me a twisted smile. "I told him that. He said the first thing they'll do is get a change of venue since I've poisoned the well against my ex over the years."

The smile melted off his face, and he looked near tears. "He has all this power and money, and he'll use it all to take Julie away if I don't do what he wants." He looked up at me with bleak eyes. "I thought it wouldn't be that bad for Noah, but you're right. I'd be destroying the kid. It's just wrong. Only there's nothing else I can do."

I looked at my old friend's defeated face and the self-loathing in his eyes until he turned his gaze away to the creek bank. Suddenly, I had a vision of him eating his own gun that made me shiver. "No!"

He never looked at me, even when I yelled, but stared out at the creek with hopeless eyes. "That man will leave me nothing. He'll destroy my daughter just to keep bad publicity away from what he wants."

I reached out and touched his shoulder to get him to turn his attention back to me. "Joe, listen to me. I won't let him do this to you. We'll find a way to stop him. I promise."

He looked at me as if from a great distance. Then he smiled sadly. "You never give up, do you?"

"Never." I shook his shoulder slightly. "Neither can you. Julie needs you to be the man you are, not what Walker wants to make of you. He can get away with lots, but he can't get away with this. This is the kind of thing a good investigator or a couple of them can catch and prove. He's got power but not that much. Not even the Kennedys had that much."

He shook his head, not to disapprove but as if to shake out the fear that had clouded his mind. "You really think you can keep him from doing this?"

"I know it. This kind of thing leaves a trail. Your ex is not the pure creature they'd need to make it work. Not when a good investigator gets on the trail. We can stop this. We will."

He stared at me and then smiled. "God help me. I want to believe you."

I smiled back at him, though it was the last thing I felt like doing. I wanted to punch something, preferably Walker Lynch's face. "Good. Now start cleaning up this mess and investigate this murder. I'll get that asshole off your back. I promise."

He looked at me quizzically for a few seconds, then indicated the car, and we drove back to town. The whole way in, I talked to reassure Joe that everything would work out right, acting calm, but I was boiling inside.

Walker Lynch. He'd hurt too many people in my life. He thought his money gave him the right to do what he wanted to other people. I had to believe it didn't. I'd take that bastard on and pull him down if it was the last thing I ever did.

I had not forgotten the address of Terry's new apartment, much as I might have wished to, but I had no intention of approaching him there. I had no intention of ever setting foot in that man's place. So I drove over to an intersection nearby and waited for his Range Rover to show up. When it did, driving decorously a couple of miles under the speed limit, I hit my siren and flashers and pulled out behind him.

He pulled right over and parked. I stopped behind him and got out with my notebook to look to the rest of the world like this was a routine traffic stop. He sat quietly, waiting for me to approach. I walked up in a calm, professional manner, trying hard to control my anger and disgust at his boss and, by association, him.

He looked up at me with a hint of a grin at the corner of his mouth and one eyebrow quirked while a light of amusement danced in his dark eyes. "What have I done, Officer? And aren't you a little out of your jurisdiction? If you'd wanted to talk to me, Skeet, there are more discreet ways to get my attention."

"I don't want your attention. Never have. I've got a message for that son of a bitch you work for. And that's your job, isn't it? Carrying his messages? Doing his dirty work?" My jaw was set hard, and my words came out clipped and forceful.

His face sobered the second I mentioned his boss. His brows lowered over his eyes, and the full lips tightened. "I don't know what this is about, but I've told you—"

I brushed his words away with an impatient left hand. "I don't care what you've told me or want to tell me. All I want from you is to relay this message to Walker."

He half-covered his mouth with his left hand while his lips twisted and he stared at me from the corner of his eyes a second. Finally he pulled his hand away from his mouth, sweeping off his hat to lie on the seat beside him, and looked straight at me, eyes wide and absolutely serious.

"Tell him that I know how he used Joe's little girl to threaten Joe and try to make him railroad an innocent kid into jail, just so he could avoid bad publicity." I tried to keep my voice low, so people would think nothing of this scene if they came upon it. Enraged shouting would only make them wonder.

He gave a puzzled frown. "What the—" Outrage filled his voice, but I cut him off.

"Don't talk. Listen and carry this message." I was speaking in what I called computer mode, an attitude with little emotional affect that I'd developed to deal with volatile street types. "Tell Walker that it won't work. Joe's going to do a full investigation of the murder, and I'm going to do a full investigation of that tramp he's bought so he can threaten Joe's custody of Julie."

Terry's eyes widened as I spoke, and he ran his hand through his dark hair, pulling it back from his high forehead with a taut arm on which the tendons stood out in high relief. "Shit!"

I interrupted again, not caring if he'd known about this or not. He worked for the man. That was enough.

"Tell him that I'm going to prove what a mess she is, and I'm going to prove that he tried to blackmail Joe with her and the threat of a custody battle in another county with him bank-rolling it."

I took a breath, and rage poured through me. This time Terry stayed silent with a grim expression, eyes on my mouth, listening to me. My computer mode was gone. You could hear quiet fury in my voice now. "Tell that bastard I'm going to bring him down, and the only way he can stop that is to kill me. And that's going to be a lot harder than he thinks, even if he uses his classified, special forces mercenary."

"I don't kill for that man or anyone!" Terry's voice was a growl, and he stretched out toward me, eyes peering out from under angry brows, all charm gone from a face turned hard and deadly. "But he has people who do. You don't want to tweak his nose this way, Skeet."

I leaned down into his face and lowered my voice even further but not the anger in it. "He tried to blackmail Joe into violating everything he believes in and is sworn to do by threatening to take his child away and put her in the custody of a drugged-out hooker who'd probably sell the kid as soon as look at her. Someone's got to stand up to this damn criminal. Because that's all he is. Money and power and charm aside, he's just a crook that someone needs to take on."

The muscle in his jaw tensed, and he rubbed the corner of his mustache with his right thumb. His eyes were glued to mine, dark and angry, and I was reminded of my first impression of this man as a dangerous predator used to walking in treacherous surroundings and coming out on top.

I stepped back out of his face and calmed my voice but kept the steel in it. "If the special forces hotshots of the world won't, I guess it'll just have to be me. And whoever he sends after me is going to find me a lot harder nut than he'll be expecting. I've survived a lot of thugs. I'm betting I'll survive him, too."

I pretended to write something in my notebook, as if giving him a ticket.

He gave me a fierce, compelling look. "Skeet, I had no idea—"

I gave a harsh laugh. "Yeah, it seems like you just don't know anything that man's doing. How convenient for you."

I ripped a sheet of paper from my notebook to give him and complete our charade, but before I could hand it to him, he kicked his car in gear and roared off, leaving me standing, holding out a piece of paper with a scribbled line on it.

I stared off at the thin silver ribbon of the river in the early-morning distance. I'd thrown down the gauntlet, and it might have been stupid. But if nothing else, it would focus Walker's malice and harm on me instead of Joe and Julie. I could handle it. I had a secret weapon, experience. I'd spent a lifetime dealing with men, some of them quite powerful, who wanted the world or their immediate surroundings rid of me, and I was still here.

I tried to put the whole case out of my mind when I got to work and focus on our weekly staff meeting, the self-defense class I teach at the Women's Center, the monthly student disciplinary proceedings, and over the course of a long dreary afternoon, the faculty senate meeting where I had my usual skirmishes with certain faculty members over the cost of the new parking garage. I left the university with a longing for a quiet evening at home with Gran and Brian. I felt I'd been neglecting them lately while I worked this case, as well as my regular job. I'd make up for it tonight because I suspected things were going to heat up once Terry gave my message to Walker.

Consequently, I was not happy to see Angie sitting on the front steps with Brian and Lady, obviously waiting for me. I stifled a grumble, told myself to be nice, and walked up to them after parking the Crown Vic, another train rumbling and clanking through town behind me.

"What's up?" I tried to keep my tone light and ordinary. Lady ran up to me, excited that I was home, and I leaned down to give her beautiful collie coat a good petting.

Angie avoided my eyes, resting her head on her tattooed arms. This was never a good sign. Angie was the original in-your-face girl. When she started avoiding your gaze, something was going on that you wouldn't want to know about.

Brian stood up, and once again I had to notice how much he'd grown. It wouldn't be long until he was a man ready to go off and make a life for himself, and that made me catch my breath. He hadn't been with me that long. I wanted him to grow up strong and happy, of course, but just not yet.

"Angie's got something to tell you, Skeet. Something you need to hear." He emphasized the word *need*, and I knew this was trouble, for sure.

I nodded, buying time. "Okay. Do we want to go inside or

do it out here?" I'd vote for inside in an easy chair with a cup of coffee or even better, from the sound of this, hot chocolate with lots and lots of whipped cream.

"Let's stay out here," Angie urged Brian, still without looking at me. My bad feeling grew.

He nodded solemnly and gestured to the porch with its cushioned wicker furniture. I was relieved that I wasn't going to have to sit on the old splintery wooden steps after a day that had left me stiff and achy already.

I had to laugh at myself. Brian was growing up and I was getting older, and I wasn't handling either very well.

I made my way to my favorite wicker rocker, with Lady shadowing my strides while the two kids walked in lockstep over to the love seat and sat together. I dropped my laptop case on the table next to me and stared at them while I fondled Lady's head.

"Okay. I'm here and listening. What's going on?"

Brian nudged Angie, and she looked into his face and then away from both of us.

"Come on, Angie. You know you need to do this." Brian looked stern yet loving. I wondered if he'd look that way when he had his own children, and I rocked a little faster when I realized that would make me a grandmother. I wasn't used to being a mother yet.

"That night," Angie started in a low voice. "You know, the night it happened."

"The night Ash was killed?" I asked.

She nodded, her burgundy hair with its blue stripe rising and falling with her head. "That night, I'd left the house." She finally looked up at me for a second. "Liz doesn't care. No one does. So I wasn't doing anything wrong."

I nodded as pleasantly as I could manage. What she said about no one caring was true, at least at her home.

She shrugged with a quick tilt of her head. "I like to just wander around outside at night. I was over by the Steens."

I tried not to react. Stalking Noah, I'd bet. I looked over at Brian. Now he was peering intently at the floorboards and refusing to engage anyone's eyes. This had to be painful for him. Lady left my side and went to him, laying her gold, brown, and black head in his lap.

Angie held up her head with her usual bravado. "I wasn't doing anything wrong," she insisted. "I saw Noah climb down a tree from his window. I thought he was coming to see me, so I followed him. I was going to surprise him from behind when he tossed a rock at my window."

It sounded to me as though this rock-at-the-window scenario had probably happened before.

Angie turned her head to face away from me. Silence built, and Brian looked up from playing with Lady's ears.

"Angie," he said quietly.

From her profile, I could see her lips tighten and her eyes close for a second.

"Only he didn't go out toward Wickbrook. He wasn't going to see me. So I kept following him because I wanted to see who he was going to see."

She looked back at me with pain in her eyes. "I wish I hadn't."

"Where did he go, Angie?" I asked gently.

"To the golf course." A single tear left her right eye, but she seemed not to notice. "He met that awful man, Ash, there. Ash held out a bottle of whiskey to him, like he was offering him a drink, but Noah shook his head. Then Ash went into the clubhouse, and Noah took a little bottle from his jacket and poured it into Ash's bottle of booze."

The antifreeze. It had been Noah.

"What did Noah do then?" I kept my voice as soft as I could. It was obvious how hard this was for Angie. I think only her fear of Brian looking down on her for cowardice compelled her to speak.

"I don't know!" she wailed, tears coming in earnest now. "I ran away because I thought he'd be mad that I followed him and call me clingy and smothering again. I didn't see. But he can't have killed him. Noah wouldn't. He just wouldn't."

Brian watched Angie, with his own pain all over his face. I nodded and motioned him toward her. He put his arm around her shoulder tentatively, and she threw herself into his arms, wholeheartedly sobbing into his chest and onto Lady's head.

So I'd just put the final nail in my friendship with Joe and made myself a target for Walker's thugs to protect an innocent boy who probably wasn't so innocent, after all. Noah might not have been the one who slammed that golf club into Ash's head, though that looked more and more likely, but he certainly was the one who poisoned Ash with antifreeze. I needed to talk to that boy.

And as far as the Walker threat went, I couldn't let him do that to Joe and Julie. I thought of Miryam's story of her rape at Walker's hands, also. It was just as well that I'd declared war on the evil creature.

After supper, I headed to the Steen house again. I'd called after Angie's revelation and made an appointment to meet them after dinner. I wondered if Noah had any intimation that his secret had come out. I thought of Elliott and his quiet assurance that neither Noah nor Chelsea could ever kill. I suspected that man had kept Chelsea and her son on a pedestal for his entire adult life. Learning that either of them was as messy and human as the rest of us might be very hard for him to handle.

I passed quiet houses and wondered if any of us ever knew the truth of what went on inside them, any more than we did with those polite faces their residents presented us each day. I would have sworn that Noah Steen wasn't a killer. A kid with a hot temper when his family was attacked, yes. A kid who'd received the shock of his life, yes. A kid knocked off his usually placid center by an adult egomaniac, yes. But a killer, no.

But there it was. Peter and Angie saw him sneak out. Angie saw him meet Ash at the golf course and pour the antifreeze into Ash's Southern Comfort. I had wrecked what was left of my friendship with Joe in defense of this kid. I'd gone out on a limb because I believed he didn't have it in him to murder even Ash Mowbray in cold blood. But, it turned out, he did have it in him to poison Ash in cold blood.

By the time I arrived at the Steen home, I was steamed. I felt I'd been played by this spoiled homecoming king who'd already broken my Brian's heart. Chelsea opened the door to me with a questioning look, and I gave her a brisk nod. The cheerful room was brightly lit, and the three of them sat as they had the first night I arrived. I suspected that was their habitual arrangement. Chelsea and Noah on the couch together and Elliott in the nearby armchair.

"I have to talk to Noah about something," I explained as I shrugged out of my jacket for Chelsea to hang in the coat closet. There would never be any tossing of jackets over chair backs in this house, no matter how warmly it was decorated.

Elliott leaned forward in his chair, suddenly alert at the possibility of a threat to his son. "What is that?"

Chelsea reclaimed her seat on the couch with Noah. The boy himself looked at me with a weary face much older than his years and nodded.

I sat and looked directly at him. "Noah, the night Ash was killed, you climbed out of your bedroom window and down that tree outside, didn't you?"

"Of course, he didn't!" Chelsea's voice had taken on that slightly shrill tone that indicated great upset. "Why would you say such a thing?"

Elliott shook his head and stood, as if to come over and lecture me. Noah stared at me with a bleak look.

"There are three witnesses who saw him climb down the tree," I said in a cold, clear voice. "And one of them saw you meet Ash at the golf course."

Chelsea sucked in air audibly, and Elliott sagged back into his chair.

"They're lying," Chelsea cried. "Everyone who's been jealous of Noah for years is coming out of the woodwork to gossip and tease and spread wild rumors about him. Now this!"

"These are credible witnesses," I told her, holding back my reservations about Peter's malice. Dante certainly hadn't wanted him to speak but had confirmed it. And Angie—the last thing in the world she wanted was to see her beloved Noah in trouble.

Chelsea opened her mouth to yell at me some more, but she was stopped by Noah.

"It's true. I didn't kill him, though," he said, leaning forward to try to make me see. "I got this message from him on my phone wanting me to meet him and talk. He kept calling me his heir. I was so mad. I called to cuss him out, but then I ended up agreeing to meet him. I just wanted to hear what else he had to say."

He turned to look at his parents. "I know you've been trying to protect me, but I was tired of being ambushed in public with all this filthy stuff he kept saying. I wanted to hear it all for once and know what I was going to have to deal with."

Elliott dropped his gaze to the floor, as if ashamed to face his son. Chelsea's face paled even more than normal, and she gave a tiny moan before stiffening and turning on me. "But he didn't do it. He didn't kill him. Noah would never hit someone with a weapon. If Ash had been smacked in the nose and fallen and hit his head to die, that might have been Noah, but to beat in his head with a weapon? Never!"

I came right back at her. "Well, your innocent son, who would never do anything cruel like that, was seen pouring antifreeze into Ash's drink that night. But I suppose poisoning is somehow more noble than knocking someone on the head with a golf club, huh?"

I watched the shock hit her like a physical blow that rocked her back on her feet. Her eyes opened so wide I wondered if she would faint on us again, but she rallied, pulling on some iron inside her. I could tell she was trying to gather strength to come to her son's defense again.

Meanwhile, Elliott had flown out of his chair and across the room to where I sat. "This can't be true. Noah would never do anything like that. Not Noah."

I looked over at the big, good-looking kid with the miserable eyes who sat behind the coffee table. "Noah, what do you say? Remember. There are witnesses."

He dropped his glance to the coffee table and addressed his words to it. "I didn't think of it as poisoning." He looked up, pleading. "I wouldn't do that. Honest. I just wanted to play a dirty trick on him. That's all. I remembered the kids who drank the antifreeze and got so sick and had newspaper articles written about how stupid they were. And I thought I'd meet him and give him some antifreeze to drink so he'd get sick and have all that ridicule in the newspapers. It would serve him right for all the crap he did to my folks."

"Oh, Noah," Chelsea moaned.

"It was just a little bit," he insisted. "Just enough to make him sick enough to go to the hospital. Not enough to kill him or anything like that."

"It was enough that if he'd passed out and not been found and no one had struck him with the golf club, he might well have died anyway. The coroner says it would have been touch and go whether he lived or died."

Noah's eyes grew huge. He shook his head frantically. "I didn't mean to kill him. I just wanted to play a mean trick on him to pay him back for all the hurt he was causing everyone. I didn't think it was enough to do more than make him really sick. Honest, Skeet!" He covered his face with both hands in a hopeless gesture.

"You were there at the scene of the crime." I looked straight at him, and he raised his face to return my gaze.

"He wanted us to play golf together. At midnight! He was crazy. He thought he could beat me. I didn't care about any of that. I just wish to hell I'd taken my clubs with me when I left. He'd already pulled them out of the clubhouse."

He shook his head at the stupidity. Whether his or Ash's was not clear. "Who plays golf at night? In the dark? He was drinking. He wanted me to drink some, but I wouldn't. It smelled putrid. When he went back for the golf cart, I poured the antifreeze into his bottle. I'd put it in a little vodka bottle I got from a friend and was going to offer him a drink, but this was even better."

Chelsea moaned as she rocked her head from side to side. Elliott stared at Noah.

The boy shrugged and looked at me with a plea in his eyes. "I just played a trick on him. Yeah, it was a dirty one, but I didn't mean to kill him. He came back with the golf cart and took a big slug out of the bottle. I told him I hated him and wanted him to leave me alone. And I left. He was drinking again when I left. I knew he'd drink all that and get sick as a dog. And that's all I wanted. When I left, he was drinking and shouting. Alive."

"Noah would never kill anyone," Elliott said in a calm, firm voice as he walked back to sit in his armchair. "He hasn't got that darkness in him. Not like me. I didn't know anyone had seen him. I followed him that night. He didn't know I was behind him. I stayed after he left and killed Ash because I was jealous and afraid he would steal my wife and son. Then I ran. I didn't realize it was Noah's club I'd used until it was too late to do anything about it. You can arrest me and take me to Joe. I'll go quietly."

Noah looked bewildered. "Dad?"

"Elliott, you will not do this!" Chelsea dropped her hands and glared at her husband.

"I'm sorry, my dear. I only wanted to stop him from what he was doing to us all," Elliott pleaded. "I never wanted to hurt you or Noah."

Chelsea stood and walked over to him, shaking her head. "Oh, stop. Do. You don't expect Skeet or me to believe this, do you?"

"Dad?" Noah questioned again.

Chelsea laid her hand on top of Elliott's head. "Dear old fool. Going to martyr yourself for your son, were you?"

Elliott looked up at her with pure misery in his eyes. "I would do anything for Noah or you. I'm sorry for all the pain this has caused. But I don't regret killing him. He was a horrible man." He picked up his cell phone from the table beside him and dialed.

"This is Elliott Steen. I want to confess to a murder. Tell Chief Louzon I'll be waiting here at home for him."

"Elliott! No!" Chelsea slapped the phone from his hand.

He looked up at her. I'd seen that look before on the faces of people who'd given up.

"I know you love us, but don't do this," she ordered. "I know you're lying, but Skeet and Joe and a jury might not. You didn't kill Ash any more than Noah did."

"I hated him so much," he said with great fatigue. "And I could see he wasn't going to give up. He was just going to keep coming with new ways to wreck our lives and hurt you two."

"Elliott," I said, "is this the truth? Because a false confession won't help anyone, and it will keep Joe from looking for the real killer."

"Dad?" Noah asked again, tears in his eyes. "Dad, you didn't kill him. I know you didn't. You're just saying this because you think I'm in big trouble for the antifreeze. Don't, please!"

I remembered that strange, calm threat Elliott had made to Ash back at the city council meeting.

Chelsea shook her head at her husband. "No, you couldn't have done this. You're too good. You have too much decency and love in you. Now tell Skeet the truth."

Elliott looked up at me. "Unfortunately, the truth is that, in a moment of passion, I killed Ash Mowbray." Elliott sagged back into his chair, looking suddenly old. Chelsea remained standing next to him with her hand resting on his head.

A knock at the door signaled Joe's arrival. Things speeded up then. Elliott repeated his confession, and Joe cuffed him to take him back to the jail after telling Chelsea how to go about trying for bail in the morning. I told her to call Marsh Corgill and get him down to the jail to represent Elliott right away.

While she was on the phone, I turned back to Noah, who looked dazed. "Did Ash say anything that might suggest anyone else was around?"

Finally taking his eyes off the door out of which his father had gone in handcuffs, Noah looked at me. "No. Well, he did ask me if I wanted some . . ." He blushed. "Some sex. He said guys my age always wanted some. He knew that. He'd see I got it. I told him I thought he was disgusting and got out of there. So I guess maybe there was a woman there?" His tone became hopeful. "Or on the way?"

I nodded. That made sense, given what I knew of Ash Mowbray. He'd have tried to use liquor, sex, and the promise of money to woo his son away from his parents. So maybe there was a woman stashed there that night. I needed to find her.

"Skeet, I know my dad didn't do this." Noah looked at me with bleak eyes. "This is all my fault, but I can't see how I can make it better. Find the real killer, please. Don't stop because of this. Set my dad free."

I nodded. "Too many questions still for me to stop looking, Noah. If someone else did it, I'll find them. If it was your dad . . ."

He shook his head in despair and turned to watch his mother as she answered Marsh Corgill's questions over the phone.

I looked at Chelsea, desperately focused on getting help to

save the husband who'd once saved her, and Noah, watching her now as if she was his lifeline in deepest ocean waters. In some ways, this family was a model of what love could do and be. In other ways, it was a stern warning about how love could twist lives.

CHAPTER 12

Tuesday morning while I worked on a report for the chancellor's cabinet meeting later in the day, I was interrupted by a call from my ex-husband. At Mary's message, I shook my head silently, sure that Charlie had run off with Marie again, and told her to put Sam through to my phone.

"Morning, Skeet." He sounded harried. "I hate to bother you, but it's about Charlie."

I sighed. I'd known it would be. "Okay, Sam. What's going on?"

Sam spoke to someone he called "honey" in the background in a softened voice. I wondered if he'd had some woman spend the night. I hoped so. Maybe it would take the pressure off me. I'd often wished Sam would fall in love with one of the women he occasionally dated, so he'd stop trying to convince me to go back with him and start all over. But he could just be calling from a restaurant. Sam used endearments to women all the time. It was second nature to him, like flirting.

"Sorry. I just wanted to answer Erika's question." His

voice was a little calmer than it had been when I answered the phone.

"Are you still at Charlie's? What's happened now, Sam?" I had visions of another stroke, though surely they'd have Charlie in the hospital and would have called me in when it happened. Same with a massive heart attack. What could have kept Sam there all night?

Sam gave a nervous laugh. "No, don't worry. I went home last night, but I took off work to come here today and sit with Erika and Charlie. I want to be here when Marie shows up this time. It's too hard on Erika to have to try to deal with that woman alone. I wanted to have a talk with Marie and with Charlie."

I wasn't sure it would do any good with either of them, but Sam wouldn't want to hear that. He thought he could charm anyone into doing whatever he wanted. Well, it had worked with me for too long a time, hadn't it?

"Has she come already? This early? Is that what this is about?"

"No, but Charlie and I have had that talk." He was silent for a second, and I closed my eyes. I had a feeling I wasn't going to like what I heard. "I thought you should know about it."

"And?" I hated it when people dithered around about bad news. Spit it out. Let me start to adjust to it and figure out how to deal with it. Don't just talk all around it without ever saying what it actually is.

"Skeet, he wants to marry her." He sounded crestfallen. So the charm offensive hadn't worked with Charlie. I could have warned him. "He seems pretty determined. And I don't see any way we can stop him unless we want to go to court to declare him incompetent."

That thought appalled me. "We can't do that. Charlie's boneheaded stupid about this woman, but he's not incompetent."

"Exactly my point. So where does this leave us?" Sam sounded exasperated and tired, and I reminded myself that most ex-husbands would not be sharing the care of my delinquent father with me. With most men, I'd have been on my own. Score a big one in Sam's favor.

I ran my hands through my hair in frustration at the whole situation that I somehow couldn't manage to make any better than it was. "I don't know, Sam. Nowhere, I guess. If he's determined to marry her, there's not much we can do. Stand up at the wedding when they ask if anyone knows of any reason they shouldn't marry and say because she's trying to kill him? I don't think so. Our hands are tied."

"It really pisses me off, especially when Erika's been working so hard to rebuild his strength and does such a great job with him." His velvet voice had become more of a growl. Sam was always the first to defend underdogs and feel sorry for working-class girls. Score another one in Sam's favor. "Why didn't they send her to us first, instead of Marie? We wouldn't be in this position now. Erika's got integrity."

Erika was an excellent nurse-aide, but I suspected Sam was so vehement because she was young and pretty. If she were older and plump, he'd take her expertise more for granted. "I know she's doing a good job. But it sounds as if Marie's going to undo all that. Damn! I'd hoped she'd just move on to easier pickings when she saw that we were trying to protect him."

"No such luck," he said. "I don't want to cut ourselves off from him, but short of that, I don't know how to stop him."

I remembered Gran scolding us at Charlie's the other

night. *Maybe he's found that shutting yourself off to love because you've been hurt is really a fool's choice. Maybe he's decided to take a chance on love and open himself up to really living.* "We can't do that, Sam. So we can't stop him. We'll just have to find a way to live with it—or talk him out of it."

He laughed a dark, unhappy laugh. "Good luck with that. I've tried my hand at it. No luck. Maybe you can do better. I don't know."

I did. Sam was the son Charlie had always wanted, the son I wasn't. If he couldn't talk Charlie out of this destructive relationship with Marie, it was damn sure I couldn't.

I swallowed my hurt at that thought and answered Sam. "So I guess we'll have to find a way to live with it. Maybe they'll take long enough that Marie will get tired of him and move on, or he'll actually come to his senses and see her for what she is."

"You always find a way to hope, don't you?" Sam had a more genuine laugh lurking behind his voice. "I've always loved that about you."

I frowned at his choice of words. We were definitely not going there. "Not always a good thing. It kept me with you a lot longer than I ever should have stayed."

"I'm sorry about that." His voice sounded truly contrite, and I regretted what I'd said. "I'm sorry about a lot of things, Skeet. I wish I could go back and do them differently. But I can't."

I knew the sad, remorseful look his handsome face would have taken on to go with that voice. It was the worst of all worlds. I couldn't forget what he'd done and let him back in my life, and he couldn't forget how he felt about me and let go of me. It was painful for both of us and wouldn't even be happening, except that Sam was determined to help with the care of the only father he'd ever really known.

"Oh, Sam." I sighed loudly. "It usually takes two to really ruin a marriage. Don't worry. It's over."

The phone went quiet for a while. The silence went on so long I began to wonder if he was still there.

"Yeah," he finally said. "It's time for me to get that through my head. Even if I don't want to."

I flat-out refused to start off my day feeling sorry for my ex-husband. "Okay. Thanks for calling about Charlie. We'll hope it's a long way off. A lot of things can happen between now and then. I've got to go now, Sam. Talk to you later."

As I tried to return to the report for the chancellor's cabinet, I couldn't help hearing Gran's voice in my head again and seeing the light in Charlie's eyes as he kissed Marie. Maybe I could draw on Scarlett O'Hara's technique and simply refuse to think about it all until tomorrow.

Later that morning I had a strange phone call from Pearl, asking me to come over to her house right away for Angie's sake. I drove over there, wondering what the emergency could be.

As I pulled up in front of Pearl's Victorian mansion, I glanced across that street at the smaller Steen house and wondered how Chelsea and Noah were holding up with Elliott in jail. Another train clattered through town, and its hooting whistle sounded to me like the murderer jeering at me for not being smarter, not seeing through his veils and machinations.

Angie answered the door, her eye makeup obviously streaked from tears. "Hey, Supercop."

She said it with no energy, and it had no zing of mockery the way it usually did. Something was obviously wrong with her. I wondered if it was simply guilt over having told me of Noah's poisoning of Ash.

"Come in, Skeet," said Pearl.

We entered the living room and settled into chairs.

"Angie's come here in great panic, so I thought you could give us the truth of where things were standing with this murder investigation." Pearl gestured to Angie to start speaking.

"Noah won't even see me," she cried. "He's just focused on his dad and his family right now."

I shook my head in disgust. "Angie, where else do you expect him to focus? His dad's in jail for murder, and his mom's desperately trying to get him the legal and other help he needs. Don't you think he might find that a little more important than all this boyfriend-girlfriend stuff?"

Pearl frowned at me. Angie hiccupped.

"Don't you think I can see that? But I was counting on Noah. And now if Elliott goes to prison for Ash's murder, Noah will have to take care of his mother, and he won't be able to marry me and take me away from Liz." Her last words were choked by tears as she started sobbing.

My mouth dropped open slightly in surprise. "Marry you? Angie, you're barely sixteen. Noah isn't even eighteen yet. You're both still in high school. What are you talking about?"

Pearl sighed and handed Angie a box of tissues. "Angie had a plan to manipulate Noah into marrying her as soon as he turned eighteen. She's that desperate to get away from Liz. She thought she could live with Noah and his parents while they finished school."

"I'll have money coming to me," Angie said with a sniffle. She scrubbed roughly at her eyes with a tissue. "My dad's will says when I turn eighteen or marry. I think it's quite a bit of money since he didn't leave any to Liz. Just the house. Everything else comes to me."

That was news. Of course, money was the last thing Liz Richar needed as sole heir to two of Kansas City's biggest fortunes.

"I thought Noah could marry me," Angie continued, "so I could get away from Liz, and I could get hold of my money and . . . I just can't stand living with that woman any longer. I know she hates me and wants to kill me."

I would ordinarily have dismissed Angie's words as an overemotional teen's paranoia, except I knew Liz hated her and had tried to kill her at least once in the past. That had been touch and go, too. Liz had almost succeeded. So I had to take Angie's claim seriously.

"What is she doing, Angie? You can always tell me. If we can come up with proof that she's endangering your life or trying to harm you, the court will allow you to live with someone else."

"But that's just it," she wailed. "I never have proof. But accidents have been happening lately that I really don't think are accidents. So far, I've been lucky, but how long will that last?"

I felt my jaw tighten. I believed Liz had almost killed Angie—and Brian as collateral damage. With no more thought than swatting a ladybug while trying to hit a fly. I knew why Angie hadn't told me about these accidents. If I knew they were happening, I'd never let Brian go over to that house again.

"I'd rather kill myself than let that bitch do me in. At least, I'd be taking the power myself." Angie blew her nose noisily.

"And doing exactly what she wants," I pointed out. "Don't you think she'd love it if you killed yourself? Tragic widow trying her best for dead husband's troubled daughter devastated when girl commits suicide."

"What can I do then, Skeet?" she cried. "Just wait around for her to finish me off? Wherever I turn, something makes it impossible for me to get away from her."

"Skeet, does it look as if Elliott actually committed Ash's murder?" Pearl's face looked older and sadder than usual. I wondered how long she'd been holding Angie's hand and listening to her woes.

"I don't know, Pearl." I shook my head glumly. "He says he did it, but I'm inclined to think that was all about protecting Noah, who was at the golf course that night and gave Ash antifreeze to drink. Not enough to kill him and probably not something he'd do if he was going to beat in Ash's head. But Elliott could see how bad it made things look for his son. I think he confessed to protect Noah."

Pearl's face turned a little grayer. "What happens if they don't find the real killer? Will Elliott be tried and go to prison?"

"That's a real possibility," I replied just as seriously. "The man is taking a terrible chance for the sake of his son."

Angie turned to me in appeal. "You'll find the real killer, won't you, Skeet?"

I had to shrug. "I can't promise that, kiddo. All I can promise is that I'll try my hardest. I don't ever want to see any innocent person going to prison for a crime he didn't commit. Either this killer's been very clever, or other people are messing things up. But sooner or later, we have to make our way through all the lies and false clues and misdirection to the truth."

Angie nodded, as if my answer satisfied her. It didn't satisfy me. I'd found my way to the truth before in situations where I still couldn't prove someone's guilt in a court of law and had had to watch the guilty walk away. I hated it, but it would be worse if that happened and someone innocent took the rap.

In the afternoon once the chancellor's cabinet meeting was over, I set myself to work on the backlog of paperwork that's always hanging over me. I had nothing else scheduled for the rest of the day, so I hoped to make a real dent in the paperwork mountain.

My cell phone rang with a number I didn't recognize. When I answered without giving my name—as I always do on the cell to unknown numbers, so telemarketers can't target it—I recognized Terry's voice with his slight indefinable accent that came from growing up all over the world with his American father before attending school in England.

"I need to meet with you somewhere people won't be able to observe us. I have something that will help Joe against Walker, but I can't be seen giving it to you."

Getting right to the point was admirable—and kept me from hanging up when he asked to meet. Meeting with Terry, especially alone and somewhere isolated, was not something I wanted to do. For ammunition in the war against Walker, I'd do it however.

"Do you remember how to get out to Karen's farm?" I asked.

He gave a little laugh. "I usually remember places where I've climbed trees to take sniper shots. At least the ones in the States."

"We can meet on that long drive she has. After it turns off the county road and before it reaches her house. No one should see us there." And it wouldn't be conducive to ideas of anything else that might pass through his head. A gravel drive in the country is not the most comfortable place for a tryst.

And that close to Karen's farmhouse, it wouldn't be a good place for an assassination, either. I tended to believe Terry when he said he didn't do violence for Walker, but he'd done plenty of it for his country and maybe others, I knew. He was a man steeped in violence, and a man who hired his skills and experience out to others. So although I had hunches that I could trust him, I couldn't let myself.

We set the meeting time and hung up. I cleaned up the last of the paperwork I was dealing with, put the rest away for another day, and set out to meet him. Some clouds were moving in, and I thought we might get a small thunderstorm.

It was badly needed. This long stretch of dry, sunny weather had come during the fall months when we would normally have received much of our year's rain. We'd been in a drought with last year's mild, dry winter and last summer's heat wave. Everyone had hoped the fall rains would save us, but they'd held off. Even a small storm would be a lifesaver for farmers, though probably not enough to stave off the full effects of drought. We needed a normal fall full of rain and a winter full of snow and icy rain to soften the rock-hard ground and refill the aquifers.

I didn't have an umbrella with me, but as I looked at the clouds, I decided I didn't really need to run home for one. If this storm actually hit, it wouldn't be a good gully washer. It might be nothing but lots of thunder and a few sprinkles. We'd had too many of those lately.

The thunder and lightning had started by the time I hit the winding county roads that led to Karen's farm. I sped up. I'd feel better about the lightning when I was sheltered by the tall windbreaks planted on each side of Karen's drive. If I had to be out in a thunderstorm, I always wanted to have taller trees or towers nearby to draw the lightning away from me. I had a Cherokee great-uncle who'd been struck by lightning in his youth and lost his hearing altogether and part of his sight.

I turned down Karen's drive and saw Terry's Range Rover waiting for me farther on at the halfway point of the drive. We'd be out of sight of the county road there and almost out of sight of the farmhouse. He'd picked a good spot. Of course.

I pulled in as quietly as you can on gravel and parked behind him. He stretched his long legs out of his car, and the rest of him followed. He stood with arms crossed, waiting for me to choose to get out and come to him. I appreciated that. He seldom pushed, unlike a lot of men. And especially in a situation like this, I hated to be pushed.

I got out of my car and walked over to him. A few spits of rain came gusting down the tree-lined road into my face, but the storm looked as if it would be just what I'd expected—thunder and lightning with very little actual rain. The wind was whipping up however.

As I came even with Terry, he reached up with one finger to the big old broad-brimmed gray fedora he wore to tilt it in a tiny salute. I'd seldom seen him without it, except the time he showed up, his longish hair tied back, dressed for combat.

"Terry," I said with a curt nod. "What have you got?" I wanted to pick up whatever it was he had for me and get out of there.

He tilted his head to the left and looked down at me. Not that much. I'm tall for a woman, but he was a tall man. He usually had some kind of mischief in his glance, unless it smoldered or became suddenly implacable, but now it was bare and open. I almost thought *vulnerable* and then had to laugh at myself. This man was never vulnerable.

"You can't ever tell anyone where you got this," he said, hands still empty. "Not even Joe. I know you don't like to take credit for other people's work, but you're going to have to pretend this is all your own investigative work."

"Why?" I didn't like the sound of this.

He crossed his arms again and stared at me with his head slightly tilted and his lips tightened. "Because I found some of this information in Walker's confidential files. It's findable out in the real world by others, but it would take a lot of time and money to do it. No one can know I've given it to you. Promise me that."

I shook my head in disbelief at the idea he'd trust me with something like that. There had to be some trick up his sleeve. Or else he was setting me up for Walker. "What's to keep me from promising and then turning around and telling Joe or someone?"

Suddenly, he threw his head back in that great laugh that opened up his whole face. "Skeet, you are the person they invented the word *honor* for. If you'd lived back in the Middle Ages, you'd have to have found some way to be a knight, even as a woman. You're that kind of honorable. 'I love the name of honor more than I fear death.' *Julius Caesar.*"

He bowed his head slightly, as if acknowledging nonexistent applause. "One of the advantages of British schools. I've a quotation for every occasion."

"I didn't think Julius Caesar was all that honorable." I didn't know what else to say to a man comparing me to a medieval knight. I suspected it wasn't the compliment most women wanted.

"He wasn't. You are." His little closemouthed smile lit up his eyes and showed off those high, rounded cheekbones. "If you give me your word that you'll tell no one else, I'll feel I have ample assurance of confidentiality."

I shrugged. "Okay, I give you my word that I won't tell anyone about where I got this whatever."

He nodded and unfolded his arms. "This file."

"I won't tell anyone you gave me this file." I didn't care. If it would help Joe and Julie and make things uncomfortable for Walker, I was in.

He reached through the window into his car and pulled up a lawyer's brown expandable file with a tied flap. He handed it to me with a tired partial smile. "This should keep Walker off Joe's back."

I took the file and opened it to glance inside. He stood silent, watching me inspect it. It was the real deal—arrest reports, plea bargains, rehab commitment orders, and other goodies. Enough to amply prove that Joe's ex was no fit mother for Julie.

The more I saw, the surer I was that stealing this for Joe and me was going to get Terry into big trouble. He might be the original danger man, but this could leave even him having to make a run for it with a target on his back. "Aren't you afraid they'll realize you're the one who took this file?"

His smile broadened as he leaned toward me, putting his face on the same level as mine. That smile had lots of things in it but no fear. "Who says I took it? Who says the original file isn't exactly where it always was without any sign of having been tampered with or copied?"

I shook my head in disbelief at his nerve. Was there nothing this man wouldn't try to pull off?

He straightened up and lounged with his legs crossed against the side of his car, his lips tightened and turned down in a frown that lowered his brows and darkened his eyes even further. "I've only done this because Walker threatened Joe's kid. I don't hold with involving family, especially children, in these matters."

He looked directly at me, his frown fading into an intense, searching gaze that held my eyes prisoner while the wind whipped some hair loose from his hat and into his left eye. Two small lines had formed at the inside corners of his eyebrows. He stared, as if studying something of vital importance.

I noticed my breathing had sped up, and I was staring back with the same intensity, trapped by some power in his eyes. I broke the connection, looking back to the file and resisting the urge to shake myself in order to rid myself of the strange weight his glance held. I concentrated on bringing my breathing back under control.

He uncrossed his legs and pulled himself up to his full height, and his face took on that almost painfully open look it had held as I drove up. "And for you, of course. I won't have you thinking that I'd be a part of something targeting a child. There are limits to how low I'm willing to let your opinion of me sink."

I stopped pretending not to watch him and openly stared in astonishment. "You can't be serious. You don't really give a damn what I think of you. This is all a game for you. You've made that apparent."

He put his right hand in his pocket and leaned forward a little, watching me with that undefended look that I'd never seen before on this man whose whole life was based on aggressive, guarded resistance. He almost looked sad as he stared at me.

As I watched, he pulled back behind his usual walls again until I began to doubt that I'd ever really seen him without them. He took his hand out of his pocket and took a long step over to stand in front of me, just a little uncomfortably inside my personal space, but I felt that if I stepped backward I'd lose points somehow, so I stood my ground. He gave me a sidelong glance and, with a quick movement, placed his hand over my right cheek and the top of my neck. My head rocked back slightly in surprise.

"You also need to understand that there's a limit to what I can do for you, Skeet. Much as I hate to admit it, right now I'm probably not someone you should rely on." The shadow of that sadness I thought I'd seen before played around his mouth.

His hand was warm and strong against my face, and I wondered why I hadn't shoved it off. I was sure I would any second now. He pulled back first, though, and shook his head the slightest bit. That movement brought the slenderest smile to his serious face and brought me to my senses.

"Then it's a damn good thing I don't rely on you, isn't it?" I stepped back now, not caring if I lost points. "I'll give this to Joe, and I won't tell him where I got it."

He just stared at me as I turned and walked back to my car. After I opened the door and set the file inside, I turned back to look at him. He stood exactly where I'd left him, with that strange not-quite smile on his not-quite sad face. It occurred to me that I'd never acknowledged the risk he'd taken to get me these papers.

"Thank you for this, Terry," I called.

The smile deepened a little, and he gave that salute with his hat.

When I passed him, he turned to follow my car with his eyes the way a sunflower turns with the sun. As I rolled onto the county road, I saw him in my rearview mirror, still standing there.

CHAPTER 13

I called Joe on my cell phone and told him to meet me at the same place as yesterday. I told him I had an idea about what he could do about Julie's birthday, which Joe and I both knew was a couple of months away. I was careful what I said over the phone because if you've got enough money like Walker does, you can buy the technology or the people, like secretaries and receptionists, to listen and overhear anything.

Then I headed out to the banks of Turtle Creek by that little eddy pool where we'd had our confrontation and waited for him to show up. I couldn't take a chance on someone seeing me enter his office or mine carrying this file.

I sat on the creek bank with my feet hanging down over the edge and listened to a train. This far out by Wickbrook, the sound of the trains was muted, but you could still hear them if you tried. Now that the thunder sprinkle was over, a little blue heron hunted in the pond created by debris on the left side of the creek. Yesterday's turtle was nowhere to be seen. I watched the heron take a few graceful yet stiff-legged steps before striking in the shallows with its long beak. Along the shoreline on the river where it emerged from the wildlife refuge, I often saw great blues and, rarely but memorably, migrating whooping cranes. I could watch cranes and herons for hours.

Joe drove up, and I pulled up my legs and got to my feet. I'd left the file locked in my Crown Vic for safety. Nothing like sitting out in plain sight with something like that, making a perfect target for some of Walker's hired muscle.

Joe got out of his cruiser as I reached my own. "What's up?" he asked in a wary voice. "Strange message. Are we doing spy stuff now?"

"Right now we are, but I hope this is the end of it." I unlocked my door and reached inside to take out that accordion file. I held it out to him. "I think you'll find everything you need here to do battle with Walker and win. I suspect you can even keep him from the whole thing if you judiciously let him know just a few of the things that you and your law enforcement friends have investigated and learned."

He gave me a questioning look and took the file, opening it to thumb through it. "My God, Skeet! It's everything I'd need to stop this. How in the hell did you get it? So fast?"

This was the part I didn't like, but I'd given my word. I shrugged and looked away from him. "I called in some favors. You know how things work with cops. Friends have friends who have friends. I was surprised how quickly I had what you needed, too. I thought it would take much longer, but here it is. The good guys come through for each other."

He looked at me, eyes suddenly suspicious. "You didn't tell these guys why you were looking for this stuff, did you?"

I shook my head. "Have no fear. None of my law enforcement pals know anything about your situation." Which was true. Terry was neither law enforcement nor a pal.

He stared at me for a second and then looked back through the contents of the file before looking up once again. His face had shed the weight of years it had begun carrying. He still looked tired as hell, but he didn't look beaten down and defeated any longer. As a matter of fact, he looked happy, if confused.

"Damn, Skeet! This will do it. Walker can't use her against me if I have all this. Thank you! God, thank you!" Now his hazel eyes shone and his voice was choked.

I hoped he wasn't going to cry, and I wished he'd stop thanking me. I hadn't done a damn thing. It was all Terry, but I wasn't allowed to let him know that. I shook my head and waved both hands side to side, looking away from his glistening eyes. "I didn't do much except put the word in the right ears. That's all."

He started to speak and had to clear his throat. I turned away and walked over to the edge of the creek bank where I'd been sitting earlier. I thought I'd give him time to get himself together without my staring at him. I'd never want anyone to see me all choked up and weepy, even if there was good reason for it because I'd been scared to death.

The heron had moved to the other side of the little pool and was studying the shallows beneath it with an eager eye, holding its head in readiness for the next chance to strike. I wondered why I was drawn to the killer birds—herons, cranes, hawks, and eagles. Then I remembered how much I'd always loved hummingbirds. *Walela* was one of the few Cherokee words I knew. That made me feel better. They were brave little warriors when their territories and families were threatened, but they were not predators.

Joe walked over to stand beside me as I studied the heron's beauty.

"Have I wrecked our relationship for good?" he asked while he stared out at the creek as well.

"I don't know." I continued to watch the heron strike into the water and catch something small and wriggling. "I don't really think we had one, Joe. I thought we had a friendship, but then it turned out that you were just pretending to accept me because you knew that was what I wanted to hear. I thought we had this honest, deep friendship, but it was based on deception on your part, so I was wrong."

He didn't reply for a few seconds. The silence between us would have been companionable once—or at least I would have thought it was—but now it held strain and pressure. I realized that as different as they'd always seemed, supposedly easygoing Joe and manipulative Sam had something in common. They both wanted to force me to feel something I didn't—or didn't want to—feel. I couldn't believe how blind and stupid I'd been. In a way, Joe had been a smoother operator than Sam even, because he'd fooled me so well for so long.

"I guess it probably does look that way to you," he finally said, "but that's not the truth of it. I didn't put on a front for you, at least not consciously. Of course, I wanted you to like me and more, so I tried to set my best foot forward. Then that Terry guy showed up."

I turned to him and opened my mouth to protest about his stupid assumptions that Terry and I had anything going on, but he finally looked at me and held up his hand to stop me.

"I know. I know now you're not seeing him any more than you're seeing me or Sam in that way, but at first I thought so. And I realized I'd let myself get put in—what do the young guys call it? The friend zone? That's all I was going to be because I'd been too nice. That's what my young single officers talk about with their friends. And I realized they're right. I'd been a fool."

"Bullshit, Joe! I don't buy that friend zone crap." I hated that term and the way I'd heard guys use it. "I've heard guys going on about it before, and what it's really about is that they just want to get in some woman's pants and they pretend to be her friend to get there—and get pissed if they can't. Pretending to be a friend to get sex that some woman doesn't necessarily want to give isn't honest. In fact, it's really pretty shitty."

Joe looked horrified. I guess he never figured that I'd call him on what all that really was. "Hey, I wasn't trying to do that with you. I wasn't some horny young dude just looking for sex. What I wanted was the whole ball of wax—love, sex, marriage eventually. Certainly a romantic relationship that's a whole lot more than just sex."

I waved him off vigorously with both hands. "I don't want another relationship that isn't based on a solid friendship and mutual respect. I tried the other way with my marriage to Sam, and it was a disaster. If I ever try to have another romantic relationship, it'll be with someone who's a solid, proven friend, who respects me for who I am—and doesn't just say what he thinks I want to hear. To con me and manipulate me. That's not a friend. I want what I thought we had. But it turned out I was dead wrong."

Another uneasy silence settled over us for several minutes. I watched the heron hunt with stillness and patience. Joe stared at the creek's ripples or the heron or something I couldn't see.

He finally turned toward me, but I kept my eyes on the heron. "I guess I have been a fool, but not the way I thought I was. I screwed up exactly what I wanted. Isn't there some way we could start all over again, Skeet?"

The heron stilt-walked to the side of the little shallows that it had started from. What would Gran say? Was that a sign? Start over? Go back to the beginning? I'd lived too long away from Oklahoma and those traditions. I was afraid I was too separate from my maternal heritage to interpret the everyday signs the Creator provided for us, just walking as blind through the world as the people who didn't even know about them. I didn't want to be that way.

We stood in silence as I watched the heron and wondered. Finally, I decided it was either a sign or I'd take it as one. I looked over at Joe, who watched me with a hopeful expression on his face.

"The only way to start over is to really begin at the beginning again and see if we can build an honest friendship. No promise or guarantee, though, that it will ever be anything other than that, Joe. That's all I can offer right now."

His face fell for a second. Then he took a deep breath and smiled at me with a slight nodding of his head. "Okay. I can see why. Let's try again from the start. I'll put the rest of it out of my head for now and just try to focus on a real friendship."

I looked at him. He looked a lot worse for the wear because of what he'd lately been through. He'd never be as shiny as Sam, but I'd thought before that he had a solid honesty that I could trust and rely on. We'd see if I'd been right or not. I knew I'd be more skeptical about Joe—at least for a while. It wouldn't be the same, but maybe we could develop a more honest friendship now.

I gave him an abrupt nod. "All right. We'll try it and see."

There didn't seem to be a lot to say or do after that, and I think we both felt awkward standing around after just talking about all those emotional issues. We separated and walked to our cars.

I gave him a tiny wave as I headed back into the heart of the town, and he gave me a smile in exchange. I had no idea how this would work, and if we could actually start again after having come to this point, but I conjured up the memory of the heron moving back to its starting point and felt more sure than ever that it was a sign and I was reading it correctly and we needed to try. Maybe I wasn't just walking through the world blind like the *yonega*. Maybe I hadn't lived so long away from the People that I'd forgotten everything I learned as a child. Maybe I was starting over in more than one way.

Wednesday morning I'd spent time with my night shift and morning shift officers at changeover and consulted with my sergeants from both shifts about a personnel issue that had been troubling all of us. I'd finally just settled at my desk with my second cup of office coffee for a morning of solid work on the paperwork mountain that always threatened to overwhelm me if I left it for too long when my cell phone rang. Another unfamiliar number. I answered with "Who is this?"

"It's me, your dad." Charlie's voice had that barely suppressed mischief that I'd come to dread. "This is Marie's cell phone."

"All right," I said, trying to buy time to figure out what sort of reaction I needed to take.

"Me and Marie are getting hitched this morning." Charlie sounded as if he'd been bursting to tell me that. "At ten o'clock on the fifth floor in the Jackson County Courthouse in KC. If you want to come, you're welcome, but don't try to stop us." He paused for a second. "Sam said he's coming."

I took a deep breath. I'd hoped to have months before this moment and that enough time would elapse that Charlie would come to his senses. But here it was.

"I'll be there, Charlie."

"I'm . . . I'm real glad, Skeet. I'll see you there." And he clicked off.

I sat for a few seconds staring at my cell phone. I was trying to get my mind around the idea of Charlie getting married to anyone, let alone to that damn Marie. It seemed it was going to happen whether I could find a way to deal with it or not.

I dialed Sam.

"You going?" he asked when he picked up the phone.

"Of course. How can I not?" I ran my hands through my hair in frustration. "Sam, what are we going to do?"

"Go to a wedding, I guess. Just don't expect me to kiss the damned bride!"

I laughed. "Hardly. Though I'm sure she'd love it."

He made retching sounds. "I wouldn't."

"I guess we ought to take them for an early lunch afterward. But where?"

"Where else? Gates. That's where your dad always wants to go for everything."

Gates Bar-B-Q was not an appropriate place for a wedding lunch. There was simply nothing fancy at all about Gates. It was a shorts and flip-flops, jeans and T-shirt place. The kind of place where you eat on plastic plates with plastic silverware and they yell at you as you walk in the door, but it had great barbecue and was Charlie's favorite restaurant.

"You're right. It's got to be Gates."

"You're taking this better than I thought you would, Skeet. I'm surprised."

I gave a bitter laugh. "It's just because I'm in shock. I probably need a brandy and a blanket." I was sorry the minute I said it. Mentioning a blanket gave him an opening for one of his double entendres and an offer to crawl under it with me. I closed my eyes in frustration at my stupidity.

"Okay. I'll see you there." He hung up, and I was a little puzzled that he hadn't done his usual thing. He must be as shocked by this turn of events as I was, shaken off his usual behaviors. Whatever it was, I'd gladly accept it.

I set my paperwork aside and told Mary that I'd be at the Jackson County Courthouse if I was needed, then headed out, totally on automatic pilot. I was still back there sitting at my desk, though, trying to get my head around the idea of Charlie getting married.

As I left Brewster proper, I finally began to take in where I was going and why. I might have hyperventilated a little driving over the Broadway Bridge. I also might have cursed loudly over and over in the car where no one could hear me as I drove into downtown Kansas City.

I stepped off the elevator in the Jackson County Courthouse onto the fifth floor twenty minutes ahead of time. Sam was already there, of course. A benefit of living in the city. Questionable at the moment.

Charlie and Marie sat together on a bench in the hall, holding hands like geriatric high school students—except Marie wasn't geriatric. Only Charlie was.

Charlie beamed when he saw me get off the elevator. "Hi, Skeet. Glad you could come. Bet you never thought you'd see me tying the knot again, did you?"

"I think you're safe with that bet, Charlie."

I walked over to where Sam leaned against the wall opposite them, arms crossed over his chest, and took up a similar position against the wall myself with my own arms crossed. It occurred to me that we looked to outsiders like two stern parents regarding a delinquent teen.

Marie was a plump bleached blonde, and for this day she had her hair done up in ringlets that looked like they belonged on a twelve-year-old. Her faded blue eyes peered out from heavy eyeliner and blue eye shadow that made her look like a designer raccoon with dangly earrings. With circles of artificial pink on her rounded cheeks and more of the same color on her mouth, as well as an eyelet-and-ruffles dress with spike heels, she looked as if she was trying to be a cross between a hooker and a schoolgirl. Sam and I had estimated that Marie was actually about my age, which made her young enough to be Charlie's daughter, but apparently that wasn't enough of an age gap for her, and she had to try to make it look even more ridiculous. Either that or Charlie had developed a thing for little girl hookers, which I didn't think was the case.

Charlie, on the other hand, was dressed in his good, funeral suit, which I thought more than appropriate. Someone, probably Erika, had slicked down his scruffy white hair neatly, making him look more than ever like a mischievous little boy turned suddenly ancient. Which was probably the best actual description of Charlie's personality.

I'd adored my father as a kid and been devastated when my mother could no longer live with him and, taking me, left to move in with her mother outside of Tahlequah, Oklahoma. But I'd long since come to see why my mother couldn't live with his irresponsibility, drinking, temper, and rash, self-destructive impulses. I'd run to Brewster to get away from them myself, only to have him reel me back in with his illness and stroke.

Now, here we were, and it occurred to me for the first time that I could just leave him to his new wife when this was over. No more sharing care with the ex-husband I'd wanted out of my life. No more struggling with my father's unruly, abrasive personality. I could finally walk free of those entanglements I'd fled to Brewster to escape. If only I didn't think Marie wanted him dead as soon as possible with his little bit of money in her greedy paws.

A short, thin balding man in shirtsleeves called out Charlie's name and directed us into the judge's chambers. The ceremony was short, perfunctory, and legal. Sam and I had to sign as witnesses afterward, and I wondered what Charlie would have done for witnesses if we hadn't shown up. Round up strangers from the courthouse hallways, knowing my father.

We congratulated them afterward. I even went so far as to shake Marie's hand.

"You'll have to call me Mom now," she said with an awkward laugh.

"I think not," I told her with a big forced smile. "I already have a mother. I suspect I'll stick to Marie." I didn't mention that I didn't call my own mother "Mom" or Charlie "Dad." That wasn't any of her business.

Charlie's face was gleeful when Sam told him we were taking them to Gates for a wedding lunch. "You hear that, Marie? The kids know how to do us proud."

I thought Marie looked considerably less delighted. And I couldn't blame her. Gates is not the place you get all gussied up for. She'd probably hoped for one of the fashionable restaurants at one of the downtown hotels.

Sam drove the newlyweds in his car to Gates since Marie wasn't sure she could find it. I snorted at that. How could you miss? Straight south down Main Street twenty blocks and you were there. I hit it first and waited for the wedding party in the parking lot, thinking how festive we did not look, Sam in KCPD uniform, me in black pantsuit, Charlie in his funeral suit. Only Marie looked as if she was at a wedding celebration.

We walked in to the sound of several different voices shouting. "Welcome to Gates! Can I help you? Can I take your order?" Marie shrank back at the vocal onslaught.

We walked up to the counter to place our order—Charlie for a long end of ribs with baked beans, Sam for his double deck combo (a sandwich with beef, ham, and turkey) with fries, and me for a burnt end sandwich with potato salad. Obviously confused, Marie stood staring at the menu boards above our heads, trying to decide what to get while a chorus of voices kept shouting, "Can I help you? Can I take your order?"

I knew how disconcerting it could be on your first visit. I'd been a kid when Charlie first brought me to Gates, and the constant shouting of the counterstaff combined with the strange names of the dishes had left me paralyzed and near meltdown. It was clear to me that Marie had never been here before and was in pretty much the same state. I should have been nice to her. She was my stepmother now, Charlie's wife. I knew what she was going through, and I could have suggested a simple order to her that would get her out of the cacophony. I'm not proud of the fact that I didn't. I just left her to her own devices.

"C'mon, Marie. Order. You're holding up the show here." Charlie's voice was sharp. He hated to look bad in front of others, and standing staring while not replying to the constant loud requests for an order marked anyone as a novice and ignorant of the ways of a Kansas City institution.

"Why don't you order for me, honey? I don't really know what's good or not."

Charlie snorted. "It's all good. It's Gates. Best barbecue in the world."

I shook my head. So he was starting up that old argument.

Sam grinned. "Hell, Charlie, you know B.B.'s is better—plus they've got all those blues greats playing live."

"Good blues, but the best barbecue is Gates. Isn't it, Skeeter?"

"Charlie, you know I'm a Jack Stack fan. They've always been my favorite." I tried to think of how many times Charlie, Sam, and I had sat in Gates with Charlie trying to force us to say Gates was the best barbecue. Had to be in the hundreds of thousands by now.

Kansas City is barbecue town. We have lots of barbecue restaurants, the best in the country, and Kansas Citians have their local favorites. The truth is that it's hard to get bad barbecue at any local KC barbecue place. Gates, B. B.'s Lawnside, Jack Stack, Rosedale, Danny Edwards, LC's, Arthur Bryant's, Smokehouse, Oklahoma Joe's, Zarda, Brobeck's, and R.J.'s—they're all good in sometimes subtly different ways—and not a comprehensive listing at all.

By this time, we'd found a seat at a table with our drinks. Sam turned to Marie, who'd been silent as we wrangled back and forth about our favorites. "What's your favorite barbecue place?" he asked politely.

Marie shrugged. "I'm not from Kansas City, you know. I don't have a favorite barbecue place. I'm not very big on barbecue."

We all stared for a moment.

"How long have you been in Kansas City?" I asked, trying to change the subject.

"Five years," she replied brightly. "It's my home now."

Sam tried to hide a snigger with a fake cough.

Charlie looked at her aghast. "Five years? And you haven't eaten at Gates or Jack Stack or B. B.'s?"

"Charlie," she said with a smile that could cut flesh, "I don't like barbecue. I find it hard to digest."

I tried to toss her a lifeline. "What are your favorite Kansas City restaurants?"

She shook her ringlets. "I like national chains. You know, like Perkins, Pizza Hut, and Denny's. That way you always know what you'll get when you order something."

I watched Sam's and Charlie's eyes widen and realized mine were probably doing the same.

Sam gave his head a little shake. "You don't mean you only eat in chain restaurants, do you?"

Marie looked around at us and seemed to realize that she'd said something troubling. "Well, I like Applebee's, too, okay? That's Kansas City, isn't it?"

Applebee's national headquarters was, indeed, located in Kansas City, but it was hardly a local KC restaurant.

"Sheesh!" Charlie shook his head, while Sam and I tried to avoid looking at Marie.

One of the Gates staff brought our plates and platters and bowl, and we dug in, except for Marie. She picked up the single beef sandwich Charlie'd ordered for her and took a tiny, tasting bite.

"Oh. It's awful spicy." She dumped it on her plate. "I just don't think I can eat this, Charlie."

"That's okay," I said quickly. "Charlie will clean it up for you, won't you?"

He'd been about to say something angry, but now he

laughed. "I used to do that for you, didn't I? Whenever your eyes were bigger than your stomach."

"You sure did." I laughed. "I always thought you ordered me the bigger one just so there'd be some left over for you."

He shook his head with a sly chuckle. "Didn't know you were on to me all those years ago."

"I need to visit the ladies," Marie said daintily. She looked at me, as if I should join her. Fat chance of that.

She left the table, looking around trying to find the restrooms. I could have pointed her to them, but I stayed where I was.

Sam's cell phone suddenly rang, and he headed for the door to take the call outside. I took another bite of the burnt ends. Not as rich as Jack Stack but still delicious.

"Skeet," Charlie said. "I been wanting to talk to you." He had licked his fingers and was now wiping his hands with the wet towelette from the little packet they gave.

I swallowed my last bite of potato salad. "Well, I'm here."

He leaned forward on his elbows, looking at me seriously. "I been watching you, and you're making the same mistakes I made."

I shrugged. I didn't know what mistakes he was talking about. I hadn't gotten canned from my job in disgrace. I wasn't a loud, obnoxious drunk. Most of the time I didn't even drink—with his behavior as a caution flag in front of me. I tried to control my temper and did a better job than he did, I knew.

"Well, I am your daughter. What mistakes are we talking about?" I took my moist towelette out of my packet and began to wipe my hands as well.

"When your mom left me, I shut myself off. No one was

ever going to get a chance to hurt me again. Just like you did after you and Sam split. Only I was hurting myself worse than anyone else could have done to me, and I didn't even see it. Until I woke up old and sick and alone and miserable. I realized I didn't want to live like that anymore. I realized I'd ten times rather take a chance on getting hurt than live that way again."

I paid close attention to my hands with the towelette, making sure I wiped around each finger's cuticle and under the edge of each nail. I didn't want to hear what Charlie was saying, and I definitely didn't want to look at him while he said it. I started over with the cuticles again.

"I know you think Marie's no good for me. Maybe you're right. I don't know. But I know I'm taking a chance on people again. I'm not going back to being that old man in a hard shell."

The towelette was pretty much used up by that time, so I carefully folded it again and again before laying it on my plate. The chorale of voices continued to shout their refrain of welcome and help. I looked over at the woman working against the backdrop of red-painted brick in the carry-out section nearest the door. At that moment, I envied her.

"You're carting around a pretty hard shell yourself, Skeeter. Not going to let anyone get close. Not Sam. Not that police chief in your town. Nobody. You keep going the way you're going, and you'll end up one day with no one around and no one wanting you. You think I couldn't have had another wife after Coreen? Women always liked me, and there were some real nice women who wanted a chance with me. But after a while, even they gave up. After a while, everyone gave up. Don't go there, Skeet."

I finally looked up to meet his eyes. "I'm not you, Charlie.

I have people in my life. People that I let get close to me. I don't necessarily need a man, a husband."

"Oh, yeah. You say that now while Sam's still chasing after you. And that police chief in your town. It's easy to say that now when you've got your pick of good men. What are you going to do when Sam gives up and finds someone else and so does everyone else who's wanted you? What are you going to do when Brian's grown and gone to his own life and you're living one that's lonelier and lonelier and trying to hide it from everybody including yourself?"

I wanted to say, *I should be so lucky as to have Sam find someone else and leave me alone—and probably Joe, too. Men are more trouble than they're worth.* But I didn't. I don't know why. Maybe I was afraid Sam would walk up and hear me and get his feelings hurt.

"I'm not you, Charlie," I repeated like a mantra.

He shook his head. "You're just exactly like me. Stubborn and hardheaded and going to do it your own way, no matter what anyone tells you." He smiled at me, tilting his head to the left. "All I'm saying is, think about it. Don't wait until it's too late or almost too late for you. And don't die a lonely old crab in a thick, hard shell."

I sighed. "Charlie, I am so different from you that it's not even funny. If anything, I have too many people in my life. I'm not likely to have a chance to die old and lonely."

At that moment, Marie came sashaying across the room toward us. Charlie's face broke out in a huge grin.

"I know you and Sam don't approve. But I'm going to be happy, Skeet. I'm going to get back some of that happiness I let pass me by during all those years. You wait and see. And you need to think about doing the same."

He stood up as Marie came to the table, and Sam came walking back into the room.

I could tell it was time to say our good-byes and go separate ways. I needed to head back to work. I'd take paperwork any day, much as I hated it, over listening to my old man pontificate on how I needed to let love into my life.

If I had my way, love wasn't getting anywhere near me.

CHAPTER 14

Back in the office for the afternoon, I finally took a break from the paperwork mountain to check my list of questions on the Ash Mowbray killing. I still needed to talk to Harvey about his tie pin, as well as to Chelsea, and I needed to talk with Peter about the theft accusation from his ex-partner and how his flash drive had ended up at the crime scene. It was clear to me that someone had planted most of those items there to confuse things and cover for the real killer. How to tell one from the other was the problem. But talking with the owners to find out who could have had a chance to take their items might lead me to some answers.

As if drawn by my organized thinking, Harvey Peebles called my office. When I told Mary to put him through, it turned out that Harvey was all shaken up after a questioning by Joe in which he'd learned that his tie pin had shown up at the crime scene. I smiled to think that Joe had lost no time to take hold of this case, now that Walker's plan was neutralized. He was really investigating. Harvey begged me to meet him at the Herbal.

I agreed to meet him because I wanted to know who could have stolen his tie pin to leave with Ash's body—or whether Harvey had finally been pushed to the last extreme by the aggressive Ash and in one mad impulse brained him. I'd seen it happen with passive, nervous types like Harvey before. One deadly impulse acted on when pushed to the limits.

So I walked down to the courthouse square under cloudy skies, in air that was finally developing a hint of autumn chill, to join the town's mayor at the Herbal for some of Dolores's great coffee and pastries.

Dolores is the secret weapon in my campaign to keep Gil Mendez from leaving my department for KCPD or the feds. At least, I hope she is. Gil's crazy about her, and they've started dating. I think he's serious, and she's built her thriving business right here in Brewster. Maybe that would be enough for me to keep him for a few more years. I can be so selfish sometimes.

I found Harvey in the back booth already drinking coffee, a small man with graying blond hair and big political ambitions, I suspected. I slid in opposite him. Dolores had followed me over and taken my order for coffee and a cranberry scone. When she left, I turned to Harvey, but I had to wait a few seconds to ask my questions while a train thundered over the tracks a block and a half away, its whistle screaming a warning to any traffic nearby. When the whistle ceased, I leaned over the table toward him as he adjusted his glasses and took a sip of coffee after blowing across its surface to cool it first.

"So tell me everything, Harvey." I've learned not to be specific in my questions when dealing with some types of people. They'll usually tell you more that way.

"I didn't even know my tie pin was gone until the next morning when I couldn't find it to put into my tie." He wouldn't meet my eyes, and I wondered what he was trying to hide from me. "I thought I'd lost it in the council chambers in all that riot and mess the night before and asked Dee to check into it to see if the cleaning staff found it."

I nodded as I made notes. In my mind, I replayed the wild scene in the council chambers. Bea had grabbed Harvey by his tie and shook him like a rattle. The tie pin could easily have come loose and fallen to the floor. If that was when it happened, anyone there could have seen and picked it up, especially Bea and the others in the immediate area. If that was when it happened rather than Ash grabbing it at the scene of the murder. I knew that Dee was Harvey's long-suffering and totally loyal secretary. I wondered if she would lie for him about this—and immediately knew she would.

Dolores brought my coffee and cranberry scone.

"Aren't you having one of Dolores's treats?" I asked, knowing Harvey had a weakness for her cheesecake.

He shook his head vehemently. "Oh, no, I couldn't put anything into my stomach right now. I'm too upset."

"I can certainly understand that, if you've just been questioned in a murder case," I said.

"I don't know why Joe is questioning me." His voice took on an ill-treated whine. "If you ask me, I've been hounded for all this disaster with Ash when I was only trying to do what's best for the town. It's not as if I was benefiting in any personal way from the situation." He looked at me out of the corner of his eyes, as if trying to judge what I thought of what he'd said. "Wasn't Ash killed with Noah Steen's club? Joe ought to be questioning him."

"He already has, Harvey." I lifted my notebook page, as if referring to an earlier entry. "Who knew Ash was going to be on the course that night?"

His face flushed. "Well, it was hardly a secret. He told Walker and me, and he was loud about it, so anyone could have heard him. That man was always loud. He was a disaster. I can't believe I was fool enough to let Walker talk me into . . ." His voice trailed off, and he looked at me as if to ask if that was enough.

I returned his look and kept silent.

He shook his head, as if trying to bring his thoughts or his tongue under control. "I don't know who else he told about it. He wasn't keeping it a secret, though. I imagine anyone could have found out if they'd wanted to."

I looked at him with interest. "Who was around you when he was talking like that? Who could have heard?"

He threw out his hands in a gesture of helplessness. "We were at a bar over in Girlville, the Otter Slide. It was full of people. I can't remember anyone in particular. It was packed."

The Otter Slide was a bar that catered primarily to students, meaning probably all those people were people with no motive and uninvolved in the whole Ash situation. But it made me wonder why Walker, Ash, and Harvey would meet in a student dive—unless they didn't want anyone concerned with the town's business to see or overhear what they were doing.

"He said he was meeting a woman. Someone he hadn't been with in a long time, but God, she was a pistol back in the day. Still takes care of her body. A woman like that, she doesn't really get older. She just gets hornier and better." He looked suddenly defiant. "Ash said all those things. I didn't. I wouldn't. Wouldn't ever talk about a woman that way. You know me, Skeet."

"Yes, I do, Harvey." I finished scribbling his words down. "Someone from his past, you think?"

"Oh, yes, definitely." His voice had grown more confident. "I figured it was Chelsea he was talking about."

I looked up at him with interest. "Did you?"

"Well, yes." He dropped his gaze from mine and tried desperately to find somewhere else to look. "I mean, she'd been his lover when she was a teenager."

I nodded and pursed my lips as I wrote in my notebook. "And you thought she'd be willing to meet him at night at the golf course?"

He looked nervous. Harvey was always afraid of making the wrong decision, and now I had him doubting his assumption that Ash's woman was Chelsea. "Who else could it have been?"

I thought of Bea talking about Ash and the women he did yard work for—and more in some cases, like hers. How many older women in town had Ash slept with during his teens?

I laid down my notebook and took a bite of my scone. "This is delicious. Are you sure you won't have anything, Harvey?"

He shook his head violently. "I couldn't put anything in my stomach right now." He looked down at the table and peered up at me from under his eyebrows. "Skeet, what do you know about anonymous letters? You know, the kind where the letters are cut and pasted from a newspaper or something."

I sat up, alert. "Have you received one, too, Harvey?"

"You mean someone else has?" he asked with a kind of relief. "Who?"

"I can't tell you that, but I do know of one other person

who's recently received a letter like that. Have you still got the letter?"

He shook his head. "Oh. Oh, no. I trashed it as soon as I read it. Vile thing." His eyes glanced to the right and down, as if to escape mine.

I leaned across the table to get his attention. "What did it say?"

He shrugged and still avoided my gaze. "Oh, you know. 'I know what you did.' Stuff like that. I didn't pay it any real attention." He fidgeted in his seat, his eyes flitting around the room, as if looking for something to fix upon.

"If you get another, please save it. It might help us figure out who's sending these. I'd bet other people that we don't know about have received them as well."

His face brightened. "You think so? Of course. It must be." He rubbed his palms together and then clasped his hands on the table before me. "Skeet, I've heard there were other things left with the . . . the body. Is that true?"

I nodded. I wouldn't tell him what, though he'd only have to ask around town to find out.

"So . . . so I'm not the only suspect?" He looked so hopeful that I was glad to be able to give him a positive answer, and he excused himself to leave shortly afterward, thanking me all the while.

After he left, I could drink my coffee and savor my scone in peace. I thought of the wide variety of items scattered around that crime scene and realized there was nothing to incriminate Walker, even though there seemed to be something for every other suspect we had—Noah, Chelsea, Peter, and Harvey. Well, I guessed there was nothing for Bea or Elliott, either. There went my theory that Walker had killed Ash and scattered around things to incriminate everyone else and then black-mailed Joe. Actually, it still sounded pretty good.

On my way back to the office, a light drizzle had begun, and the train that had rumbled through town earlier now moaned in the distance far to the north. I regretted my decision not to take my car. I shivered in the chill drizzle and decided to stop in to talk with Peter about his flash drive and the accusations of his ex-partner—and warm up a little while waiting to see if the rain would stop. But only Dante was in the shop.

"Peter hasn't wanted to come into the store lately," he said. "It's like he's hiding out in the house, afraid to come out." His forehead wrinkled with worry. "I don't know what to do with him. I wish I knew what was causing this. Do you think it's because of all this mess with Ash's murder? I've been hearing all sorts of things about that lately."

"What kinds of things?" I asked.

"Well, I mostly hear from Pearl and Bea, of course, because they're my only friends in town, other than Peter."

His face drooped in momentary sadness, and I realized how difficult and lonely life in this small town must be for him. He erased the sad face and replaced it with one determined to be cheerful.

"But I sometimes hear things from customers when they come in as well. They're getting friendlier. These things just take time. Someone said yesterday that Ash had been heard bragging he was going to meet a woman that night. Pearl said it was Chelsea, that Ash wouldn't leave that poor woman alone, and he probably tried to rape her, so she had to club him in self-defense."

"Pearl said that?" I was skeptical that Pearl would actually accuse Chelsea of having killed Ash. I wondered how much of it was Dante's dramatizing to fill what was becoming for him an empty life.

He shrugged. "Well, actually it might have been Bea. She was here, too, when we were talking about it. I think she was the one who did say it, actually." He smiled at me sheepishly. "Peter's the one you want for exact wordings. I just remember the general gist of things. Except Peter's not seeing anyone these days." The sadness rolled over him again. "Sometimes I think he barely even sees me. At least he hasn't shut me out completely, but he won't leave the house. He acts like he's hiding from something, but I don't know what it could be."

I suspected I did. "I think I'd better talk to him at the house then. I need to talk to him about his flash drive. It was found at the scene of Ash's murder."

"What?" Dante's face lost color. He stared wildly for a second before settling into a determined look. "I'll go with you. He might not open the door if he knows it's someone else."

Dante put a sign on the door and locked up the shop. We walked out the back and across the alley to the back door of the small bungalow right behind the shop. Dante unlocked the back door and let us in.

"Peter," he called. "Sugar, we need to talk with you about some things."

Dante cocked his head to listen for a reply. The house remained silent.

He looked puzzled. "He's probably upstairs. He likes to work at this lovely antique desk in the bedroom." He shook his head. "Either that or he's gone back to bed."

He looked over at me. "I think he's become clinically

depressed. I've been trying to get him to see someone, but of course, he won't hear of it. A sign of weakness. He's sometimes terribly traditional hetero-masculine for a gay man."

I tried to look sympathetic. I knew depression was a serious problem, especially for men who wouldn't get treatment the way women usually would. That was why male suicides tended to be far more successful than female. And in the case of suicide, success is not good.

A shudder ran through me, and I wondered where it came from. Perhaps that last thought in connection with all of Charlie's talk earlier today. Or maybe the feeling I'd had that Joe would kill himself if I couldn't find a way to pull Walker off him. Still, it left me feeling wary as we walked through the silent house.

From the appearance of their shop, I would have expected the house to be overstuffed with fancy antiques and fripperies, but it was sparsely furnished. Every piece of furniture seemed specially chosen for the spot where it stood. I didn't know anything about antiques and home decorating, but I had the suspicion that each chair and table was probably quite valuable.

As we neared the stairway, Dante tried calling out again, with no response. "I don't understand. Peter isn't usually a heavy sleeper."

My earlier bad feeling intensified. "Let's get upstairs to that bedroom. He might be sick or hurt."

Dante's eyes widened, and he began to take the steps two at a time, calling with a new concern in his voice. "Peter! Peter, love, answer me."

I raced up the stairs behind him and followed as he turned left and darted to a room two doors down the hall. He threw open the door just as I caught up with him and pulled out my cell phone.

On the bed lay Peter Hume, unconscious. On the ornate, gold leaf–embossed table to his left, a bottle of pills lay empty on its side. A fifth of Jameson's stood next to an almost empty glass as well. A substantial amount of the whiskey in the bottle was gone.

"Peter! Oh, God, what have you done?" Dante rushed to the figure lying sprawled on top of an antique quilt.

I gave the address to the dispatcher for the ambulance, praying it wouldn't be delayed as it had been so often lately, and checked Peter's pulse to report it to them—still there, thank heavens, but weak and thready. Dante knelt on the floor next to the bed, calling Peter's name and moaning. I pulled him to his feet and sent him down to unlock the front door for the EMTs.

I called Joe. "You've got a suicide attempt. Or at least, it sure looks like one. I'm treating it as a crime scene, though, and you might want to get here to preserve it from the mess the EMTs are sure to make trying to save him. It's one of your suspects in the Ash Mowbray murder. Peter Hume of the flash drive left at the murder scene."

"Damn, Skeet! What is going on in this town lately? I'm on my way." Joe hung up as I heard the ambulance siren outside the house. For once, the incompetent sheriff's office hadn't delayed in sending it out.

It looked like Peter Hume had lucked out, and medical help would get to him in time. I looked at the pill bottle lying on the table. Prescription in his name. Diazepam. I knew that one. Valium. Take enough of it with enough alcohol, and you could be pretty sure you wouldn't wake up—unless someone found you before it did all its work.

Dante led the EMTs into the room and pointed. "There he is. Please save him." He wasn't crying any longer, but he looked a decade older.

I moved out of the way for the experts to do their job. I hoped that we'd found Peter soon enough. But since I was who I was, I couldn't help wondering if this attempt was connected to Ash's murder. Had Peter killed Ash? Was that why his flash drive was found there? Did guilt and fear then send him over the edge? Or was it simply fear that he'd be thought guilty because of the flash drive and the threats he'd made? I'd seen fools try and actually succeed in killing themselves before, simply because they were afraid they'd be thought guilty of crimes they hadn't committed.

Dante hovered over the EMTs, his large hands held out as if he wanted to force them to save Peter.

I wandered over to the desk that he'd mentioned earlier when we first entered the house. He'd said Peter liked to sit there and write, and I saw papers lying on its surface. Perhaps I'd find a note to explain all this.

As I stopped directly over the small elegant desk, I saw that the two sheets of paper were filled with cut-and-pasted letters from other printed materials. The discarded envelopes lay beside them, addressed in the same way.

Dante had seen me move and followed. "That's that anonymous letter. He didn't burn it." He reached for it, and I intercepted his hand.

"Leave it. Joe's on his way with crime scene techs. They'll want to test these letters and the envelopes for fingerprints. No sense putting any more on than Peter already did."

"He got another one. Is that what made him do such a stupid thing?" He turned to stare back at the bed where the EMTs had slid an IV into Peter's arm. One sat with a stethoscope in his ears, monitoring Peter's pulse and blood pressure, and the other was setting up the gurney to transport him to the ambulance. "Hateful person. Who would do such a despicable thing? To Peter, that crusty old sweetheart?"

I pushed him in the direction of the bed when the EMTs started transferring Peter to the gurney. "Go with him to the hospital. We'll find out who sent these."

I stayed in the corner by the desk as the three of them made their procession out and down the stairs. I took a pen from my pocket and moved the letter enough so I could read it without contaminating evidence.

The first one read: *I know what you did. Don't think you can get away with it.*

The second one read: *I know what you did. You'll have to pay to keep me quiet. I'll tell you how soon.*

Pretty generic. Toss out an "I know what you did," and the average person can come up with several reasons to feel guilty and fearful that someone knows what they did. Not something I'd pay money for or try to kill myself for. But then, I lived a pretty boring life.

Still, I couldn't be sure from this that the person who sent these actually knew anything at all about what Peter might or might not have done at any time in his life. These letters could have to do with Ash's murder or with the allegations of Peter's ex-partner or with something else altogether and probably trivial.

Joe showed up and we waited for the crime scene techs together; the whole time I ran over everything Dante had said to me. On my way out of Peter and Dante's house, I called Chelsea and asked if she'd drop by my house before supper so we could have a quick discussion about Ash and her without Noah or Elliott overhearing.

Could Dante's imagination combined with Bea's shrewd guess have given me the actual solution to a murder that wasn't really a murder? Had Chelsea been forced to kill Ash to defend herself from more of his sexual assaults?

The rain had stopped by the time I arrived home, and Chelsea was already waiting for me in the living room with a piece of Gran's carrot-pineapple-pecan cake and a cup of coffee that she'd turned beige with cream. Waste of good coffee, if you asked me.

Gran sat on the couch across from the big armchair where Chelsea sat upright on the very edge. I was almost afraid to hear what Gran was chatting to her about. Chelsea looked supremely uncomfortable and had eaten only the tiniest sliver of her cake, I could see. That particular moist, tender cake is one of Gran's specialties and one of the world's great cakes. To take a tiny nibble of it and stop required iron self-control, an eating disorder, extreme emotional upset, or maybe all three.

Gran stood and said, "I've got dinner to make. I'll leave you two to your conversation. Brian was asked to Angie's for supper tonight, and Angie looked so pitiful that I said yes when he couldn't reach you because you were at an emergency."

I nodded. "Mary told me he'd called when I checked in on the way home. That's fine, Gran."

Chelsea held out her full plate of almost completely uneaten, delicious cake to Gran. "Thank you for your hospitality, Mrs. Whittaker. This was wonderful."

Gran looked at the crumb that had been eaten, sniffed

loudly, and carried it out to the kitchen with her, while I physically restrained myself from saying, "I'll eat it if you don't want it," the way we did as kids.

I set my laptop bag on the floor next to the couch as I dropped onto the warm spot Gran had just vacated. "Thanks for coming by, Chelsea. There are some things I wanted to get straight about your relationship with Ash, and I figured you'd rather not discuss it in front of Elliott and Noah."

"Thank you. You're absolutely right about that." Chelsea sat straight upright with her cream-contaminated coffee untouched in the cup at her side, her hair in smooth waves around her flawlessly made-up face, her yellow silk blouse the perfect cheery accent for her gray pin-striped suit with a skirt just long enough to cover her knees when she sat but short enough to show most of her trim calves.

Being around Chelsea always made me aware of my hair that I'd probably run hands through at some time during the day and my black pantsuit (of which I had many different versions) worn off the rack without tailoring. Only the thought of my bright purple lace-top hand-knit socks gave me any feeling of distinction—and they were meant to be invisible beneath my slacks.

I sighed and got on with the work I'd come to do. "Chelsea, Ash was planning to meet a woman at the golf course the night he was killed."

She gave me a brittle smile. "And all of my kind friends here in my hometown are saying it was me?"

I nodded. I still wasn't sure I liked her, but I'd come to respect her a great deal in recent days.

"Is this why I'm getting anonymous letters? What more do I have to look forward to? Do you think Harvey will agree to set up some stocks on the square that they can lock me into?" She tried to make her tone humorous and sarcastic but there was real pain behind it.

"Anonymous letters?" I jumped on her mention of those.

"Well, actually, only one." She pulled out of her purse a Ziploc plastic bag containing an envelope with the telltale cut-and-pasted lettering. "I brought it for you. As far as I know, I'm the only one to touch it, so if there are fingerprints other than mine, they should be of the person who sent it."

Of course. Chelsea, with all she was going through right now, would be the one to save the anonymous letter and give it to someone in law enforcement. My admiration for her sense and courage grew.

I took it from her and put it in my laptop bag. "You may be relieved to know that you're not the only one to get one of these." I gave her a smile. "This is at least the fourth that I know of, so far."

"Do you mean there's malice going on beyond all this having to do with Ash and his death and my disgrace?" She gave me another frozen smile. "I would have thought all that trouble and heartache was enough for even the most greedy of gossips."

"There's never enough for some people. I think they like to make others suffer when something bad happens, so they can find ways to say it could never happen to them." I sighed. "But speaking of gossip, Ash was planning on meeting a woman the night he was murdered. Was it you?"

She stared straight at me, her slim jaw firmly set. "What do you think, Skeet? Do you think it was me?"

"I think it could have been." I tried to soften my words with a hint of a smile. "I don't think you'd have chosen to meet him, but I could see him blackmailing you into it."

She gave a short bark of laughter. "How? He'd already done everything that I'd humiliated myself to avoid."

I watched her with sympathy. "By threatening to tell Elliott or Noah what you'd done under duress."

Her face blanched, and she sat in silent thought, the tiny lines at each corner of her mouth and eyes the only sign of the strain she was feeling. "Yes, I suppose he could have threatened to do that." She looked up at me with bleak eyes. "That would have been just his style, wouldn't it?"

I had to agree. "Did he? Did you? Go to meet him, that is?"

She looked down at the floor for a second before returning her gaze to my face. "No, I did not, Skeet. But I don't know how to convince you of that. I realize that, under the circumstances, things don't look great for me right now. Though, at least, it might get my dear, foolish husband out of the predicament he's put himself in, trying to shield Noah." She made an effort at a cold, controlled Chelsea smile that wavered for a second before collapsing completely.

Immediately, her hands covered her face. She sat in total silence without moving. I realized there was an emotional earthquake taking place somewhere inside her, but she showed no sign of it, other than the hands shielding her face. I remembered when she'd cried in my office without sound or trace of tears. I'd never have known it if her son hadn't remarked on it. I wondered where and how this woman had learned to hold everything inside so deeply and tightly that she could cry without making any noise and sit in front of me in some kind of emotional meltdown without a quiver or whimper.

She took a long, deep, shuddering breath and lowered her hands. She was obviously trying not to shake, trying very hard, yet a tremor racked her body as she sat in front of me. She rubbed her dry eyes, as if scrubbing away traces of nonexistent tears.

"That man has never been anything but a disaster to me," she said in a strangled voice. "From the moment he first laid hands on me when I was just a girl. He destroyed my life then. I had college and a life of success ahead of me. He took it from me and left me pregnant and alone while he went off to have that life of college and success that I was supposed to have."

She tried to smile, but her mouth froze in a rictus. "But I rebuilt myself and my life, thanks to Elliott. And it was all worth it because Noah was such a joy. Until Ash walked back into town to destroy everything I'd gathered and jerry-rigged into a life from the fragments left after he exploded my first one."

I nodded, never taking my eyes from her face because I had a sense that they were a lifeline of sorts for her, and if I moved them, she might collapse totally.

"He forced me to touch him and do things that made me vomit and scream in pain. He used me, as I realized he'd been using me when I was so young and in love. He was a revolting man. I was glad to hear he was dead. I'm still glad he is. And yet he continues to haunt me and endanger my child and my marriage and ruin my life, even from beyond the grave. How can I stop him, if even death didn't do the trick? What can I do?"

Another tremor ran through her body. It was eerie to watch her sit so controlled and still and then see her body start shaking as if some motor within her had switched on.

"I suspected he was bad when we were in high school. He got money from these older women, Bea Roberts and some others, and the things he said about them, making fun of them—it was just disgusting. I didn't like it, but I thought I was in love with him then. He had me convinced that I must be. So I didn't want to see anything bad about him. I told myself he was just making it up, and they weren't really doing those things, and he wasn't really doing anything with them, either."

She looked at me with haunted eyes. "I wasn't meeting Ash the evening he was killed, Skeet. If there was a woman there, it was probably one of those older women he'd romanced so long ago. He was probably extorting something from one or another of them. I never intended to be in the same room or space with him ever again. Then he died, and I thought I was home free. Only now I wonder if I ever will be."

She stood up slowly, as if she were years older than I knew she was. "If there's nothing else right now, I've got to go home and feed Elliott and Noah."

I stood with my hand held out slightly as I might for an older woman like Pearl, concerned that she might take a fall. She seemed so much more fragile than the strong, controlled woman who'd come in my door. "That's fine, Chelsea. You go ahead and go home. I think you've given me a direction in which to look."

I walked closely behind her all the way to the door, ready to catch her if she should show signs of faltering. By the time she'd reached the threshold, however, she'd recovered her erect posture and strength with her head held high. Unless someone looked at her face, which looked as if she'd just come out of hell, she could have passed for her old self.

I closed the door on her, sure that she'd make it safely home, though I hadn't been a few minutes ago. What a price she'd paid for a crush on the wrong boy in high school!

I headed out to the kitchen for a cup of coffee and some

of Gran's no-nonsense conversation. I needed both right then. After dinner I would pay a visit to Bea Roberts, and this time we'd talk seriously about Ash Mowbray and the extra services he provided for her and other bored housewives when he was just a teen.

CHAPTER 15

The meteorologist on TV was predicting a cold front and a big thunderstorm. "Depending on how this storm moves before it hits the metro area, we might see some freezing rain and sleet but no significant accumulation in this part of the state."

Gran laughed. "*Osda!* This is that blizzard I've been telling you was coming. Going to break your drought up here this winter, starting now. No accumulation? Bull. We're going to get eight to ten inches of snow on top of ice. You watch."

She looked at the kitchen windows and tsked. "We never got those windows and doors winterized."

I flipped away her concerns with one hand. "Come on, Gran. Don't worry. We won't freeze to death. If the heating bills are a little higher, I'm good for it."

She shook her head in disapproval. "Throwing money away like some *yonega.*"

There wasn't much I could say to that. Hadn't I just been thinking how far away I'd grown from the traditions and ways I'd been raised with?

I pulled out a chair and sat down with my cup of coffee.

"Gran, I've been thinking about that. Just the other day, I was thinking about how you taught me to read the signs around me every day and how I've maybe lost the knack for that. I have to live in a different way from what you taught me—because of my job and just to fit in up here, but I think I want to take advantage of having you here with me to try to relearn some of what I used to know. You know, the stuff you taught me when I was a kid."

Gran looked at me with her mouth in a twisted smile. "You don't do it like they do." She gestured with her shoulder out the window to the town beyond. "You don't go somewhere special one day a week or a year and be Indian. Being Cherokee is something you live every day, all the time. You're real good at reading signs all around you. That was always one of your gifts. That's why you're so good at your job. You've been doing it all this time."

I wondered if I looked as puzzled as I felt.

She snickered at me. "You don't have to be wearing a costume or feathers in your hair or some damn thing like that. You don't have to be dressed like some powwow queen. It's what's inside, Skeet." She reached over and poked me in the chest.

I laughed and felt a little lightness inside me where I hadn't been aware of feeling heavy. "Okay, but I want to work on putting more of it into my life. On a conscious level. I remember some of your teachings, but I worry about the ones I've forgotten."

I felt stupid and awkward saying it, but I said it anyway. "I don't want to lose all my culture." It sounded as dumb to me as I'd thought it would.

Gran smiled, though, and nodded. "That's good. You know,

the Nation set up satellite communities in the cities where lots of Cherokee got sent in the relocation movement the government was so big on in the fifties and sixties. We've got great communities out in San Francisco and San Diego. Denver, too. Turns out there's a sizable satellite community set up a couple of years ago in KC. We should go meet with them."

She got up and poured us both more coffee. "It makes sense. The land and the culture's down in Oklahoma, but the jobs are out here in the rest of the world. We can't bring the land along, but we learned way back with the Trail of Tears that the stories and traditions and language were what really mattered. You can have those out here, too."

I needed to back off. I'd had the idea of Gran teaching me informally the way she'd done when I was a kid. This idea of some group of strangers was way too much. "I don't know. I'm not a big joiner, Gran. I wouldn't know any of those people. What do they do? Have meetings? I have enough of those in my life."

She snorted. "Don't be silly. They have potlucks, lots of good food. And folks come up from the Nation to teach about the traditions and art and history. They even have language classes."

She looked off into the early evening darkness and then back at me. "I won't be around forever, Skeet. When old folks like me die out, so will the language, if young ones don't pick it up. They're offering it in the schools down in the Nation now, but that means your whole generation and the one before yours missed out. That was back when they told us we hurt our kids if we didn't speak only English to them. Promise me you'll learn Tsalagi, Skeet. Learn your native language."

I hated to even think about some time when Gran wouldn't

be around, but I was caught by the force in her eyes and her voice. I had the feeling that she'd charged what she said with some of the personal power she'd always claimed we directed unthinkingly when we pointed our fingers. Her strong, old hands were clasped on the table as she leaned toward me, but I could feel that power in the air as if she had her index finger pointed directly at me, and I knew that whatever answer I gave would be something I'd be bound by and would have to live with all my life.

The silence stretched until I broke it finally with a little bow of my head. "I will, Gran. If they've got audiovisuals to teach it in the schools, I ought to be able to get it to learn here at home. But I can't promise I'll be any good at it."

"*Wado. Osda.*" I knew those words, at least. Some of the first you hear as a kid. *Thank you* and *good*. And *elisi* for *grandmother*. I hoped she wasn't going to start rattling off Cherokee to me, though, because that was about the extent of what I could do right now.

I stood up to break the spell. "I've got to go talk to Bea Roberts tonight. I think she might know what woman was meeting Ash Mowbray the night he was killed."

Gran looked out at the dark evening again for a second as I took my cup to the sink. "Let me ride along with you," she said. "I don't like the feel of this night."

I grinned at her. "Going to protect your armed police officer granddaughter?"

She shrugged and stood, looking small and old and clasping her arms around herself. "Maybe I'm scared to be alone here."

I had to laugh out loud. This tough old woman had nerves of steel. I'd watched her use a hoe to kill rattlesnakes that showed up too close to her grandchildren. When she was in her late fifties, she'd snuck up behind a burglar with her grandson's baseball bat and knocked him out to wait for the police she called right afterward.

Everyone up here in Missouri thought I was who I was because I was Big Charlie Bannion's daughter—and it was true that he'd been a legendary cop in his time. But I was who I was as much or more because I was Amelia Ward Bushyhead Whittaker's granddaughter and—some elders had said when I was little—her heir.

"Sure, come on," I said, still smiling. "I'll keep the boogeyman away from you, Gran."

I'd figured out my strategy by the time we pulled up in front of Bea's cottage. Gran and I would just be paying an early evening social call. I'd turn the conversation to Ash and his past. I'd seen the other day that Bea was eager to talk about those days. I knew Gran would catch whatever conversational balls I tossed her.

The lights were on within, and I could see Bea's yellow Buick land yacht parked inside her open garage. I'd have to remember to caution her to close up the garage when we left. We paused at the curb by my cruiser for Gran to wrap her shawl around herself more tightly while a train wailed its way toward downtown. The temperature had dropped severely since the afternoon, and I could tell that the TV weatherman was right. Quite possibly, Gran and her prediction of a blizzard might also be right in a few days. I made a mental note to turn the furnace up when we got home.

As we walked up to the front door, I could hear some kind of turmoil inside the house, as if someone had tripped and fallen, taking over a lamp or table with them.

"What was that?" Gran said.

"I don't know. Maybe Bea fell." I knocked on the door.

I heard someone cry out, "Help! No, don't!"

I tried the door, but it was locked. I pounded heavily. "Open up! Police! Open up!"

More crashing came from inside the house, along with another cry.

I remembered the open garage door. I told Gran to go back to my car and lock herself in, as I headed around the side of the house for the garage, calling 911 to report a possible robbery and assault in progress. I squeezed past Bea's old Buick and stockpiled boxes and garden tools. I had a hunch the door might not be locked since the garage was still open. If it was locked, it should be easier to kick in than the front door.

Sure enough, the door was unlocked, and I slipped inside after pulling out my Glock. The sounds from the front of the house had stopped, so I took care as I made my way through the kitchen, not wanting to be jumped by Bea's assailant lying in wait for me. As I came into the dining room, I found Bea on the floor next to a chair that had fallen over. She was unconscious, her left wrist bleeding copiously. The right wrist had cuts on it that were bloody but didn't seem to have been sliced through in the same way. A pair of glasses lay on the floor next to that hand.

Much as I wanted to stop to take care of that bleeding wrist, I knew my first responsibility was to make sure the attacker wasn't still in the house waiting to jump out and finish the job. I cleared the surrounding rooms as quickly as I could. In the room at the back of the house, I found Harvey Peebles struggling to try to open the glass door to the patio.

"Hold it right there, Harvey!" I aimed my gun at him. "Drop that knife!"

Harvey turned at bay, his face desperate, and threw the knife at my head. I threw up an arm to deflect it and kept moving toward Harvey. He turned around and kicked frantically at the glass of the door, causing cracks to spread all over the glass. I came up behind him and held my gun to the back of his head.

"Down on the floor." I moved back as he turned around to face me. "Now. Facedown. Hands behind your back."

His whole body sagged and he began to sob. "Skeet, it's not like you think."

I gestured slightly with the gun. "On the floor. Now."

He threw himself on the floor, still crying. I moved around with my back to the cracked glass door, which still had the burglar bar at its base holding it secure. No wonder he couldn't open it. I handcuffed his hands behind his back.

I heard someone outside the door to the interior of the house. "Skeet, are you okay?" It was the old woman who was supposed to be safely huddled in my locked police car.

"I'm fine," I snapped.

Gran showed up in the doorway, holding a shovel almost as tall as she was in both hands, metal blade up as if it was a weapon. And in her hands, it probably was.

I shook my head and called in for a city officer, telling them the situation and emphasizing the need for a rush on the ambulance.

"Harvey, you heard me tell them who the criminal was, right?" I asked.

He nodded and his sobs gained new, wailing energy. "It wasn't supposed to be like this. I didn't want to kill her. She was making me do it. Anonymous letters and blackmail. And

I had no money left to pay her with. I'd sunk it all in that damn mall project."

I ignored him. "So you know there's no way you can get away. Now we're going to help you to your feet, and you're going to walk into the dining room and sit quietly while we try to keep Bea from bleeding to death and changing this from attempted murder to murder one. Okay?"

He nodded without stopping his bawling. "Don't let her die, please, Skeet. I'm not really a killer. Not really a bad man."

Gran and I got him to his feet. Then I sent her on ahead with her shovel while I prodded him through the house as quickly as I could.

In the dining room, I shoved Harvey into a chair where I could keep an eye on him. Then I grabbed napkins off the table to try to stanch the bleeding from Bea's wrist.

As I knelt on the floor and worked on Bea, Gran hurried over and laid down the shovel on the floor so she could kneel by my side. "That looks bad."

"I think we can keep her from bleeding out if the damn ambulance gets here in time. He wasn't as efficient about these cuts as he could have been." I remembered the ambulance's arrival earlier in the afternoon at Peter's house. "It came right away this afternoon, so maybe someone good is still on dispatch tonight, as well."

"It's hard to kill someone," Harvey whined. "No one talks about how hard it is. It's not an easy thing to do. I don't know how anyone ever manages to do it."

I knelt beside Bea for minutes that just crept by, pressing against the wound with all my might and wondering at the way he spoke as if he hadn't successfully brained Ash. Harvey had struck her on the head with something. I could see the bruise and lump rising before my eyes. That would explain her unconscious state.

My eyes danced around the room, returning to my weeping prisoner in his chair every few seconds.

He moaned. "Don't let her die. Please, Skeet. I don't want to be guilty of murder."

On the floor, not far from where the chair lay, a heavy glass had fallen without shattering, although its liquid contents soaked into the carpet. Fresh herbs lay as if tossed by the handful onto the carpet. Mint and lemon balm by the smell of them. An old-fashioned wallet fat with cash sat in the midst of the herbs. A heavy brass candlestick lay on the floor with a maroon taper loose on the floor beside it. These last matched the candlestick with candle still standing on the table. I wondered if the candlestick on the floor was what he'd used to knock Bea out. Judging by the sounds we heard as we arrived, Bea had fought against Harvey more bravely than I would have expected from what I knew of the fussy little collectibles seller.

I settled my hands more firmly against her wound. I was determined not to let her slide into death. Gran placed her wiry, old hands on top of mine with firm pressure. I could almost feel her energy pass through my hands into Bea.

"She'll make it," she said.

When sirens sounded in the distance, my breathing eased. The ambulance. Not delayed for ages, after all. Gran was right. Bea should make it.

But Harvey had intended for her to die tonight. Slashing her wrists left me wondering if he hadn't heard of Peter's suicide attempt and decided to try to make Bea's murder look like a suicide. I wondered what the scene would have looked like in the morning when she was found if Gran and I hadn't come by tonight to spoil the plan.

Gran left me to let the EMTs in through the front door.

"So Bea was writing the anonymous letters and blackmailing you?" I asked Harvey.

"I listened to Walker Lynch and invested secretly ahead of time in his mall project. I invested money that wasn't mine. Estates I was administering. I don't know how she found out, but she sent me letters saying she knew what I did and then told me to bring her money."

I looked at the ashen face of the woman beneath me and realized she probably never knew the real facts about anyone she sent letters to. She just counted on them panicking and paying. But everyone handled it differently. Chelsea ignored it and turned the letter in to the authorities. Peter tried to kill himself. Harvey tried to kill Bea.

I wondered if Bea had taken Harvey's tie pin and placed it by Ash's dead body. If she would blackmail, would she kill?

I thought about that fat wallet I'd noticed. "You didn't pay her then?"

"Of course not. If I'd had money to pay her, I wouldn't have had to do all this to try to silence her," Harvey said, outraged at the suggestion.

Someone must have paid her. Something was catching at the back of my mind. Something I knew that would make sense of all this. But what?

As the paramedics took over Bea's care, I worried at what was nagging at the back of my brain, but came up with nothing. Joe's evening-shift officer arrived to take possession of Harvey. He said Joe was on his way over. Gran and I would have to give statements. I'd see if we couldn't do that at the hospital. I wanted to make sure Bea made it and to check on Peter, as well.

But I knew what I would do as soon as I arrived home. I'd make hot chocolate with lots of whipped cream, put on some smooth jazz, and pick up my knitting.

It was time to unravel this mess.

By the time we were free to head for the hospital, I'd called and arranged for Annette to give Brian a ride back to our house since we were detained at the scene of the crime. It was raining again and starting to freeze and ice over. That worried me for Gran, who could hardly afford a fall at her age, so, over her protests, I drove by home first and had Brian help her into the house.

I was glad of it when I saw how slick the sidewalks were, once I parked at the hospital. I almost fell on the way in, saving myself with some particularly embarrassing acrobatics that I fervently hoped no one witnessed. The wind was picking up, and the rain had turned to sleet. It was likely to be dangerous by morning, I knew.

I stopped by Peter's room first, where I found Dante holding his hand and murmuring to him as he lay in the hospital bed.

I knocked on the partially opened door. "How's our patient? I understand he's going to be okay."

"Skeet!" Dante's face lit up. "Peter, look who's here to see you."

Peter didn't look as joyful at my presence, but then he looked pretty washed-out from what he'd been through. "Skeet. Am I in trouble?"

I laughed. "Not anymore, Peter. You were in a lot of trouble, though, when Dante and I found you. I'm glad to see you've pulled through that."

He looked shamefaced. "That was stupid of me."

"I'm glad to hear you say that." I settled on a chair next to Dante. "You know you've got an awful lot to live for, not least of which is this handsome fellow here." I indicated Dante with a nod of my head. "Want to tell me why you pulled that stunt?"

Peter shrugged slightly. "I thought I was going to be ruined and lose everything, especially Dante."

I looked questioningly at him.

He sighed. "Before I came to Brewster, I was in a long-term relationship and we owned a successful business together. I had put up most of the money for it, and we'd both worked hard to build it into something. Then my partner found some young rough trade—"

"Peter," warned Dante.

Peter glared and then relaxed, nodding. "He found a younger guy and left me, stealing the business out from under me first, while I was unaware anything was going on. I learned about it because a mutual friend warned me, so I was able to clean out our joint account just before he took that, too. That way I had some money to start over here. He couldn't press charges against me because of what he'd done, and I couldn't press charges against him because of what I'd done. And that's the way things were. Until . . ."

"Until you got an e-mail from J. D., saying he'd given all that information to Ash so he could publicly accuse you of being a thief, right?"

He nodded unhappily. "Then Ash died, but I kept getting these anonymous letters, and then they wanted money. I could see my whole life going down the drain—once more. Black-mailers never keep those secrets. I-I just didn't think I could go through it all again."

Dante patted his hand and murmured, "Never. Never."

I nodded. "Well, you know, the blackmailer's caught, and that's all over. If J. D. decides to try anything again, you should let Joe know. I think you'll find the town is on your side, Peter. I know Dante is."

Dante, who'd wanted nothing more than for Peter to feel secure enough to tell him the details he already knew, beamed at us both. I left them quietly cooing at each other and headed down to find out how our blackmailer was doing.

As I walked down the hall to Bea's room, I could hear a train in the distance and the rattle of sleet against the windows. I shivered and pulled up outside the room where Bea sat propped up in her bed, with one of Joe's officers sitting outside her door. A precautionary measure I was glad to see. We had no idea who else was out there who might want to silence Bea permanently.

"Skeet Bannion!" she cried when she saw me. "They say I have you to thank for saving me from that brute, Harvey."

I entered and sat down beside her bed. "Bea, I'm glad to see you still here. It was a little touch and go there for a while."

She pointed cheerfully to a bag of blood above her on the IV stand. "They're giving me some more blood tonight, and then I should be able to go home sometime tomorrow."

I looked at her, puzzled. "Bea, I imagine you won't be going home. Joe's going to arrest you for blackmail."

She shook her head. "I've already told him he can't do that. I didn't know anything. So how could it be blackmail? I needed money because my bank was taking away my extension on repaying my loan because they thought the mall would go through and the shop would go under. I didn't have that money—I'm always on a shoestring—and they all had it. And thought they were better than me because they did. Besides, only Pearl gave me any money. If I ask her to, she'll say she just gave me money as a favor. Harvey didn't give me any money. He tried to kill me. And that's a whole lot worse than blackmail, isn't it? Even if it was blackmail, which it's not."

I shook my head. "Bea, you sent those anonymous letters. And you left Harvey's tie pin at the crime scene, didn't you?"

Her chin jutted out stubbornly. "That's not against the law. How was I to know it was a crime scene? I just thought Ash was passed out drunk. And it's no crime to discard Harvey's tie pin somewhere. Ugly old thing. Also, there's no law that says you have to sign your name to a letter."

I wondered if she actually believed this hot air she was blowing or just hoped I would. "They were letters that said 'I know what you did' and 'you'll have to pay to keep me quiet.' That's extortion, blackmail, and it's a serious crime."

She batted away my words with her right, less heavily bandaged hand. "But I didn't know anything. So it's not. I'll get a good lawyer, and he'll explain it all to you. I mean, I sort of knew with Pearl. I figured if Ash was sleeping with all the rest of us and going to her for advice, he was probably sleeping with her, too. And sure enough, she paid right up. But then she comes from a fine family, doesn't she?"

"So that's why Pearl paid you?" I'd wondered if the fat wallet hadn't come from Pearl, with those fresh herbs on the floor.

She shrugged. "I think so. Why else would she need to?"

I was incredulous. "So you don't know, really?"

She smiled in what she obviously thought was a charming way. "Well, I couldn't let them know that I didn't really know whatever it is they feel guilty about, so I kept everything very vague. They really did all the work. They did their own black-mailing, don't you see? It wasn't me."

She was still protesting her innocence when I headed for home, getting worried now about how slick the streets would be.

It was late when I finally got home. Brian was asleep when I arrived, but Gran had stayed up to see me make it home safe. I made hot chocolate for myself while Gran headed to bed.

As I arranged myself on the couch with Lady at my feet and jazz playing softly on the stereo, Gran cautioned me, "Don't stay up too late. If it doesn't come to you, just let it come in your dreams."

I nodded, but I didn't feel as confident of solving this in my dreams as Gran did. I'd stay up until I figured things out with my conscious mind. I picked up Miryam's pink mohair scarf to knit. It was a fairly simple lace pattern, a four-row repeat I'd long since memorized, so it took no real attention away from the problem-solving.

I ran over all the items found at the scene with Ash Mow-bray's body. I'd often felt that if I could understand who had actually left them there to confuse the scene, I'd know the murderer. Noah Steen's golf club that had killed Ash. We now knew that Ash himself had brought that out to the scene. Ash's bottle of Southern Comfort that had been poisoned with anti-freeze. We now knew that Ash brought the bottle and Noah added the antifreeze.

Then there were the pieces that were only questions. Chelsea Steen's charm. Peter Hume's flash drive.

Harvey's tie pin Bea had admitted to dumping at the scene. I remembered the end of the unruly council meeting when one of Joe's officers had had to rescue Harvey from a group of irate citizens. Especially Bea Roberts who had a grip on Harvey's tie and wouldn't let go. That must have been when his tie pin was acquired. Had Bea been the woman Ash was going to meet and who arrived after the murder, or was she the one who brained Ash with a golf club?

Peter's flash drive. If he had kept it in that neat, modern office in the shop, only his intimates and Dante could have taken it. And they didn't seem to have many intimate friends in town. Dante was totally isolated, except for good old Pearl and Bea. And Peter and Bea were quite close and partners in the fight against Ash. Bea again.

Chelsea's charm. She'd said she usually kept it with her in her purse. Someone could have taken it out when she stood up in the council meeting. She'd left her purse at her seat when she came to the front to speak. But wouldn't they be afraid to do that in public? Or could it have happened another time? When she passed out at Pyewacket's and the guys had to carry her out to the car? Her purse had lain on the table, ignored, until Pearl picked it up to take to her. Did Pearl take the charm out before she delivered the purse?

And why did someone go to all the trouble to toss around all these "clues" that pointed to such different people? If you were going to frame someone for a murder so you wouldn't have to pay for it, wouldn't you just put out items incriminating that one person? It was as if someone couldn't make up his or her mind about which person to frame. Or . . .

What if the idea wasn't to frame someone else? What if the idea was just to keep suspicion away from you without really endangering anyone else? That would be a different kind of murderer. Someone too scrupulous to incriminate another for his crime but not too scrupulous to whack Ash over the head a few times with that golf club.

That train of thought led me back to my old question: Who didn't have incriminating items tossed at the murder scene? Walker Lynch, Elliott Steen, Pearl Brewster, and Bea Roberts.

It could have been Walker. He could have done it himself or had one of his thugs do it. Not Terry. I didn't think Terry—

I knew it couldn't have been Terry because if he'd been sent to kill Ash, he'd have done it in some clean, efficient way that left no evidence at all. And what did that say about Terry Heldrich? Or about me, for that matter? No, I wouldn't go there.

Walker certainly had a motive to kill Ash. As did Elliott and Bea. Dante and Pearl, not so much. But wait. Dante was Peter's partner and worried about Ash's effect on Peter and the business. So maybe he had a motive, too.

Pearl didn't, of course. The mall would have no effect on her livelihood, though I don't think she was a big fan. Of course, she wasn't a big fan of Ash's, either. She apparently had been when he was young, but she'd not been happy to see him return—at least, not in the way he had returned. And then Bea thought she'd slept with Ash when he was a kid. And she may have. She'd paid Bea a lot of money for some reason.

I dropped a yarn over and hissed under my breath before going back to pick it up and resume the pattern.

At that moment I felt a tiny shift in the back of my mind where that itch had shown up earlier. Why would Pearl want to kill Ash? She was practically the only person without a motive. Except . . . except she'd been an older woman who knew Ash, even if he didn't do yard work for her. And she'd given him money for school. Had she really been giving him money because he was her secret lover? Bea thought so, Pearl certainly paid her blackmail. Could Pearl have been the woman that Ash was meeting the evening he was killed? The one he spoke of so cruelly to Harvey?

Still takes care of her body. Doesn't really get older. Just hornier and better.

Pearl appeared much younger than she really was because she took such good care of her body and stayed so active.

Pearl could have stolen the charm from Chelsea's purse and the flash drive from Peter's office. And I could see her leaving all those "clues" to take attention from herself without actually pointing definitely to any other person.

Apparently, Pearl had received an anonymous letter like the others. Even if the wording was generic like Peter's, Pearl's own guilt would cause her to read threatening knowledge into it. Peter's guilt over his theft from his ex-partner had. Pearl's guilt over Ash's murder would have done the same, but Pearl wasn't the type to commit suicide, and she had money to pay off Bea. But she was smart enough to know that this was just the beginning. Bea would want more and more.

There were unanswered questions, but the more I thought about it the more I felt I was on the right track. Though she was old, Pearl was strong—all that gardening and golf. She could well have been the woman Ash was meeting that night. She could have clubbed Ash from behind, especially if he was woozy and impaired from the antifreeze and booze. But would Pearl kill to keep the town from learning she'd seduced a high school athlete when she was, what? Fifty-something? She'd seemed truly disgusted with Ash, but that was because of the new knowledge that he'd impregnated young Chelsea and abandoned her.

Wait! That would have been at the same time that she was having sex with Ash. Had she thought she was the only one? Had she been in love with that young teen who probably reminded her of her own long-lost love? Had she expected him to come back for her when he was successful and older? Did that explain why she was so vehement that she'd never have given Ash money for school if she'd known he'd gotten Chelsea pregnant?

Setting aside my knitting, I had to shake my head to clear it. I'd go to bed now, but tomorrow morning I'd pay Joe a visit and give him everything I had and knew and had figured out. There were holes of evidence to plug, but if they knew what to look for, they'd find it.

I felt a little sad. I liked Pearl. But I hated murder. Even the murder of someone as revolting as Ash had turned out to be.

Well, it wouldn't be me arresting Pearl once the final proofs were in. That would be Joe's job, and he was welcome to it. But I was glad that Chelsea, Elliott, and Noah Steen would sleep better when it was all over. I'd come to feel a real fondness for that small devoted family. And on that brighter thought, I went to bed.

CHAPTER 16

I woke to driving snow. Gran had been right, of course. The TV weatherman's "slight accumulation of freezing rain" had turned to an inch of ice in the night and then to snow in the early hours of the morning. The ground and street were already white, as was the sky and air around us. Visibility was going to be a bitch out on the roads today.

The furnace was blasting, and I was glad of the heat as I showered and dressed. Today was a day for thermal underwear, a red hand-knit alpaca sweater with a drapey cowl neck that I could pull up over my face in a pinch—a gift from Karen—my thick hand-knit red wool boot socks, and my Columbia boots ordered from Backcountry and rated for minus-25-degree temps. I'd add hand-knit scarf, hand-knit gloves with flip mitten tops, and my hooded jacket designed for mountain climbing. Not that I'd do anything like climb mountains for fun, but it's made to be sturdy, water-resistant, and cold-resistant, and that's what I want in a winter coat that I've got to work in.

I stomped out to scrape the car and defrost it. When I came

back inside the house, Brian informed me that his school was closed. This didn't surprise me. I was relieved at their good sense. I wished the university would be so smart. We, of course, prided ourselves on almost never canceling classes, which left faculty, staff, and students risking their lives to get in.

It made no difference to me. Police are essential personnel. When everyone else takes off because it's too dangerous out, we and the EMTs, nurses, doctors, hospital personnel, and firemen are always still on duty. Not to mention the public works guys who'd already been out on the streets and highways all night and would continue to work around the clock until the storm was over and the streets were all passable.

Still, all our jobs were easier when everyone else stayed home. School and business closings kept cars out of the way of the snowplows, kept the accidents and injuries down, kept the roads in better shape for emergency vehicles, just made life easier for everyone all around.

I headed out to hit Joe's office at the city police department on my way in. I knew he'd be in early because of this weather, too. I could talk to him about the case and give him the information I had that indicated Pearl was the murderer before driving off to my real job, leaving all the rest of the dirty work in his hands, now that he was back on the job, thanks to Terry. And I was glad of that.

The snow was piling up but it was the layer of ice underneath that was the real problem so far. Intersections where the snow layer was disturbed and thinned out tended to be untrustworthy. I saw a number of cars and trucks that had spun out at intersections and sometimes into wrecks. Fortunately, it looked as if everyone involved was basically uninjured, but I could imagine the toll this would take on Joe's small department. Everyone would be called up off-shift.

He might have to ask for some help from my department, even though we were different jurisdictions. Probably later today, unless something drastic happened on campus, I'd be able to help him out.

The wind picked up and the snow began to fall in heavier gusts as I parked in the city police lot. I had to push my way against the force of the wind, crystals of snow stinging against my face and collecting around my nostrils, as I walked around the corner of the building and through the entrance into blessed heat and clear air in the lobby of the municipal building. Joe's office was midway down the hall, and I warmed up with every step.

Once in his office, I began to regret not bringing some of our good coffee from home. Still, I accepted a cup when Joe offered. It would be hot, and my insides could use the heat as much as my mind could use the caffeine.

"Bitter out," I told Joe as I hovered over the steam rising from the cup. "You've got some nasty intersections out there with lots of spinouts."

He nodded. "We've already been getting calls. I may need to ask for some help if this keeps up for too long."

"Sure." His attention focused back on his desk, and I cleared my throat a little. "I came by to talk to you about Ash's killer."

His head picked up and he stared at me alertly. I took a deep breath, a gulp of coffee, grimaced, and began to tell him what I'd figured out the night before. He listened, mostly in silence, asking an occasional question. When I had finished, he agreed with me but pointed out we didn't have everything a prosecutor would need, and I had to agree with that. So we discussed the best ways to get the kind of proof that would stand up in a courtroom, and we made a plan, one that would be mostly Joe's to implement. It was time for me to leave this case. Joe was back on the job and needed to be fully in charge.

We'd pretty much finished discussing the Mowbray case and were just passing the time. I was avoiding going out into the storm for a few more warm, dry minutes. Joe's secretary knocked and opened the door to announce that Brian was outside. I leaped to my feet, certain that something had happened to Gran, while Joe told her to send Brian in.

He came in with snowy patches on his head and melting down his face. "Skeet, Angie's gone. And I think she's in trouble."

The tension that had pulled me taut relaxed. It was nothing to do with Gran. And Angie was always in trouble. "What now, Bri? And how did you get here?"

"Gran brought me in her truck." He looked on the verge of tears. "Angie called me this morning to tell me she was leaving to go live in Mexico with Pearl Brewster."

I jolted alert again, and Joe jumped to his feet. "When? Why?"

"She just can't stand that Liz any longer. She wasn't supposed to tell anyone, but she said she couldn't bear to go without telling me good-bye, so I'd know she was really okay."

"When are they leaving?" I repeated.

"They already left. I told Gran and she drove us in her truck over to Pearl's—that's where Angie called from. We found the door unlocked and they'd already gone to the airport. I couldn't think why Pearl would do this for Angie, but I found this." He held out his gloved hand with one of those anonymous letters I'd seen at Peter's clutched in it.

This one could have been the other's twin. *I know what you did. Don't think you can get away with it. You'll have to pay to keep me quiet.*

Hadn't I thought last night that Pearl was smart enough to know that Bea would keep coming back for more and more money? She'd paid off Bea while setting up a plan to flee.

"Where's Gran now?" I asked.

"Out in the truck. She doesn't want to risk the icy sidewalk to get in here." He looked sheepish. "I said I'd help her walk, but she says she's too old to risk bone breaks."

I cringed at the thought of Gran falling and breaking a hip, which always seemed the precursor to death for elderly folks. "Absolutely. You head back out and go home with her now. I'm making it your job to see to it she gets safely back in the house without falling, okay?"

He straightened up to his full height and nodded solemnly. "I'll do that. Are you going after Angie?"

"We'll get Angie and Pearl," Joe said, while grabbing his big sheepskin jacket. As he shrugged into it, I zipped up my own jacket again and we headed out. On the way to the door, Joe instructed his secretary to make calls to the airport.

We took Joe's car because this was his case in his jurisdiction. We didn't even have to discuss it. We just headed for his cruiser. The wind-whipped snow didn't make talking easy, anyway, crusting into ice around our lips. It did make us speedier on our trip to the car, though.

It took time to clear the windows, though we both worked at it. Joe hadn't been inside that long. The snow was really mounting up now. As he pulled the car out of the parking lot, I noted that the snow was piling into drifts because of the wind. Never a good sign, especially if the snow kept up for long, and there was currently no sign of letup.

"She's trying to make it out before they close the airport for the storm," Joe said, as we headed out of town for the airport.

I nodded, peering out at the whirling white air around us. "They won't have closed it yet, unless the ice is building up. They fly when it's snowing. It's the ice buildup that stops them. I've always found it weird to go flying out through snow. Scary."

The defroster blasted on high, but streaks of refrozen melted snow crossed the windshield with the wipers.

Joe shuddered and grimaced. "It's always scary. I hate flying. Wish they hadn't destroyed the trains. America's railroads were the envy of the world, but we gutted them, and now you can't get to most places in this country by train. Damn shame!"

The air outside just looked like a snow tornado until the snowflakes came driving at the windshield and turned into recognizable clumps of individual flakes just before they hit.

"Are you afraid of flying, Joe?" I asked, teasing.

"Just don't like it," he said in a defensive tone. "I avoid it whenever I can. But I can fly."

I smiled at the image of big, strong Joe huddled in his seat, clinging to the armrests like so many passengers I'd seen who pathologically feared flying.

"Why on earth is Angie with Pearl?" Joe asked, to change the subject. Maybe he'd seen my smile.

"She's miserable as hell with Liz. And who wouldn't be? We had a talk about it a few days ago. She's desperate to get out of there, but there was nothing I could do legally to help her." I sighed. "She must have gone to Pearl about it. Teens have always gone to Pearl, according to Elliott."

I thought about that for half a second. "I wonder if it's not that—inside, she's still that teenage girl who lost her love in such a horrible way. Maybe she never really matured out of that place, even though she learned to put on a grown-up front."

Joe shook his head slowly. "Why take the girl with her, though?"

I shrugged. "It changes her profile. She's no longer an old woman alone. She's now a woman with a daughter or grand-daughter." It made sense to me. It was what I'd have done in her place. "I'll bet she has Angie's arm tattoos all covered up and a big, warm hat hiding her weird hair. Angie can look older than her age, and Pearl doesn't look as old as she is. With a little help, they could pass for mother and daughter. Not at all what the cops would be looking for—if Angie hadn't softened enough to call Brian."

Right after we left town on MO-9, Joe turned us onto MO-45 heading for the junction with I-29, which would then take us to the Kansas City International Airport.

Visibility was bad. Snow whirled in the air, whipped around by winds that seemed to come from two directions at once. It was hard to tell where the highway ended and the countryside began now that we were out of town with its curbs, sidewalks, and buildings. Here, the road was the only real landmark in a landscape of fields. The snow covered everything and drifted, changing outlines and shapes and playing tricks on the mind in the dim light the clouds and falling snow left to the world. I knew things would change once we connected with I-29 where strip malls and communities had cropped up along the interstate, but once you got very far off the interstates, it was still just country around here.

Joe leaned into the windshield, trying for better vision in

the almost whiteout conditions. I found myself leaning forward as well, trying to help him see, willing the car to stay on the highway and not wander off into fields that would bog us down.

Outside the car, the wind whined and moaned like a living thing. Once, it almost fooled me into thinking it was a dog lost out there in the snow and cold, crying. Joe had his flashers on to make us more visible to anyone coming our way. There was no sense in using the siren. It would just get caught up in the wind.

"I-Twenty-nine," I said, barely distinguishing the sign warning of the junction.

Joe nodded and took us down the slowly spiraling ramp to leave the state highway and join the interstate. I noticed an SUV spun out to the shoulder halfway along the ramp. I didn't see anyone near it. We couldn't stop to pick up its occupants, but if they'd been around, I'd have called it in to dispatch and a highway patrol car could pick them up. It looked, though, as if they'd spun out in the night on the ice and already gotten a ride into town.

"I think they've shut down flights by now," I said, looking at the sky. "But who knows how long ago Pearl and Angie got there? We may still miss them, even if the whole place is closed."

"We're behind someone," Joe replied. "I'm following their tracks to keep on the road, and they can't have passed here too much before we did, or they'd be drifted over and covered."

"Good." I sat back for a minute, relaxing the tension I hadn't been aware of in my neck and shoulders.

"Doesn't mean it's Pearl," he added, "but I can't imagine who else would be out here in this stuff."

With my glove, I rubbed a clear spot in the fogged-up window on my side, but the scene outside the window was still obscured by wind and snow. As we merged onto I-29, clusters of buildings with lights showed ghostlike in the distance off to the sides of the highway. That sense of driving alone in a completely empty and abandoned landscape disappeared. A few other cars also appeared, sharing the snow-covered highway with us.

This highway had seen more of the public works crews than the state highway we'd just come from, so Joe was able to speed up some. I began to be hopeful that we might catch Pearl and bring Angie safely home.

I didn't fool myself. I knew why Brian had come to me about her flight with Pearl. He expected me to get Angie back safe and sound. I didn't know how I'd face him if I couldn't manage to do that.

That thought haunted me as we drove the seven miles to the airport. Joe's secretary had called and learned that the only airline that flew to Mexico from KCI was Frontier Airlines at Terminal C. A plane for Puerto Vallarta had been scheduled to leave that morning. Joe drove us toward Terminal C through the blowing snow.

Normally, the road that circled to all three of KCI's terminals and back out to the highways was full of traffic. Not this morning, however. The weather had apparently kept people from trying to fly out. Either that, or they'd already learned that all flights had been canceled. I found myself desperately wishing that Pearl's flight to Puerto Vallarta had not been one of the last ones to take flight before the weather shut things down.

Joe parked in front of the doors to Frontier in Terminal C.

This was a huge security no-no, and immediately a TSA agent, padded out like the Michelin man in a black down-filled uniform, showed up, motioning us away. We got out of the car and Joe showed his ID and explained that he was trying to stop a fugitive.

The TSA agent shook his head. "Everyone who's going is gone. We stopped all flights this morning about an hour ago."

"Did the Frontier flight to Puerto Vallarta take off?" I asked, suddenly afraid to hear that it had.

He shook his head. "No international flights going out of here today. We told the extra agents we use on those not to even come in this morning. A couple of women weren't happy and decided to drive to Texas and Mexico in this stuff. I couldn't talk them out of it." He laughed harshly. "They'll be stranded by the side of the road out in Kansas. This shit gets a lot worse as you go west."

"What did they look like?" I asked, hoping it was Pearl and Angie and that we weren't chasing them in the wrong direction.

He shrugged. "Older woman and younger. Couldn't say much else. They were all wrapped up in this weather. Except the younger one had a bit of that godawful fake blue hair sticking out under her hood. My kid's been wanting to do pink, but the wife and I are holding the line on that shit."

I looked at Joe and he nodded. That had to be Pearl and Angie.

"I-Twenty-nine to MO-One fifty-two to I-Seventy?" he asked the guard.

The TSA agent shrugged. "That's really the only way to do it in this stuff, and it'll be tricky on One fifty-two. Snowplows may not have been out there yet today."

We thanked him and jumped back in the car, which was

already icing up. I couldn't believe the way today was going. We were on our way out into the boonies in the middle of a blizzard on a country road that probably hadn't been plowed. And I could only hope that the guard was right and that Pearl ran into trouble on that lonely road.

We were able to do the first few miles back on I-29 before we had to exit onto MO-152. Even the exit ramp had drifts of snow. It was pretty clear that this state highway hadn't seen a snowplow since sometime in the night. There were remnants of two tire ruts in the snow in front of us, though, and that was good news. Had to be Pearl and Angie making a run for Texas and then Mexico.

This would take them to Topeka, Kansas. From there, they could make it to Wichita, and from Wichita, they could easily get to Oklahoma and then Texas, right on down to the border with Mexico. A simple crossing and then they were home free. At least, for a while.

Angie was still a minor, so even though she was voluntarily with Pearl, this was technically kidnapping once Pearl crossed into Kansas, and the feds would get involved. That made extradition from Mexico much easier.

"This is all for nothing," I told Joe. "The feds will bring her back for kidnapping, and we'll be able to hit her for murder. I can't see what she hopes to gain."

He took his eyes from the road to look at me for just the slightest second before turning back to trying to decipher our way through the storm. "Maybe she hopes to lose herself in Mexico somehow. It's a big country. I wouldn't count on her going to wherever she has a ticket. I wonder how much cash she took with her."

"Also, she doesn't know anyone's on to her yet—for the murder or for taking Angie." I found myself leaning forward over the dashboard, searching for signs of the tracks before us and on the edges of the highway.

Once again, we were out in the countryside, surrounded by fields that didn't look that different from the road underneath the layers and mounds of snow. I could tell the road had seen a plow sometime in the night because it appeared marginally flatter and lower than the piles of snow in the fields around it, but that difference was rapidly disappearing. In the distance way off to my left, I could see a light. Probably a farmhouse over there. I tried to keep the location in my head. It might be important if we ended up stranded out here.

It took us forty-five minutes to drive four more miles. The farmhouse light was long gone. There was nothing but whirling snow-filled air surrounding us, an occasional dark clump of trees scattered like giant's toys across the landscape.

The tracks ahead of us had veered closer and closer to the edge of the road. Joe wasn't making the same mistake, but he'd slowed to a crawl now. I followed the tracks up ahead with my eyes and spotted a darker mass off to the side of the road.

"Look," I said. "Someone's swerved off into the fields and gotten stuck."

Joe made a sound halfway between a grunt and a groan. It meant we'd have to go trudging across all this to the car to see if it was Pearl's and hope they'd had the sense to stay with it. He stopped where he was, not daring to move to the shoulder for fear he'd not be able to get traction to move out again when we were ready. He left his police flashers on, as well as his lights, and set flares on the ground around the tires. I hoped all that was enough to warn anyone else crazy enough to be trying to drive this road in these conditions that there was a police car stopped in front of them.

I gathered his Maglite, a blanket, a long pole, and a coil of rope from the trunk of his car while he set the flares. I didn't know what else we might need out there. He took the coil of rope over his shoulders and the Maglite. I threw the blanket over my left shoulder, took hold of the pole like a walking staff, and we set out for the car mired in the snow-covered field. As we drew closer, it appeared dark and still. I recognized Pearl's car and felt very much afraid that Angie and Pearl had not stayed with the car but were out slogging through these larger snowdrifts in the fields, growing colder and wetter and more fatigued by the minute and setting themselves up for hypothermia, which could be deadly.

As we drew closer to Pearl's car, we could see the deep ruts she'd dug, gunning the engine to try to pull out. We could also see the double trail of footprints, being filled in by wind-whipped snow as we watched, leading off across the field toward a shadowy mass in the distance. I couldn't tell at first whether it was a copse of trees or a building. No light shone from it. The closer we came, though, the more it resolved in my vision through the scrim of whirling snow into a deserted and broken-down barn.

"At least, she had sense enough to head for shelter," Joe muttered. "It won't keep them warm, but it should keep most of the snow out."

"Pearl's always had good sense," I said, continuing to trudge toward the car and the footprints. "Except for anything to do with Ash Mowbray."

"All those years alone," Joe answered, breathing hard in

the cold, "they'll leave you a little screwy and vulnerable after a while."

I looked at him in surprise.

"I imagine," he added quickly and stepped up his pace, though he was already having trouble breathing.

I was breathing heavily myself, but not as much as he was. I ran for exercise, while he golfed. Made the difference in stamina. And, I had to remind myself, Joe was almost ten years older than I was. That could make a difference, too. I might not be so tough in ten years, either.

That was a grim thought. I redoubled my efforts, losing troublesome thoughts in the sheer force of concentration required to keep me upright and moving at that foolish, faster pace through drifts of snow that were freezing into ice-covered mounds.

We didn't speak again as we fought our way toward the barn where Pearl's and Angie's footprints led. But I couldn't shake Joe's remark about how years of being alone could lead to emotional vulnerability. I thought of what Charlie had said about marrying Marie. He knew she was probably a disaster, but he married her anyway. *Save me from that kind of fate, please,* I prayed silently to Creator.

"I think the snowfall is letting up," Joe said when we were halfway to the barn. "It's mostly the wind now."

When I looked around, it did seem as if the blowing snow was coming from the ground around us as much as it was coming from the sky above. It wouldn't make it a lot easier getting to the barn, but it should make getting out better, especially if we had a prisoner in cuffs to deal with. I hoped that both Pearl and Angie would still be mobile and not injured or with frostbitten extremities. That meant we'd have to stay out in this with them, risking similar damage to ourselves, until emergency vehicles could make the trek.

I could see the barn more clearly now. Some of that was a function of being much closer, but some was due to the lessening snowfall. With the snow in the air coming primarily from the wind blowing the drifted snow around, the air was clearer and visibility improved.

One of the barn's boards was broken near the ground, creating a large hole. Probably enlarged and used by some wild creature like a big raccoon or bobcat, maybe a coyote. We didn't have much in the way of predators left out here to worry about. Bears, wolves, and cougars had long since been killed off. Whatever it was had probably fled when the double barn door was pulled open on one side, as it had been recently, leaving a wide, curving swath of smoothed-out snow and sticking partly open on a mound of it that had gathered in front of the door as it was pulled back to close again.

Joe indicated the door with his hand as we approached. I nodded and moved slowly to the other side, so we were flanking that partly open door as we came nearer and nearer to the barn. He stopped about ten feet from the opening and aimed the Maglite at its darkness, nodding at me to speak.

"Pearl, it's Skeet. We're here to help. You don't want Angie hurt in this weather, do you?"

"You are not here to help, Skeet." Pearl's voice came from within, shaky but still strong. "How stupid do you think I am? You're here to stop us from trying to make it to freedom. That's something very important to Angie and me."

I decided to try to appeal to Angie instead. "Angie, I need to take you back, hon. This isn't the way to solve your problems."

Angie's face showed in the light beam aimed at the doorway. "There isn't any way to solve my problem, according to you and the law. Let us go, Skeet. Please."

"They can't, Angie." Pearl's calm voice came from farther back within the barn. "They've come to arrest me for killing that swine, Ash Mowbray. Haven't you, Skeet? Joe?"

I let silence hang in the air for a moment.

"You see, child. They didn't come for you, except incidentally." Pearl's voice held warm sympathy and deep fatigue. "Go with them. You're only in a very little bit of trouble, unlike me. I'll stay here. They can take my body back when I'm finished with it."

"No, Pearl!" Angie cried, looking behind her. She turned back to me. "She's got a little gun, and I think she's going to shoot herself."

I took a deep breath. "Pearl, you wouldn't do that in front of Angie, would you? Think what that will do to her. Do you want her to live with that trauma and feeling of guilt? The way you have all these years over Darrell?"

"I should have listened to him," Pearl cried. "He knew my father would punish him, but I wanted what I wanted when I wanted it. And because of me and my father, he died."

"And Ash played on that, didn't he?" I took a quiet step or two forward each time I spoke. "All that guilt and emotion."

Joe made a quiet move forward as well, holding the light steady on the doorway and Angie's face.

"He looked so much like Darrell when he was young," Pearl said from behind Angie. "It . . . it was confusing. I'd been dreaming about Darrell all those years, and then it was like he was alive and in my arms again. I think I went a little crazy then."

"That's understandable," I said, moving again.

"But I wasn't crazy when I killed him!" she yelled. "That was the sanest thing I ever did. It was good for me, for Chelsea, for Noah, for Elliott, for the whole town. That man was a menace to everyone. I'm not sorry."

She paused for a second and then said with less vehemence, "I heard about what Harvey did to poor Bea. I knew she had to have left Harvey's tie pin because I sure hadn't. It was like she was helping me. She'll be all right, won't she?"

Angie's face looked more and more horrified as Pearl spoke.

"Yes, she's going to make it," I told Pearl. "She'll have some interesting scars and may lose some use of her left hand, but she'll live."

At that, Angie moved slowly out of the doorway toward Joe and me. "I . . . I think you're right, Skeet. I think I'd better go home now."

I walked toward her, as did Joe to my left. Angie looked behind her into the darkness where Pearl stood or crouched with a gun in her hand. "Is that okay? Can I go with them?"

Pearl heaved a big sigh. "Of course, Angie. I'd never hurt you. I don't want to hurt anyone else. Not now that that animal, Ash, is dead. This is the end of the line for me."

I didn't like the sound of that, but my first priority was to get Angie out of any line of fire, so I moved forward and grabbed her by the jacket sleeve and pulled her behind me as I moved between her and the door of the barn. Joe came over and stood next to me, with Angie sheltered behind our backs.

"Don't do anything stupid, Pearl," he said, shining the light in and picking out her coat-swaddled form, with a gun in one hand hanging down and her pale face above it, reflecting the light.

She threw her head back and laughed that incredible earth goddess laugh I had always loved. "It's a little late for that warning, don't you think, Joe? After all the stupid things I've done that can never be undone."

I took a step toward her. "Pearl, it's not the end of the world yet."

"It is for me, Skeet," she said in a sad voice, all trace of that life-giving laughter erased.

"A good lawyer could help you make a defense of temporary insanity. You've got the money to get a good one. As long as you stay alive, you've still got a chance at some kind of life." I moved another step forward with every few words until I was at the edge of the stuck-open door and could put my gloved hand on it.

"Temporary insanity? I guess you could call it that. Going back fifty-some years. Maybe they'll just say I never should have been allowed out of Menninger's." She lifted the hand with the gun, but without aiming it anywhere in particular. "I closed myself off for too long. And when Ash came along, I was ripe pickings."

She gestured toward me with the gun, and I felt Joe tense behind and to the side of me. "You can't imagine now while you're young and at the height of your life what it's like to realize you've been a stupid, vulnerable old fool. To know that you've let yourself be used and tossed aside. That's temporary insanity. It's also called loneliness. Too often, we inflict it on ourselves."

"Pearl, you have a choice to make here," I said in my calmest voice. "You've done a lot of harm. You can do more by shooting me or yourself in front of Angie and traumatizing the poor kid, or you can decide to do no more harm and let me have your gun. We can take you back to town to get you a good lawyer."

She stood in the light that Joe still shone on her steadily, gun in her raised hand. After a long, long second, she dropped it to the ground. "No more harm, Skeet. Angie's already had to deal with enough, and I don't want to hurt you. You're doing a good job of that yourself." She shook her head. "Go ahead and take me in. I don't care anymore."

Joe and I moved forward. I secured the gun and Joe put cuffs on her. I wrapped the blanket around Pearl's shoulders instead of Angie's because the elderly fall prey to hypothermia faster than healthy young teenagers do. We called in our location and situation and arranged to meet EMTs and prisoner transport back at the airport. Then we walked Pearl and Angie back through the snowdrifts to Joe's car.

We were all shivering as Joe blasted the car's defroster and heater while he ever so carefully turned the car around in the road and headed back the way we'd come, under a sky that had cleared of falling snow and was just filled on occasion with bursts of wind-driven snow from the drifts beside us.

I shivered as much or more than the others, hearing one thing Pearl had said ring over and over in my head—*I don't want to hurt you. You're doing a good job of that yourself.*

CHAPTER 17

By evening the main roads were cleared of the snow, though they were lined by big drifts made larger by the plows, and some side roads were still in bad shape in Brewster, which didn't have the larger public works department of the city and its huge suburbs. The wind had died down and only occasionally picked up snow from the drifts to fling about in the air.

We'd brought Angie and Pearl back to town and finished all the paperwork by noon. I checked in with Frank and Gil on campus, and finding everything was under control, I took the afternoon off and went home to warm up and spend some time with Gran and Brian—and try to avoid all the voices fighting for space in my head.

Gran's words, *Maybe Charlie's found out something important that you haven't learned yet. Maybe he's found that shutting yourself off to love because you've been hurt is really a fool's choice* fought with Joe's *All those years alone, they'll leave you a little screwy and vulnerable after a while.* And Charlie's words, *You keep going the way you're going, and you'll end up one day with no one around and no one wanting you—don't die a lonely old crab in a thick, hard shell* danced around Pearl's *I closed myself off for too long, and when Ash came along, I was ripe pickings.* And again and again, one remark of Pearl's tormented me, *I don't want to hurt you. You're doing a good job of that yourself.*

Early in the afternoon, Sam called to ask if I'd meet him for dinner at Waldo Pizza in Kansas City because he wanted to talk with me about something important. Ordinarily, I'd have refused without any thought. I'd spent four years avoiding situations that might rekindle Sam's hope of breathing new life into our dead marriage. But I'd been inundated with those voices and I took a minute to answer, adding up all Sam's good qualities and giving him some points for the efforts he'd made to change over the years.

If I didn't want to end up alone, maybe I should try to make it work with Sam again. At least I knew his faults and what to watch out for. I wasn't crazy in love with him like I had been when we were first married, so he wouldn't have the power to hurt me that he'd had then, when I learned he'd been unfaithful. It might be a way not to be alone without really being so vulnerable to being hurt and crushed. It wouldn't be dangerous like those crazy feelings Terry stirred in me, which were probably the equivalent of Pearl's temporary insanity with young Ash.

So I ended up saying yes to Sam. I know it surprised him as much as it did me. It was just all those damn voices in my head, giving me no peace. We agreed on meeting for a late dinner after he got Charlie to bed.

And then I had to think about all kinds of things. Like what to wear. Did I want to try for looking seductive or not? Oh, hell, no, we didn't have to move that fast! I finally settled on black pants and a purple cashmere sweater that I'd really enjoyed knitting and always got compliments on when I wore.

As time to leave came closer and closer, I began to regret the whole decision. I wasn't ready for this, and I knew it. What if I couldn't go through with it and had stirred up Sam's hopes for nothing? I didn't want to do that to him. He didn't deserve it.

When I left for Kansas City that evening, I was a basket case. I might have called and canceled at the last minute, except for all those voices swirling around in my head. I didn't want to end up screwy and vulnerable to someone destructive like Ash or Marie the way Pearl and Charlie had.

Waldo Pizza is a fixture in the Waldo neighborhood of south Kansas City, where Sam and I had lived when we were married. We used to eat there once a week and sometimes more often. I liked their pizzas, and Sam liked their wide selection of beers. I thought I'd be sucking down some of those imported beers tonight, just to calm my nerves and keep me from jumping up and running to the car to head for home.

I hadn't been there in the years since we divorced, but walking in the door was like stepping back into that past—when I was young and happy and stupid. Sam had snagged a big booth for us in back, and he waved me over. I could see the playing cards still glued to the ceiling for the magician who worked the rooms some nights. Some of the waitstaff were people we'd known back when we were regulars, and that delighted me. The music was eighties power ballads, and the heavy bass and drums set my head to bouncing in time as I walked back to Sam.

Maybe this would work out the way I had thought. We could slowly work toward rebuilding a relationship. There was no need to jump into bed right away. Though I suspected he'd want at least a kiss. And the thought of kissing this man, who'd once been my heartthrob but was now more like a close cousin or some other extended family member sharing care of an elderly parent, made me freeze in my steps for a second.

Breathe. And sit down. And order a beer, I told myself and moved forward.

I slid into the booth opposite Sam, who smiled at me.

"I'm glad you agreed to this, Skeet. It's hard to talk about some of these things over the phone or while we're both at Charlie's." He indicated the menu. "What do you want?"

A waiter had joined us, and I ordered a Negro Modelo while Sam got a Heineken.

I looked at him and asked, "Should we just get the old usual?"

He grinned and said, "It's still my favorite."

So we ordered a sausage, red pepper, artichoke heart, and kalamata olive pizza on their traditional crust.

He asked about the day's events, and I told him. By the time I'd finished all that, our pizza had arrived, and I was halfway through my second beer.

"You're drinking more than I've seen in a long time," he said, staring openly at the bottle in my hand.

I avoided his eyes. "I'm probably still a little shaken up from today."

He nodded. "Yeah. All that adrenaline. It's hard to get rid of." He smiled again. "You'll be able to sleep tonight, though, after the beers and pizza."

I smiled and looked down at the piece of pizza on the plate in front of me. "Yeah, I imagine I will."

I was on my third beer and Sam on his fourth before he started to talk to me about what he'd brought me out here for.

I didn't normally drink, so the outlines of everything around me were starting to fuzz a little.

"I've got to say, you've been real good about being patient with me all this time. I know I've been a pain, always trying to make time with you again and never giving you a minute's peace from it." He held his beer out on the table in front of him and looked at me with serious eyes. "I know I haven't made it easy for you, Skeet, and I regret that."

I tried to smile at him and thought I might have succeeded. I knew I should have reached out and patted his hand or something, but I couldn't bring myself to do it. "It's okay."

He shook his head. "No, it's not, and I know that." He gave me a sad smile. "And I want you to know that I do finally realize how far out of line I've been."

I nodded. This was a good beginning. Maybe this really would work, after all.

"Anyway," he continued with a full, golden, Sam-in-all-his-glory smile, "it's not going to happen anymore. I just want you to know that."

I nodded again, smiling a little in response to his smile. I'd forgotten how gorgeous Sam could be.

He leaned over the table toward me eagerly. "I've got such great news, and I hardly know how to tell you about it. I'm in love, Skeet."

I nodded. I guessed he really did love me if he hadn't been able to stop after all this time and discouragement. There was certainly something to be said for that. I smiled back at him.

"I knew you'd be happy for me." He gave a nervous laugh. "It's Erika, but you've probably figured that out by now."

My smile slipped a little while my mind tried to catch up and make sense of what he'd just said.

"She's really something special," he went on with excited

enthusiasm. "Some of her experiences in making the trek to get here are incredible. She's got real courage and a big heart, and she's smart."

"And cute," I heard myself say and wondered how I managed it.

He grinned again. "Yeah, real cute. You sure know me, Skeet."

The waiter came back, and I ordered another beer, thinking there probably weren't enough beers in the world to help me understand this. Suddenly, all those voices were back in my head, telling me I'd end up alone and at the mercy of some crook like Ash or Marie.

"Anyway, I've asked her to move in with me," Sam went on. "She's not sure she wants to do that yet, but I'll win her over to it. She just wants to take it slow."

I nodded. Yes, take it slow. I probably needed to go home, and I'd have to take it slow because I'd had too much to drink.

He continued to talk about Erika and their plans, and I smiled and nodded and thought what a fool I was that even Sam didn't want me anymore. It felt as if the evening would never end.

But it finally did. Sam walked me to my car, concerned about how much I'd had to drink.

"It's not like you, Skeet."

I smiled again. That smile had been pasted on my face for so long that it was probably permanent now. "We had something to celebrate."

He laughed. "Yeah, I guess it's pretty good news for you, too. To know I'm finally going to be out of your hair. But I'll still help with Charlie, of course."

"Of course." I continued to smile. I doubted I could stop it at this point, even if someone stabbed me. "He's married now, though, so I think she'll be taking care of him instead of us."

He tucked me into my car and watched as I drove off, fiercely concentrating on staying in my lane and keeping my speed steady and legal. No need to end tonight's humiliation with the embarrassment of a DUI.

I didn't start crying until I was on the highway heading out of the city, and then it was that horrible gulping, choking, out-of-control sobbing that I hated.

What a fool I was! So sure that all I had to do was reach out and pick up Sam. And why in the hell was I crying anyway? I didn't really want him. He was just the easy answer. Only not so easy, after all.

I drove through the night, sobbing and laughing at myself before I started sobbing again. I knew the alcohol was playing a large part in my whole breakdown, and I regretted drinking it. In preparation for having to get close to Sam. That sent me off in more paroxysms of laughter.

By the time I hit the streets of Brewster, I didn't know what I wanted to do, except I didn't want to go home and face Gran and hear more about how I'd made a fool's choice shutting myself off from love.

And at that thought, I gave a defiant twist of the steering wheel and went down another street, heading in a direction I'd sworn I'd never take. If I was supposed to stop shutting myself off from love, there was one place I knew I could go.

I pulled up in the parking lot of Terry's apartment complex, shaking my head and muttering, "Don't do this, Skeet. You'll live to regret it."

I left the car and remembered to lock it, wiping the tears off my face and still muttering that I would regret what I was about to do. But I knew I was going to do it anyway. Even if I was wobbly as I walked across the icy parking lot to the outside stairs and climbed them to stand outside his door.

I kept shaking my head in warning to myself, even as I knocked on his door. As I stood there, waiting for him to answer it, I noticed myself shuddering, and I almost turned and ran. But I didn't. I waited for the door to open.

He was barefoot and hatless in jeans and T-shirt, and he frowned when he saw me.

That sobered me in an instant. I don't know what I'd expected, but a frown was not it. I looked past him into the living room and saw the blonde with the Jaguar sitting on the couch, staring at us, her legs curled up, barefoot as well. I saw the glasses and bottle of wine on the coffee table.

I turned and ran. Terry called my name, but I kept running and half-fell, half-ran down the stairs. I hit the button to unlock my car and was inside with the power locks on and the ignition started before he made it down the steps.

I roared out of the parking lot, fishtailing a little on the ice, as he ran on bare feet after me, and if there were tears on my face, they were probably just ones I'd missed earlier. I had people who loved me. Gran and Brian were waiting for me at home. I had friends I could count on in this town—Gil, Karen, Annette, Miryam. I wasn't Charlie in some old crabby shell. I wasn't crying over that mercenary. And I wasn't saying yes to romantic love or anything remotely resembling it ever again. If that damn Cupid came around me one more time, he'd find himself staring into the barrel of my gun.